I0585584

ഇ The Early Years ക
Book 1

Ron Mueller

<u>**Fiction Series**</u>
The Taelo Series
The Early Years
The Golden Feather
Journey of Discovery
Dangerous Passage
Condor Clan Slingers
Circumvention
The Journey of Sages
Future Leaders Journey
Taelo Collection

A Taelo Story
White Swan and Quiet Pheasant
The Child's Name
Floating Cloud
Quiet Rabbit
Busy Bee
Little Otter & Talking Wren
Broken Spear
Burley Bear & Meadow Flower
Taelo Story Collection

The Alex Evercrest Series
The River Front
The Girl on The Grill
Missing
Maggot
Racist
Votive Candles
Windy City
Country Road
Pool of Blood
Sins of the Daughter
Body Parts
The Skull Collector
The Vanishing
The Shadow Fighter
Moonshine
Grief's Trajectory
The Magic Touch
Northern Lights
Alex Evercrest Heroine
Alex Evercrest Collection Two
New Direction
A Family Affair
Disruption
The St. Lebuinnus Church Murder

A Brian O'Neil Novel
Hawaiian Phoenix
Moon Curser
Death Broker

The Problem Solver Series
Solutions
Drug Lords
Border Crosser
The Problem Solver Collection
<u>**Science Fiction**</u>

The Savitar Series:
Journey's End
Savitar
Confluence
Savitar Series Collection

Bram Nielson Series
The Fold
The Message
Fold Wormhole
Negative Fold
Ripples in Time
Bram Nielson Collection

<u>**Single Science Fiction Books:**</u>
Current Past and Future
The Event
The Door
Viajante 7

https://www.remwriter95.net/

Ron Mueller

ℬ The Early Years ℭ
Book 1

By: *Ron Mueller*

Around the World Publishing LLC
Cincinnati, Ohio

The Early Years ©

Ron Mueller

ISBN 13: 978-1-68223-187-6

The Taelo ^M Series

The Early Years
The Golden Feather
Journey of Discovery
Dangerous Passage
Condor Clan Slingers
Circumvention
The Journey of Sages
Future Leaders Journey
Taelo Collection

Distributed by Ingram
Eagle By: Teekaygee, Dreamstime.com
Picture By: Hien Mueller
Cover Design By: Ron Mueller

Dedication:

My Thanks to

Richard Hart.

His dedication to Taelo,

made Taelo into a series,

and

He insisted that the story get better.

Ron Mueller

Taelo Series Introduction

Taelo and his Clan lived forty thousand years ago and were among the first to begin settling the Americas.

The story of **Taelo** ***The Early Years*** begins with his naming and takes the reader through Taelo's and Golden Hawk's early years until they are recognized as full members of the Clan.

They constantly contribute to the well-being of all around them. They are known throughout all the Elk sub-clans as being good luck to have around!

Taelo's actions lead to the adoption of an older, different kind of people called the ***Others*** into the Elk Clan.

The *Early Years ends* with the successful hunt by a hunting team having both male and female hunters for the first time. The success of the team flips the culture on its head!!!

In, ***The Golden Feather,*** this same team takes the next step in their development.

They first travel south into the Andes of South America.

They meet the peoples living in those areas.

On their return they go into the far North Coastal area where the Elk Clan originally had its home.

Their actions once again change the culture of the Elk Clan!!

Introduction

In ***Journey of Discovery***, Taelo and Golden Hawk travel from the Pacific coast to the Atlantic Ocean and see the wonders of nature and discover many new species of animals.

The "Mount" allows them to travel faster and farther than they thought possible.

Bears, Wolves, Sharks, and Alligators all take their turn in challenging Taelo's team !!

In ***Dangerous Passage,*** Taelo and a new mix of members travel back across the ice bridge into Asia.

They first battle very aggressive giant bears.

Then they must overcome natural challenges.

Finally, they meet the Blue Eyes. In the battles that follow Taelo, and his small team overcome the brute force of the much larger blue-eyed enemy.

On their return they lead the White Bear Clan back home!!

In **Condor Clan Slingers** the team returns to the Andes to aid the Condor Clan in their battle against an aggressive Warrior Clan.

They change that clan by having the women lead the battle.

They rescue the sacrificial Condor bride.

They forever change the Condor Clan !!

In **Circumvention** Taelo pursues the belief that the world is round !!!!!

His team follows him from the Pacific coast around the world and back to the Pacific coast.

He proves his concept and along the way the adventures his team experience are mind blowing !!

A true explorer in the earliest of times!

In The **Journey of Sages**, Taelo takes the wise and older leaders
for a journey around the Pacific.
The Journey is filled with challenges that the leaders of the Elk
Clan and the Clan of others had never imagined.

> Ocean currents the could not control.
>
> Volcano eruptions
>
> Cannibals that wanted more than to chat!

The last adventure is the **Future Leaders Journey**.

These future leaders meet the fierce warrior of Africa, the
face tiger bigger that the saber tooth the have experience in their
homeland.

They experience the man-eating fish in a river so wide that
they cannot see across it.

****

Taelo and Golden Hawk ,his cousin, are exceptional individuals

that demonstrate what an open and inquisitive mind can

accomplish.

These books are meant for parents to read or at least discuss
with their children. There are many opportunities to explain
and reinforce the central concept of "treat others as you wish to
be treated."

Additionally, the books are written to challenge and develop
the young reader's vocabulary. Every five pages they should be
asking about the meaning of a word !

Introduction

1 Wonders in the Stream

oft white puffs floated across a clear blue sky. Just below the clouds a huge eagle glides effortlessly on the updraft from the valley below. The mountains surrounding the valley, still capped in snow, was a display of variations of green grasses, new leaves against the backdrop to the dark green pine trees standing like sentinels guarding the white crown above.

It was spring.

It was the Elk Clan's naming ceremony. This was when the child selected an object that was then used to give the child a name.

It was his turn.

Rougher, older hands replaced his mother's gentle ones. He was carried into the center of the circle. All the naming objects were lying on the rim of the circle surrounding him. From the beginning there was only one object of interest to him.

He made his choice immediately. Instinctively he looked up and stretched his hand to the sky. In his small hand was the claw of the eagle.

High in the sky the eagle's almost exuberant cry reverberated across the valley. Swiftly the eagle went into a silent dive. Her agile claws closed firmly on her prize. She, on strong wing strokes, rose high back into the sky and disappeared down the valley.

He remembered the quiet weeping of his mother, White Swan, her tears falling on his cheek, the strong arms of his father, Grey Fox Running, encircling them. He remembered snuggling in the middle in a feeling of warmth, safety, and contentment.

He had chosen the talon of the eagle, and the eagle had chosen him.

He became Taelo (Tā low), the talon of the eagle.

His cousin had selected the wing of a golden hawk.

He was named Golden Hawk.

The cool morning air moving softly across his cheek woke Taelo from his recurring dream. He opened his eyes and through the dark grey of early morning, he could barely see the trees outside the tent opening.

He crawled out and gazed up to the crumbling rocky cliffs towering above the small lazy Flint River, the rocks at its base formed a long sloping skirt down to the river.

The clear water of the small river gurgled down numerous small rapids and meandered down to a wide-open valley just beyond where the Clan was camped.

He gazed across the camp to the point where the cliffs ended, and the valley opened.

A quiet satisfaction warmed him against the cool morning air. The Clan was camped in one of his favorite places.

He walked to his cousin's tent. It was their naming day.

He arrived just as Golden Hawk stepped out.

Taelo hugged Golden Hawk and wished him a happy seventh naming day.

Taelo and Golden Hawk both saw the early morning fire at the Weaver's tent. The Weaver's fire was their most visited morning camp.

Golden Hawk picked up the rabbit they had skinned and hung up the previous night.

The two would trade it for a morning meal and with luck they would hear a new story from the Weaver.

This morning, they saw him sitting by his small fire. The Weaver, an old warrior no longer capable of hunting, was the Clan's net maker. His many stories captivated Taelo and Golden Hawk.

"Good morning, Grey Weaver, may we join you for breakfast," Taelo inquired politely.

They decided a breakfast of berries, boiled egg, and a tough, bread-like muffin, provided by the old hunter, would be just the thing.

Grey Weaver grunted his greeting and began to serve the two a morning meal. He was pleased to have them at his fire. The two were considered good luck and welcomed throughout the camp.

The action of the eagle on the naming day for these two was still discussed every year.

Grey Weaver felt privileged to influence and develop these two. He taught them many important skills through the stories he told. The Clan had enjoyed fruitful years since the birth of these two. They seemed to bring good luck.

Taelo listened to another story from the Weaver as he and Golden Hawk slowly ate their breakfast. The coolness and freshness of the air and the quiet of the camp, Golden Hawk at his side, gave him a warm complete feeling.

After breakfast Taelo returned to his own campsite and waited restlessly for his mother to pack some food for snacks and lunch.

The family was going to Taelo's and Golden Hawk's favorite swimming hole up the Flint River by a huge sandstone rock that had been washed down stream in some long-ago flood from the upstream cliffs.

The two families could sit comfortably on the flat slightly sloped top of the rock and there was still enough room for Taelo and Golden Hawk to dive into the deep pool of cool clear water surrounding the flat-topped rock.

Just downstream of the rock they had tied a rope to the limb of an old tree that extended out over the water.

They would dive off their rock platform, swim to the bank, climb up to the first oak limb and swing back out into the pool.

Then they would climb the rock to dive again. This round robin of diving and swinging would go on for most of the day.

The naming day family outing was a custom they all looked forward to.

When everyone was ready, he and Golden Hawk ran out ahead.

The way to the river went by an immense old rambling limbed mulberry tree.

As they approached, Golden Hawk was pulled to the tree by the large dark purple mulberries so dense they were pulling the limbs low. He and Taelo scrambled into the tree, and each claimed a low limb running parallel to the ground to stand on. They each began to eat the purple jewels of sweetness that were as big as their thumbs.

"To get the best ones, you must climb up on the branches and pick only the largest mulberries," Red Oak, Golden Hawk's father called out encouragingly.

Taelo and Golden Hawk walked fearlessly out along the large low branches using both hands to pick the succulent dark purple berries.

Hundreds of mulberries at least three times the length and size than those found on the younger mulberry trees hung within reach on each side of their branch. It was the ultimate treat enjoyed only in early summer.

Taelo meticulously picked one of the long, multi-lobed berries and carefully put it in his mouth. He slowly squeezed the berry to the top of his mouth and savored the sweetness that spread across his tongue and infused his mind with sweet wonder.

He knew these mulberries were meant to be savored and enjoyed in slow motion. He closed his eyes each time he put one of the mulberries on his tongue. The sweet juice teased the taste buds and instilled him with a peaceful contentment.

Taelo watched as his mother, White Swan and his aunt, Quiet Pheasant, efficiently picked berries from the lower branches as they talked quietly.

Red Oak and his father, Grey Fox Running ate a handful of berries and then sat down on the trunk of a large old tree blown down in some past storm.

Taelo heard his father, "If we are going to get any swimming done today, you better come down so we can get to the swimming rock."

This caught Taelo's attention, and he looked over to Golden Hawk.

They began to laugh at each other when they saw the purple around each other's mouths and on their hands.

"Last to the water is a turtle," Taelo called out as he scrambled down from his branch and took the lead running toward the rapids.

They were laughing merrily as they again ran ahead of the family toward the river. They were only a short distance down the trail when they spotted bushes with translucent golden ripe goose berries dangling in the morning sun. These berries were gigantic. They were about the size of a small bird's egg.

"Look at these jewels," Golden Hawk exclaimed as he popped one the size of a blue bird's egg into his mouth.

The two had been by here a few days ago and had totally missed them. Taelo held up one of the smooth golden orbs to the sun. He could almost see through the tiger striped translucent skin.

"Wow look at these beauties," Taelo commented to Golden Hawk as he dropped the large succulent orb into his mouth and carefully popped it. "They are delicious."

The two had picked and eaten a handful of the delicious bubbles, by the time their parents caught up to them. Gooseberries were not quite as sweet as the mulberries, but their refreshing tangy sweet flavor was as much a treat as the mulberries.

Once again, the procession stopped. This time they all took part in picking a bag of gooseberries. After a few more gooseberries, Taelo and Golden Hawk concentrated in filling the bag White Swan had pulled out.

This time the two were first to say it was enough.

They ran off together towards the river.

They were now on the flood plain of the Flint. This area had been swept clean of its leaves and forest floor covering and except where the brush or willows had captured debris, the floor was sand swept around several old elm trees surrounded by open grass and a few smaller ones trying to reach up into the sunshine.

The two reached the bank of the small river. The clear cool water at this point tumbled lazily down a series of small rapids.

A person could cross at almost any rapid and remain dry. Here rapids punctuated the transition of the cliff's switch from the left side of the river to the right side of the river.

Across the river, the land transformed from a steep hill to the high cliffs dominating the valley for the next few miles downstream.

The cliff was punctuated with two distinctly different types of caves. One was a large room with two entrances. The opening facing the Flint was a large oblong square. The back opening slanted upward and came out on top of the cliff. The cave had a hole in the center of the roof forming a perfect chimney for the fire circle below it. This cave was used for the meetings of the elders.

The other cave was a long narrow tunnel going back into the cliff for a good two hundred spear lengths before coming to a room where half a dozen people could fit.

Though the opening of this cave was very large, it quickly diminished in size to the point where only small boys like Taelo and Golden Hawk were able to crawl through the very narrow area to reach the room.

The cave had been put off limits for the children after several became trapped and had to be rescued. However, almost all the young boys still made the journey to the back room in the cave.

Taelo and Golden Hawk regularly went back and enjoyed the solitude they found there.

Their thoughts were now on a day of playing in the river. They had been outfitted with old foot coverings intended to be used in the water. Their only other clothing were the two leather flaps tied to their waist.

The rapids before them extended up-river a good stone's throw. The water flowing through the placid pool upstream made a tumbling, gurgling journey down multiple paths to a spear deep pool of rippling but calm water that was the closest swimming hole to the camp.

At this time in the morning, they were still the first, but Taelo knew that soon the other Clan kids would be arriving to swim.

The quiet they now enjoyed would be broken by the shrieks and laughter of swimmers chasing and playing in the water with each other.

He and Golden Hawk eagerly raced out into the rapids and jumped into the pool on the far side at the base of the rapids.

They jumped from a big round boulder into the four-foot-deep pool around it.

They were frolicking in this pool until the rest of the family caught up.

Grey Fox Running called to them as he waded out into the rapids and walked up stream toward the calmer waters at the top, "Today we are going to teach you how to catch crayfish."

This caught Taelo's and Golden Hawk's interest and they immediately ran up stream toward their fathers.

They were forever chasing the crawfish and catching them, so they wondered what they were going to learn.

"Follow me to the rocks upstream, where the water runs smoothly and quietly passes the rocks in the stream," Grey Fox Running spoke quietly as he took out a long thin stick from his backpack. Red Oak held a similar one in his hand.

Their curiosity peaked, and they quietly followed their fathers.

Quiet Pheasant and White Swan stayed on the bank on a trail running parallel to the river. They were enjoying the sight of the fathers and sons playing together. The two sisters cherished moments like these.

Their husbands were great fathers, but they were two of the top hunters in the Clan and almost always away hunting. Times like these were rare and therefore special.

"Once those two boys learn how to capture the crayfish, we will lose them for the rest of the summer. They will relentlessly pursue their new-found skill," White Swan commented to Quiet Pheasant.

"Yes, they will work on this until a new skill or game can be added to it. They are so intense in perfecting what they learn. It sometimes scares me," Quiet Pheasant replied as she closely watched the four in the river.

"However, we will have an abundance of crayfish tails for the rest of the summer," she chuckled.

"I agree. The two learn swiftly and work together well. When they are together, they watch out for each other," Quiet Pheasant continued as the two slowly walked along to a point upstream where a fallen tree provided them a comfortable seat to sit and watch.

The two sat quietly and watched the father and son interaction as the four hunted the mighty crab.

Taelo and Golden Hawk followed and watched as their fathers walked smoothly and quietly upstream looking down into the water. Suddenly their fathers stopped. Red Oak reached slowly down into the water with the hand holding the thin long stick. He slowly lifted the edge of a large flat stone and swiftly reached down with his other hand.

He grabbed a crayfish just behind the two large claws and quickly lifted it out of the water.

As the crayfish began to reach back with its two large claws, Red Oak put the thin stick into one of the open claws and then deftly put it into the second claw. The crab instinctively closed his claws on the stick and held on.

Grey Fox Running just as quickly opened a sack, and Red Oak dropped the crayfish into it. After a few shakes, the crab let go of the stick and fell to the bottom of the sack.

"We now have one very nice snack for later today," White Swan said from her seat on the bank.

Grey Fox Running opened the bag for the two boys to look in.

"Wow look how big it is," both said in unison.

"Would one of you like to try to catch the next one," Grey Fox Running asked.

"Yes, Yes," both cried out in unison.

Grey Fox Running took out two additional thin sticks about two feet long.

OK, I have been standing here quietly because there is another crab, as big as the one we just caught. Taelo and Golden Hawk, you two will work together. One of you will reach down and lift the rock up. The other must be ready to grab the crayfish by the body.

It is extremely important that the two of you work together otherwise the person holding the crab will get a nasty pinch. The stick must be put into the claws of the crayfish before it can pinch the hand holding it.

Later when you get better, each of you can do it by yourself the way Red Oak just did. This time you will work together," Grey Fox Running instructed quietly.

"I will pick up the crayfish. You pick up the rock and then keep the crab from pinching me," Taelo spoke up as he stepped up to the right of his father.

Golden Hawk stepped up to Grey Fox Running's left side as he slowly stepped back to give them both more room. There at the edge of the rock the two boys could see the two claws of a very large crayfish. One claw was almost twice the size of the other.

"This one lost a claw in a fight and is now growing a new one. The small claw is more dangerous than the big one because it can reach farther back, so get that one first then engage the big one," Grey Fox Running said as he stepped back farther.

Golden Hawk bent and slowly raised the rock. A gentle swirl of sand lifted with the rock and was slowly washed away by the clear, gently moving water. The crab was exposed and waiting for the water to clear before making its getaway.

Taelo swiftly plunged his hand down into the water and grabbed the large crayfish where Red Oak had grabbed his and lifted it out of the water. He could hardly hold onto the crab as he lifted it up.

Just as he thought the crayfish was going to pinch him with the small claw, Golden Hawk put his twig in, and the crayfish bit it instead. Golden Hawk then quickly fed the end of the branch into the large claw.

Together the two boys dropped the crayfish into the bag Grey Fox Running offered. To the surprise of everyone, it was at least twice the size of the previous one.

"Congratulations, the two of you have caught one of the largest cray fish that we have ever seen," Red Oak said as he looked into the bag and passed it around for the others to look inside. He then took it over to White Swan and Quiet Pheasant.

"This is the largest crayfish I have ever seen. It's a miracle that those two were able to capture it without getting pinched," Red Oak said quietly to White Swan and Quiet Pheasant.

Even though the swimming rock was only a mile or so up the stream, it took over an hour to reach it.

Taelo and Golden Hawk were on the hunt for more crayfish. They caught six more and the group was ensured of a wonderful lunch of roasted crayfish tail. It was hard for the two boys to stop hunting. They were hooked on catching the cray fish, but they were also looking forward to a rare day of swimming and frolicking with their parents.

"There will be no safe crayfish for the rest of the summer," White Swan said in a knowing tone.

She knew the two boys would pursue their new-found skill relentlessly until they found a new skill to add to their collection.

The huge wedge of the swimming rock came into view. Its point was wedged up into the bank and its flat top leaned slightly toward the water.

Just upstream a small clear stream ran into the river. This was water from a spring just past the other bank of the Flint. Its source was a natural spring bubbling up from the ground at the base of the cliff. They would use it to drink and would take several bags back to their camps on their return.

The steep bank of the river was rich black dirt dropped by flood waters over the years.

A slick mud slide was easily made by splashing water up on the bank.

For the rest of the day, the boys went swimming, diving from the rock, sliding down the mud slide and swinging out on a braided rawhide rope out over the water.

The mudslide kept them busy for a short period and then they took up swinging out on the rope. Then it was diving from the rock. The two then started the cycle all over again. This went on until a late afternoon lunch caused them all to gather on the swimming rock.

Lunch consisted of freshly roasted crayfish tail and wild onions. White Swan and Quiet Pheasant had used the gooseberries, onions, and mulberries to make a seasoning to go with the freshly caught crayfish. They put this on the crayfish as they roasted them over the hot coals of the small fire.

They also had a snack of fresh mulberries and gooseberries. All of this was washed down with some crystal-clear spring water.

Taelo savored the succulent crayfish tail. It was one large piece of white meat. The magic taste his mother had crated did not escape him.

"This is unbelievably delicious. I have never had anything so good," Taelo complimented his mother and aunt.

"This is absolutely wonderful. I did not think that we would eat so well today," Red Oak commented as he finished his second helping.

Everyone chimed in their agreement.

Everyone was sitting on the swimming rock relaxing and drying off in the late afternoon sun. Quiet Pheasant was just going to announce the time to go home, when high in the sky a loud piercing scream reached her ear.

Everyone looked up at a huge bald eagle. It let out a loud second cry and then turned upriver.

Everyone silently watched the grand sight.

Again, Quite Pheasant was about to speak, when a different and much closer cry reached her ear.

Coming up the river was a golden hawk. It dove toward the water at the edge of the swimming area and pulled up a large trout.

As it went over the rock, it dropped the fish.

Golden Hawk was astonished as the fish dropped between his legs.

There was a moment of stunned silence. This was just not real.

Golden Hawk and Taelo gave a cry of surprise and then scramble about as they captured the large trout and together were holding up their prize. It was large enough to be a meal for all of them.

"This is truly a sign that our sons have strong totems watching out for them. Their totems have come by and wished them well and even left a gift.

Let's go home and enjoy the gift given to Golden Hawk," Red Oak spoke up as the adults looked at each other and up at the sky as the two totems flew out of sight.

No one spoke of the impossibility of such an event.

The trip back home went rather quickly. The two boys ran ahead down along the trail on the bank of the stream as the two couples followed at a normal pace. They talked quietly about what had just transpired.

For the rest of the summer the two boys spent their days playing in the rivers and streams of the various valley's through which the Clan traveled. Taelo and Golden Hawk would roam the streams and rivers catching their crayfish lunch and then bringing the extra home for White Swan to cook in soups and other dishes.

That first season, Taelo and Golden Hawk became known for supplying the camp with crayfish. They always returned from the rivers and streams carrying a bag of crayfish. They were generous and repaid their many morning breakfast providers and gave some to everyone in the camp.

White Swan and Quiet Pheasant never turned down the boy's offering. If there was too much food for the day, they would season and smoke the meat. The crayfish would be welcome treats in the coming winter.

2 Talking to Cave Bears

*T*aelo learned from his father about the dangers of bears. Bears were constant competitors when the salmon made their run. The bears were always given the rapids they chose.

The bears were also very territorial and when the Clan wandered into a bear's territory, they would leave it as quickly as possible.

Taelo and Golden Hawk listened to the Weaver tell stories of how a bear should be handled.

The Weaver advised that the best way to handle a bear was to let the bear have what they wanted. But if you had to face the bear, then it was best not to run away because the bear despite its size was very fast.

It was best to slowly move away into the thick dense part of the forest that provided a thick dense cover that would make it difficult for the bear to get through.

Hunting a bear was a recognized way for a young man to transition from boyhood into manhood.

Even then, they were only hunted if the Clan thought they needed the meat and the hide. The hide provided the best cold weather covering and jackets.

Taelo and Golden Hawk went out one day and tracked one of the Giant Brown bears. They spent almost all day following the bear through the mountain pine forest.

They watched the bear as it stood and reached high up on a pine as thick as the fire ring at their lodge was wide. It clawed its mark a good foot above a previous scar on the bark of the tree.

It let out a roar and then peed on the trunk. She had declared this her territory and had left her scent.

When the bear began to sniff the air, they both immediately began a retreat. They first followed the Weavers advice but then fear gave wings to their feet and they ran at full speed taking turns looking over their shoulders to make sure they were not being chased.

Several days later, Taelo and Golden Hawk agreed to join the group of children being organized to go out to pick blue berries. Usually, they would not have done so but both White Swan and Quiet Pheasant had suggested they help watch out for the younger children.

Three Clan mothers led the kids on the hike out to the hills where the blueberry bushes were thick and loaded.

It was a pleasantly warm and sunny day, perfect for berry picking. The clouds overhead were cotton puffs of various shapes and sizes causing kids to see the heads of dogs, or a swimming fish floating by in the sky. The sun was warm but there was a light breeze making the day fresh and invigorating.

It was a fine outing with a constant flow of chatter and joking.

The kids ran about shouting and chasing butterflies, picking meadow flowers, and chasing each other. Taelo and Golden Hawk were content in following the group and talking about which berries, they liked the most.

They all followed a small gurgling stream, a step wider than most of the kids could jump, up a wide sloping valley to the blueberry patch on toward the top lip where the ground flattened out. It was surrounded by large trees on the approach side and many small paw-paw trees around its far side.

The many head high bushes with dark bluish leaves were loaded with dark, almost black blueberries of various sizes. Everyone was to fill their bags with these purple, bluish-black jewels.

Most of the kids eagerly rushing into the area were shorter than the blueberry bushes and they disappeared as they scattered to pick and eat the berries. An equal number of berries went into their mouth as went into their bag. The mothers knew this would happen and were happy to see it.

This saved them from picking the extra berries the youngsters were consuming.

The morning passed without incident, everyone picked and filled their bags, ate their fill, and was generally enjoying the day.

Taelo and Golden Hawk spent their time keeping track of the kids who disappeared as they went ever deeper into the patch.

The sun was at its zenith when everyone gathered out in the valley for a lunch of cold goose, some bread like buns and cool water from the small gurgling spring.

Then after a short rest, the group was once again out in the middle of the blueberry bushes picking berries.

High in the sky an eagle let out as loud scream. Taelo looked at Golden Hawk and then saw the large female cave bear and her single cub coming into the same blueberry patch.

The arrival went unnoticed by the rest until the bear, upset by the chatter and the noise of the kids around her, let out an ear-splitting roar. Everyone froze where they stood. They had all heard stories of the dangers of an angry cave bear.

Instinctively the mothers nearest to the meadow, hastily led the children out away from the blueberry patch.

The bear stood on her hind legs and pawed the air as she once again let out a roar. She was at least two full spears high. She was one of the largest anyone had ever seen.

This was her blueberry patch, and her angry ear-splitting roar was letting the intruders know it.

Taelo and Golden Hawk were on the opposite side of where the mothers were frantically moving the children out of the patch.

This movement and the noise being made by three crying youngsters caused the female cave bear to let out another ear shattering roar heard back in the camp almost a mile away. The giant brown bear was extremely agitated and angry. This was her territory, and invaders were not to be tolerated. She was on the verge of charging at the intruders.

By now the mothers were rushing everyone they could out of the thicket and down the hill.

On the opposite side of the thicket, separated from the fleeing group were three of the younger children. Their crying made them the center of attention of the female bear.

Taelo and Golden Hawk instinctively moved to where the children were standing. Taelo quieted them down and told Golden Hawk to slowly lead them out of the patch.

Golden Hawk began to lead the children away from the bear toward the edge of the blueberry patch.

Taelo stood between them and the bear. He raised his arms high into the air high as possible. He was following the Weaver's instruction on how to face down a bear. The part worrying him was about not showing any fear.

He hoped the stories he had listened to were true. He did not feel very large or very brave in the presence of a bear four times taller than he.

He recognized this as the bear he and Golden Hawk had tracked. He remembered how high her mark was in the tree. He stood a mere half a spear and with his hands in the air he might reach to three quarter of a spear.

Her mark was at least two spears high.

Taelo began to speak to the bear in a loud but calm voice.

"Great mother bear we did not mean to encroach on your blueberry patch. Let me give you the wonderful blueberries I have picked. I have all I need and want to share them with you.

My mother expects me home soon. It is time for me to go. You do not want to get into a shouting match with her. When she is mad, she can roar almost as loud as you. If you were to hurt me, she would come after you. So, if you excuse me, I will quietly leave," Taelo said as he threw his bag of blueberries at the large bear and waved his arms and got her attention.

Taelo stood quietly with his arms raised and watched the giant mother bear before him. He tried to show no fear though it permeated his entire being.

He wanted to run!

The bag he threw hit her in the snout. She roared and took a few steps toward Taelo who was slowly moving away from the three children as Golden Hawk led them back into the woods.

The smell of the berries distracted her. She and her cub stopped to eat them.

Taelo had counted on her eating the berries. He was not sure what he would have done if she had charged him immediately. He hoped this would calm her down and allow time for everyone to leave the area.

Golden Hawk successfully used this moment to get the children out and around the patch.

"Yes, please enjoy the berries and then follow me. I will show you the best berries so you can enjoy them with your cub," Taelo spoke confidently as he moved further into the blueberry thicket and away from the retreating group of children and mothers.

He was moving slowly toward a thick stand of small trees. These would provide him a barrier. The bear would have to break through the small trees if she decided to chase him. He would be able to easily navigate the thicket, but the bear's size would prohibit her from easily following him.

At least he hoped this was the case!

One of the more, brave mothers had returned to the edge of the blueberry thicket and watched in wonder as the giant bear quietly followed Taelo with her cub close behind.

She found it inconceivable to think about doing what Taelo and Golden Hawk had just done. She had never witnessed such self-sacrificing courage. She knew this would be a story she would tell many times in the years to come.

Taelo kept up a calm conversation with the giant bear and pointed out the bountiful blueberries. As if understanding, the mother bear, and the cub began to eat the blueberries Taelo had pointed out.

The lone mother at the edge of the thicket could not believe the bear was doing what Taelo instructed. It was as if the bear understood his direction.

Finally, when Taelo thought he was close enough to the thick stand of small trees, he dropped down into the blueberry bushes and scurried away.

Once in the thicket of small trees he stood and slowly walked back around the blueberry patch to the other side. It was a relief for him to watch the Mother bear and her cub as they continued to eat blueberries. It was clear that the mother bear no longer had anything more on her mind.

He went down the hill to where everyone was reunited and making a hasty get away.

Everyone looked up into the sky as once again the eagle let out a scream and glided away down the long valley.

"That was an unbelievably brave thing for you to do," the mother who had observed him said as she looked at Taelo with awe and a quiet respect.

In her mind he was a warrior not a child. This was a tale, others who heard it would find hard to believe but she would tell all the elders. She would proclaim and give the credit of the bravery shown by both these two young men.

She would tell the story of Taelo talking to the mother cave bear.

Taelo tried to explain the rational of his actions.

"The mother bear, just like you, was only worried about the well-being of her cub. She was as frightened of us as we were of her. Had we shown fright or otherwise caused her more alarm she would have attacked us. She just had to be comforted and to know we meant no harm. She had to see we were not hunters. She could not understand my words, but she knew the meaning by the tone of my voice," Taelo replied.

This seemed reasonable to him, and he was glad to have listened and thought about the stories told each winter by the older hunters and by the Weaver.

He would need to thank the Weaver for his story on how to face a bear.

A few days later, Golden Hawk and Taelo were up early and once again sitting at the Weaver's breakfast fire.

The Weaver thanked Taelo for crediting him with teaching the two on how to face a bear. He laughed and said he was glad that it had worked and would have missed them for breakfast had it not.

The story of Taelo talking to the cave bear soon made the rounds of the camp and everyone once again looked at Taelo and Golden Hawk with new interest.

The Weaver was especially happy to have the two boys for breakfast.

Golden Hawk laughed and looked at Taelo and pointed out that the Weaver had just told them that the two of them were lucky to be alive.

The Weaver laughed and asked if they wanted to hear a story on how to handle a dire wolf.

Little did he know that later his dire wolf story would once again serve to save Taelo and Golden Hawk.

Quiet Pheasant and White Swan let them know how proud they were of the bravery they had shown in rescuing the children. They both expressed concern that they not become overconfident and become a dinner for some other bear.

White Swan and Quiet Pheasant initially wanted to admonish the two for taking such a risk, but they recognized that the two had kept a level head and reacted in the most appropriate manner. Their quick action had saved the lives of the three children.

They were sure Taelo and Golden Hawk were guided by the voices of the ancients. There was no doubt in the hearts of the two mothers that these same ancients had guided and watched over them and that their totem watched over them as well.

As mothers, they knew their role was to ensure these boys grew safely and were well taken care of. They were not to be limiters but enablers.

By custom, the children saved by Taelo and Golden Hawk owed both for their lives. The families of the three children came by to thank them for saving their children and to see what they in turn could do to reward Taelo and Golden Hawk.

The two knew that they must accept some form of recompense otherwise they would shame the families.

The two boys had decided to ask for something reasonable and symbolic.

They asked each family to gift the tongue, tail, and hump of a buffalo to White Swan and Quiet Pheasant. This was the most valued pieces of meat from a buffalo, and it recognized their mothers as well.

They expressed the fact that these gifts would be enjoyed by them both and would balance their account.

That night as she lay next to Grey Fox Running, White Swan shared her concern about Taelo's fearlessness and his habit of taking immediate action.

"I was proud of both Taelo and Golden Hawk today. They accepted the praise in a modest fashion, and they found a way to have each family thank them in a way that will not be a burden.

They were very wise and understanding.

However, I worry. Taelo knows no fear. You must speak to him and let him know he must be careful.

As soon as possible you must also make sure you teach him how to hunt and handle weapons. You must show him how to handle himself in all dangerous situations," White Swan said quietly.

She and Quiet Pheasant had decided they would never be able to protect the two but needed to make sure they could take care of themselves.

"Yes, I will talk to him. He may be fearless, and he is wise for his age. He knew not to show the bear fear. Instead, he showed the mother bear his confidence and I am sure the bear saw a figure of immense size.

His quiet voice soothed the worried heart of a protective mother.

He did everything exactly as he should have. I am not sure there is anything I can teach him about how to handle such a situation.

But Red Oak and I will train both boys on how to handle the tools of the hunt," Grey Fox Running replied quietly in words he felt were coming from another dimension.

3 Herding Salmon

*T*aelo and Golden Hawk watched as the silvery flashes of quivering muscle propelled the fish up the rapids as they made their last swim to the place where they were born. They were the survivors returning from the sea and returning from where they had started out as small fingerlings. Now they returned to their beginning to ensure the next generation of their kind. They would lay and fertilize their eggs. There would be no sense of graciousness, no sense of virtuousness, it was all a deep life force that drove the cycle of survival.

Taelo and Golden Hawk watched the bear, the eagle and the hawk all take their share of the persistent, seemingly endless numbers of the fish.

This year they felt they had grown strong enough to pull in the dying giants and planned to be part of the Clan members that would be called the gatherers and would pull the fish from the stream and take them to the cleaning area.

3 Herding Salmon

Taelo and Golden Hawk stood behind the older gathers and listened to the instructions being given. This was the start of the annual gathering. It was the most important food gathering the Clan did each year.

The Clan leaders organized the gathering into nine groups. The gathers brought the fish to the cleaners. The cleaners cleaned and passed each fish to the slicers who would cut meat from the bones.

The slicers in turn passed the meat steaks to the salters who rubbed the meat down with salt and sent it on to the skewers who in turn handed the fish on skewers to the smokers.

The smokers put the skewers over small, elongated smoking fires that were maintained by the wood gatherers.

The smoke-drying area looked like schools of headless fish swimming in unison over small smoky fires. The series of small fires over which the fish were suspended on horizontal poles slowly dried and smoked the fish. A variety of wood chips chosen for the flavor of the smoke were thrown periodically into the small fires. It took most of a day for a fish to be dried. As soon as one batch of fish was dried another batch was loaded. The drying went on around the clock.

Once dried the fish were bundled together in groups of four or five. This amount, when mixed in a stew with vegetables and greens, made a meal for a family of four.

These bundles were stored in baskets hanging high in the branches of the trees to prevent the various wild animals from taking them.

The Clan made good use of the salmon. This was a key source of sustenance for the winter. The Clan thought of themselves as hunters, but fishing provided them with most of the food they consumed throughout the year, and it provided much of the currency for bartering with the other Clans.

The salted fish could be stored for the entire year. This made for a very effective way to build up a food reservoir. They could not have survived most winters without their supply of dried fish.

All these groups were attended to by those distributing water and food.

The fish heads were used by the feeders to make a stew to feed the working groups throughout the day. There was no specific mealtime, instead the stew was available and eaten when one became hungry.

Taelo and Golden Hawk made their way to the stew each time they had brought in three fish.

This was a total Clan event.

Everyone worked together to keep the entire gathering running. Each worked to their level of capability.

3 Herding Salmon

The camp became one huge assembly line. As many as twenty long horizontal drying poles about two feet off the ground covered the smoking area and was the focal point that controlled the speed of the entire gathering.

The drying was continuous and those at night had the added task of keeping the wild animals away.

Taelo and Golden Hawk had in previous seasons worked at delivering the water, at gathering wood and as a smoker. This year they had decided to move up to gathering fish.

They knew they had been accepted on a trial basis and most thought they would drop out once they found how hard the gathering work would be.

In previous years, Taelo and Golden Hawk had observed the spearing technique, and the hand catching technique. They decided that they would hand catch.

Once started, the harvesting of the fish went on from morning until night.

They observed the older gatherers as they caught and carried the large salmon by the gills over to the cleaning area.

They tried this and found it was quite hard on their hands.

After taking in the second fish, Taelo went into his dwelling and came back with an old pair of leather mittens. He gave one mitten to Golden Hawk, and he kept one. The mitten protected their small hands as they carried the fish by the gills.

This idea worked so well that the two of them were bringing in as many fish as the older Clan members.

Several of the adults copied what the two boys had done and soon everyone was using their old gloves or mittens. This was an idea they all liked. Everyone had previously accepted the minor cuts and scrapes as part of the fishing process.

Now they were able to work faster and did not have to worry about getting cut.

Together Taelo and Golden Hawk spent hours wading in the shallows of the river and retrieving the spent salmon.

They took short stints in helping clean, steak, skewer and smoke them. This gave them a break from the strain of the gathering.

Taelo and Golden Hawk were exhausting themselves. Taelo kept asking Golden Hawk if he could think of an easier way to handle the fish. The two constantly talked about finding an easier way to catch and process the salmon.

Golden Hawks snide reply that they should ask the fish to swim over to the cleaning area triggered an idea for Taelo.

Taelo pointed to the fact that the fish were swimming in the stream. Why not get them to swim to a fixed pick-up point.

Golden Hawk said that sounded great but made the point that the fish, even though they were dying still struggled to escape and neither of them knew how to instruct the fish of where they should swim.

Taelo smiled and replied that they would just have to be politer and more persuasive in how they talked to the fish and asked them to go to the pick-up area.

During the next lunch break Taelo jumped up and shouted that he had figured it out. Everyone around the two looked over to see what was going on.

Taelo quietly shared his idea with Golden Hawk.

High in the sky an Eagle let out a scream.

This excited both of them. White Swan and Quiet Pheasant looked at each other and wondered out loud what the two might be up to.

"The fish are swimming in the stream, why don't we guide them with some sticks stuck in the sand to where we want them and then pick them up. This will save us a lot of effort." Taelo suggested to Golden Hawk.

After lunch, the two examined a location where a large shallow pool existed just upstream from the fish processing area. They measured this area by walking the shape they planned to lay out. Then they estimated the number of vertical and horizontal poles it would take to implement their idea. They cut about two hundred straight thin willow sticks.

By this time most members of the Clan noticed the two boys had stopped gathering fish and were industrially cutting and laying out the poles. Though they all kept working at their jobs, everyone had one eye on Taelo and Golden Hawk.

The small river was only about three feet deep at the deepest.

The vertical poles were about four feet long. The boys laid out the vertical poles three inches apart and parallel to each other. They then put the horizontal poles across them and lashed the shorter vertical poles to the horizontal ones.

They built two similarly sized long lengths and two shorter lengths. Finally, they built one short section.

Taelo and Golden Hawk were ready to try out their idea.

By this time everyone was curious as to what the two were building.

White Swan, Grey Fox Running, Quiet Pheasant, and Red Oak came over to where the two were struggling with their unwieldy contraptions and asked how they could help.

Taelo smiled and had them immediately help to put their fish trap into place.

Curiosity was running high as the Clan watched the shorter poles get pushed into the sand at the bottom of the stream.

One half of the guide began on the far side and came across and upstream in a shallow arc. The arc guided the large salmon going upstream toward the camp side of the river. The smaller fish swam right through the guide. A mirror image arc was put on the upstream side to guide the fish going down stream toward the camp side of the river.

The remaining two sections of poles went from the point where the upstream and downstream arcs met and guided the fish into a holding area in which they were trapped.

As the fish swam around, trapped in the pool, a single row of polls guided the next unfortunate fish to a dead-end channel dug in the sand beach. This was the point at which the fish were picked up and taken to the cleaning area.

Even before they had completed their fish trap, the fish began to pile up. It appeared to those watching that the fish were willingly lining up to be lifted out of the water.

Taelo and Golden Hawk exhausted themselves hauling the fish out of their trap.

In short order they had caught and pulled out more fish than the entire Clan. They could not keep up with the rate the fish came into the capture area.

When the older men saw what the boys had accomplished, several of them came over and formed a line to move the fish to the processing area. Soon all the men in the camp were helping pull the fish out of the catch basin.

The processing of the fish took a huge leap in the number of fish ready for smoking. This went on all day without stopping.

As evening approached, Taelo closed the entrance to the pool and opened a way for the fish to go up or down stream.

This was easily accomplished by removing two of the vertical poles at the end of the arc just before the fish had to swim into the catch pool.

That evening the elders sat around the fire discussing what they should do with the number of fish they were capturing. The Clan had never caught so many fish in one day. Everyone knew this new way of taking in the salmon was going to provide an abundance of fish. This was a luxury of food abundance the Clan had not anticipated.

The leaders in the camp reorganized the Clan based on the new volume of fish being caught. More processing and drying were needed.

Fewer catchers were needed but more help was needed in processing the fish and in gathering wood for the fires.

The drying area was expanded.

The next day when the camp was ready for more fish, Taelo and Golden Hawk lowered the poles they had lifted, and the fish began to swim into the pool. Everyone was amazed at the ease of the harvest.

The cleaning area was moved closer to the area of the catch. This greatly reduced the distance to carry the fish.

Everyone ended up doing less work and processing more fish.

The bottle neck now became the drying. More drying racks were set up and soon the Clan had doubled the capacity of their drying process. This meant having to gather more wood.

A number of those catching fish began to gather more wood.

The Clan had a record catch of fish. Never had they been able to capture so many so quickly. They knew they had enough fish to give a bountiful share to all the other sub-Clans and still have abundance for themselves. This would put them in good stead with all the other Clans and that season they could live without the fear of hunger during the coming winter.

Taelo and Golden Hawk had revolutionized the way the Clan caught their salmon. The salmon harvesting went on for some very productive but many fewer weeks.

This year, during the fall gathering, the Elk Horn Clan would have an abundance of salmon to share beyond what they normally would have even in the best times in the memory of the Clan.

They would also tell the story of Taelo and Golden Hawk and how they had devised a new way of harvesting the salmon. This story would be the way the other Clans would learn of this new way of catching fish.

Once again, the two boys had distinguished themselves!

The fact the two boys were making such a huge difference to the well-being of the Clan at such a young age did not go unnoticed by the elders.

Taelo and Golden Hawk enjoyed their notoriety, but they found it hard to accept that they had done anything so unusual.

3 Herding Salmon

4 Flying with Lions

Taelo and Golden Hawk continued their fearless wandering on the challenging snow-capped rocky mountains. The chain of sky-high snowcapped mountains ran parallel to the wide area that the Clan wandered as they hunted the elk, buffalo, and other game.

They appeared to be nearby but the distances to their base was measured in multiple sun rises. The many valleys, small rivers, cliffs, and foothills created an environment that pulled the two into a world of adventure and discovery.

The two wandered the rivers, valleys, and the foothills around them.

Each day they returned with enough small game to keep the family fed or to trade with their favorite storyteller the Weaver.

He broadened his stories and used them to teach the survival skills, the hunting lore, and the more esoteric concepts of dealing with other people.

The Weaver tapped all his friends and Clan members for their knowledge, so he could be ready for the questions Taelo and Golden Hawk would ask.

He became their teacher.

White Swan and Quiet Pheasant had worriedly watched their boys grow and develop for ten seasons.

They had no other children.

Like all mothers, the two constantly thought about the dangerous predators traveling the same areas as their two sons. They knew trying to limit the boys would only cause them to sneak out and take more chances.

The two prevailed on Grey Fox Running and Red Oak to teach the two young boys how to defend themselves.

Red Oak made the two boys some fixed hunting spears and some throwing spears with the same type of stone heads the men carried.

He spent a great deal of time with the flint smith to fashion some smaller but just as deadly spear heads to fit the smaller spears he was making for the two boys.

Meanwhile, every night he had the boys target practiced using spears with simple points made by burning a straight stick end in the fire.

This gave the boys a chance to gain throwing experience without losing valuable flint heads. They soon were hitting the target at every throw.

Then Red Oak tied a bundle of grass to a rope and hung it in a tree. Now he began teaching the boys how to hit a moving target. This was a challenge both boys took to eagerly. Soon they were as adept at hitting their swinging target as the fixed one.

Finally, Grey Fox Running and Red Oak taught them how to use the hunting spears to protect themselves from an aggressive attacker.

This last lesson was not about throwing but on how to use a spear to ward off an attacking animal. How to always keep the animal at a distance and to back away to keep the advantage the spear provided.

The sling was a weapon the two fathers had decided to teach the boys. Grey Fox Running made a set of slings the right size for the two.

Then he and Red Oak set out to teach the boys throwing accuracy and power. They took the boys out to hunt rabbits with their slings. This was a very useful way to learn how to hit a moving object.

In just a few months the boys were almost as good as their fathers.

The boys took to the use of the spear and the sling with an eagerness and natural ability that surprised both fathers.

They would go out in the morning and by the end of the day they would come back loaded with small game.

Their skill with the sling continued to improve.

The training for the two came just in time.

One morning, Taelo let his mother know that he and Golden Hawk were going to the cliffs rising high on the other side of the valley.

He let her know they were going to see if there were any interesting caves and if they could find some crystal and other valuable stones. The jaunt the boys were planning was a long way but was not unusual.

Both mothers urged them to be careful and to come back before dark.

Taelo showed her his spear, his flint knife, sling, and his bag of stones and reassured her that they would be back before sundown.

Taelo and Golden Hawk set out at a steady but rapid jog that most of the others their age would have found too fast but for them it was comfortable.

Taelo took in the cliffs rising several hundred feet into the air and extending for miles in a north and south direction.

Their jog quickly closed the distance and soon they were close to the foot of the cliff.

As they approached, they spotted a young mountain goat and began to follow it upward along the cliff.

The base of the cliff had a skirt of fallen boulders and smaller stones formed when the winter freeze expanded the trapped water and crack the stones that then fell to add to the growing skirt.

The goat led the boys up the face of the cliff along an almost invisible trail. With an expertise that would have impressed most of the hunters in the Clan, Taelo and Golden Hawk carefully trailed behind the goat. They kept it in sight but managed not to spook the shy animal.

Golden Hawk commented that the goat seemed to be following an invisible trail. They were able to find the footholds and continued to follow.

Neither had any thought of killing the goat. It was just their guide and a teacher of goat movement. The sun slowly traveled across the clear blue sky, and the morning approached its zenith.

Taelo made a quiet comment to Golden Hawk wondering where they would end up by following the goat.

Back across the valley, a mother's premonition burrowed into White Swan. During the previous night she had dreamed of a mountain lion chasing the two boys. The dream had bothered her, but she had dismissed it. As the sun reached its daytime zenith, she could no longer ignore her intuition. She stopped what she was doing and talked to Quiet Pheasant.

The sight of a white swan flying overhead moved White Swan into immediate action. She told Quiet Pheasant to pick up her spear and join her in finding Taelo and Golden Hawk.

Quiet Pheasant did not ask why or what was up but took up her spear, hiking bag and joined White Swan and together they set out at a fast jog toward the distant cliffs. She too had seen the white swan as it flew quietly by.

White Swan was glad the boys had told her where they were going. The two often set out with no particular direction in mind.

Golden Hawk was in the lead as they followed the mountain goat along its meandering upward route. They watched what the goat ate and they themselves would try some of the leaves or berries the goat had eaten. Soon they were able to let the goat get out of sight and then find it by trailing it by the bitten leaves and broken small branches of various bushes or by the grass which had been cropped.

Even the best Clan trackers would have been impressed!

At one point, the trail along the face of the cliff went outward and Taelo was able to look back along the trail he and Golden Hawk had just traversed.

The two were about one hundred feet up the face of the cliff on a narrow ledge just wide enough for the goat to walk along. The footing or lack thereof made it a challenge for the two of them.

High overhead a large eagle soared. She was watching the scene below.

She let out her piercing scream!

Taelo stopped to look up to the sky and then he again looked back along the way he had just come.

What he saw froze him in his tracks!!!

Behind them coming up the trail was a large mountain lion. The lion had not yet spotted the two boys, but it was clearly following the same trail.

Taelo's adrenaline immediately kicked in. They were in great danger. Quietly he tapped Golden Hawk on the shoulder and pointed to the lion. They were between the lion and the lion's favorite meal. This made them meals as well.

Taelo and Golden Hawk instinctively began to look for a place where they could defend themselves. As they watched the goat, they saw it turn and instantly disappear.

They quickly followed to that point on the path. Here the path made a sharp ninety degree turn back to the left around a point of rock.

This Taelo decided would be the place to make their stand.

He looked at Golden Hawk and told him that they would have to stand and fight the lion as it came around the bend.

The path was only wide enough for one.

Taelo told Golden Hawk that he would run full speed and spear the lion in the heart and try to push if over the edge to its death on the rocks below.

Golden Hawk knew they were in great trouble. He nodded in agreement and told Taelo that he would be behind and to make sure to leave enough room for he and his spear.

Both knew they were in great trouble. The lion was larger than the two put together.

The Clan never hunted the lion or any of its kin. They had no need, and it was just too dangerous.

Taelo prepared himself to rush the lion and to drive his spear into it as it turned the corner.

"Why should you be the one that faces the lion by yourself," Golden Hawk asked in a concerned voice?

"Because I am the closest one and there is only room for one," Taelo replied since there was no other reason.

Taelo knew that his only hope would be to surprise the lion and push it off the path with his spear.

Golden Hawk put his hand on Taelo's shoulder and asked the ancestors for their help and then stepped back.

Taelo prepared himself to attack.

Surprise, speed, and the chance he would catch the lion off guard was his only hope. He also hoped he was strong enough to push the lion off the cliff. He intended to hit the lion with all the speed and weight he could muster.

He took several deep, slow breaths.

Taelo heard the call of the eagle.

He knew this was a test and he was being watched.

Golden Hawk also heard the eagle and knew instinctively this was Taelo's moment.

White Swan heard the scream of the eagle. This both reassured her and frightened her.

Taelo's totem was near and calling.

Something significant was going to happen!!

But what was the challenge Taelo and Golden Hawk were facing?

She and Quiet Pheasant began running full speed toward the cliffs ahead. They now had the mystical power and strength only worried mothers possess.

The tension was high both on the cliff and with the two mothers who were now running at full speed.

They were now sure the boys were in danger!

Their adrenaline was giving them the boost that would have carried them into first place in any race.

In their motherly hearts, there was no fear for themselves.

The lioness already on the alert because of the smell of human, sensed something wrong as it turned the corner.

It did not expect to see the small figure rush at it with a spear. The sharp spear tip cut through the hide and drove into the lion's rib cage going between the ribs and proceeded toward its heart. The spear found its target and scored immediate success.

The lioness was dead even as she reacted.

Taelo had used all his quickness to rush forward and drive his spear into the lion. However, he was now within reach of the mighty lioness. She reached out with one claw and grabbed him by the shoulder and pulled him toward her. Taelo pushed with all his might, but it did not seem the lion was going to budge.

Then the eagle came hurdling down and caught the lion by the snout and pulled the beast out away from the cliff!!!

Instead of pulling back when the lion's huge paw clutched him, Taelo lunged in with all his might and drove the spear in as far as he could.

The lion reared up as the eagle pulled on his snout.

The force Taelo was exerting was enough to send all three off the edge of the cliff.

The eagle let go of the lion. It spread it large wings and regained its flight.

It rose upward and let out another piercing scream!!

Instinctively it knew it was done and was already departing down the valley.

As the lioness left the trail and began the quiet, almost floating descend off the cliff, her reflex pulled Taelo to her chest. Already, her life had left. The two hit the rocks some fifty feet below.

Golden Hawk was stunned by the swiftness of the events and Taelo's fall off the cliff.

He was in a state of panic!!~!~!

He watched in horror as Taelo, the lion and the eagle left the cliff and fell to the rocks below. To him it appeared the lion had hugged Taelo to its chest and protected him from the fall.

But Taelo was not answering his call!!!

Golden Hawk began a frantic descend to the rocks below.

Golden Hawk took daring leaps and jumps in his descent toward his cousin down in the rocks.

He risked everything to get down to Taelo.

He was in fear of losing his other self.

White Swan and Quiet Pheasant were now almost to the cliffs. They had heard the eagle scream. They had witnessed its dive for the cliffs and then had seen it rise and fly away.

Both were now in a state of panic.

What had happened?

Were the two boys alright?

What did all this mean?

The eagle was gone. It had left, and this was a point of confusion and concern.

Were the boys alright?

"I am not sure I can take it much longer," White Swan said between taking long breaths.

Quiet Pheasant only nodded her response and continued running at full speed.

To Taelo the descent was in ultra-slow motion. He looked back and saw Golden Hawk's surprised look.

He looked into the pale-yellow eyes of the eagle. He thanked it for its help as they all went over the edge.

The eagle seemed to blink at him and then let go of the lioness's nostril.

He had felt the claws of the lioness flex and pull him toward her chest.

The impact on the rocks knocked the wind out of Taelo but the lioness below him provided the cushion keeping him from harm.

He lay quietly taking stock of himself. Everything seemed fine. He relived the last few moments and realized he had just lived through a miracle.

His totem had helped him, the lioness had held him to her chest, and the landing had only knocked his breath away.

Suddenly he heard Golden Hawk calling his name and he slowly sat up.

Golden Hawk descended the cliff and across the rocks as if he were flying.

Taelo watched in amazement as Golden Hawk took his last giant leap to where he and the lioness had fallen.

"I didn't know you knew how to fly. How did you get down so fast," Taelo asked as Golden Hawk arrived in a breathless state and sat at his side?

"Unbelievable, you are alive, are you OK," Golden Hawk asked as he sat breathlessly down beside Taelo.

"You talk about me flying but you actually do it and don't even get a scratch."

They were both sitting on the chest of the lioness.

"I am fine. A little surprised at how this all turned out. I am not sure how we are going to explain the dead lioness," Taelo said as he examined his kill.

Just then the two looked down the slope of rocks and saw their mothers and heard their shouts. This surprised both of them.

"How did they get here?

What made them come out this way?

What are we going to tell them," Golden Hawk rapidly inquired?

"Let's not tell them about my flight down with the lioness. Let's just keep it to killing her," Taelo said quietly to Golden Hawk.

White Swan and Quiet Pheasant stopped in their tracks as they reached the spot where Taelo and Golden Hawk sat on the chest of the lioness.

They saw the spear driven into the lioness. The animal was magnificent. It was in its prime. It was at least eight feet long and more than three feet high at shoulders. The animal must have weighted five hundred pounds.

The two boys sat looking calmly at their mothers.

"We see the lioness, we heard the eagle, and we see the spear. Tell us you were not out hunting for her," White Swan said quietly as she tried to make sense out of the situation.

She was so happy to see the two that she was not really concerned about what their intensions had been.

Taelo slowly and carefully explained how they were trapped between the lioness and a mountain goat.

He pointed up to the trail along the cliff and explained the situation and how the eagle had helped him as he attacked the lioness.

He purposely omitted the detail about falling with the lioness, but he credited the eagle with helping him push the lioness off the cliff.

After a few awkward moments and the two mothers just standing and taking in the situation, Quiet Pheasant spoke up.

"We will need to get help to carry this lioness back to the camp.

White Swan and I will stay here.

You two run and get enough of the young men and women to help.

Make sure they bring strong enough poles," Quiet Pheasant instructed the two.

She had never seen a lioness this large and in full prime.

Taelo and Golden Hawk were glad to get away without more questioning. They quickly set off on a fast jog to get the needed help. This also gave them a chance to talk about how to tell their story and leave out the part about falling off the cliff.

They did not want to be restricted in their activities.

"Let's go over the story another time," Taelo commented to Golden Hawk as they made their way to the camp.

"Don't worry, I have it memorized. You did all the talking so at least we have only one story," Golden Hawk replied.

"The story they just told us is too simple. I know Taelo well enough to know he is leaving something out, but I can't quite decide what it is.

How do two boys kill a lioness at least eight times bigger than they are," White Swan said as she walked among the rocks trying to read the signs?

The signs she was trying to read did not exist. She soon realized this and looked up at the trail along the cliff.

"I agree with you. Did you notice Taelo did all the talking and Golden Hawk only spoke after the whole story had been told? Should we press and find out what else happened," Quiet Pheasant replied as she too could find no indication of what had happened?

"No, let's accept the miracle for what it is, a sign the two are protected and have capabilities well beyond their years. Someday, I am sure they will tell us the rest of the story," White Cloud said as she once again looked up to the trail the boys had been on.

A small goat stood on the trail looking down at her.

How had they gotten down here so quickly?

She knew they could not fly. Or could they fly with lions?

The camp came to life as the news spread about the lion. A group of eager young men and women went out to bring it into the camp. It was late evening when the lioness was brought in. Most of the camp turned out to look at the huge beast.

"You will have to tell me the real story the next time you stop for breakfast," the Weaver smiled at Taelo and Golden Hawk after the first explanation had been shared with the camp.

The older men who no longer could hunt came out to examine the lioness. They were surprised at the size and great condition of the animal. This was a prime specimen. It would have given a team of hunters a full battle. The fact two young boys had brought the animal down was astounding.

They looked at Taelo and Golden Hawk with new respect and appreciation. The elder's prediction that the two were meant for greatness in the future was indeed coming true.

The women gathered round and skinned the lioness.

They all commented to White Swan and Quiet Pheasant on how brave Taelo and Golden Hawk were and wondered how the two could let them go hunting at such a young age.

Both White Swan and Quiet Pheasant kept quiet. There was no way to answer such a question. Of course, they worried but they could not keep the boys from going out into the woods.

Taelo offered the skull to the medicine man. The claws were extracted and saved to make jewelry and decorations. The hide would be used by their mothers to make formal clothes for them.

In the evening around the central campfire, Taelo once again told the story of tracking the goat along the cliff side. He told of the call of the eagle and then realizing that he and Golden Hawk were themselves being tracked by the lioness. He elaborated on the part of the lion coming around the bend and how he and the eagle had worked together to catch the lioness off balance.

Many questions were asked but Taelo did not reveal he had fallen down the cliff with the lioness.

He did tell of the help from his totem, the eagle and of driving his spear into the lioness and then pushing as hard as he could to get her to go over the edge of the cliff.

He thanked the flint smith for giving his spear a sharp edge and Red Oak and his father for having taught him how to use the spear.

Taelo and Golden Hawk enjoyed the notoriety that followed but were soon looking for their next adventure.

4 Flying with Lions

5 The Clan

*T*he Clan gathering was one of Taelo's and Golden Hawk's favorite times.

Their fathers and the Weaver had all told them stories about the Clan history. His father's stories went back to a time before the Clan met in this valley.

A time before the Clan became so large that it had split into sub-Clans.

At that time, they lived in a valley with a giant waterfall. It was the first home of the Elk Clan after they had crossed the ice bridge from another land.

The onset of continuous cold winter weather drove the Clan leaders to move south.

It was at that time they first chose to split the Clan, so each sub-Clan could have their own hunting territory.

That was long ago. Now there were five sub-Clans formed from the Elk Clan.

Taelo and Golden Hawk were in the Elk Horn Clan. It was the first sub-clan.

5 The Clan

The Grazing Elk, the Shy Elk, the Swift Elk, and the Elk Hide Clan each had been formed as the clan grew through the years.

From the Weaver they learned that the Clan meeting gave the leaders a chance to balance the prosperity and the balance of the overall Clan population. If the Clans were getting too large for the area where they lived the leaders would either rebalance the Clans or periodically, they would add another Clan.

The stories of the Weaver showed the two that the Clan leaders used the gathering to ensure all the sub-Clans were prepared for and able to survive the coming winter.

The naming ceremony was always held during the gathering. Taelo often dreamt of his naming day. The day he chose the Eagle, and the Eagle chose him.

White Swan credited the gathering as a time for finding and then choosing a mate. It was a time for new romances to begin. Normally a mate always came from another Clan. In this way the Clan's make-up, strength and survivability were enhanced.

The people were of one kindred and looked forward each year to renew old friendships. This was a time to recount adventures and often to honor those lost to unfortunate accidents or hunting injuries. The histories of the elders were recalled and celebrated. It was a time of bonding and rekindling of old friendships.

The gathering place was a luxurious valley through which a small, lazy stream meandered and in one location broadened to form a small lake. The small lake boasted a few mallards and northern geese and for those energetic enough to throw their nets or go spear fishing it easily yielded a variety of fish.

It was guarded on the far side by tall dark green pine trees separating the dark greenish blue water from the light blue sky that reached well beyond the valley like a blanket to embrace the far snow peaked mountains.

This was a valley Taelo, and Golden Hawk knew like the back of their hands. There was not a spot or point in the valley the two did not know by heart. They had explored every nook and cranny as they embraced and acted out the adventures their minds created.

For the last several years the Elk Horn Clan had out produced all the other Clans by a significant amount.

They had generously shared food supplies with the other sub-Clans. This year the Elk Horn Clan was loaded with an over-abundance of dried fish, elk, rabbit, moose, and other food stuffs. Their supply of leather goods, baskets, general utensils, woven cloth, various tools, fishhooks, stone ax heads, and clothing made them the most prosperous members of the Clan. This abundance had so loaded them down to the point that they were the last to arrive at the meeting valley.

They stopped at the top of the hill to look out across the valley.

Below them the early morning air was still and the light wispy campfire parallel plumes of smoke from each family lodge rose like slowly undulating white worms straight into the still morning air and danced in what seemed an orchestrated performance.

The sun, rising over the far horizon seemed to give them life as they changed colors of pinks and yellows and mixed with grey.

It was a scene that caused the Elk Horn Clan to stop and appreciate the beauty of the scene that greeted them.

The grouping of campfires indicated all the other sub-Clans but theirs had already arrived and set up camp. The Elk Horn Clan would have to take the place farthest away from the river and up along the hillside.

Elk Horn Clan leader, Wise Owl, stood overlooking the valley below. The abundant wealth they were bringing to this gathering had greatly slowed them down. Now he stood contemplating what he should have his sub-Clan do.

There were no good camping spots left.

Taelo stood between his father, Grey Fox Running on his left and his mother, White Swan on his right. They were a close-knit family and Taelo felt a great love and affection toward both. He was now twelve seasons old and was beginning to grow.

He was seldom disciplined, not because his parents were lax but because Taelo was attuned to the requirements of their rigorous, demanding life.

It did not escape him how hard all the elders worked to gather food and to make the clothes and equipment needed to sustain the Clan.

He and Golden Hawk often talked about this and had decided to make a purposeful effort to contribute their share.

Grey Fox Running commented that because they were late, they would be camped farthest from the lake.

We will be the sub-Clan with the most wealth, but we will be doing the most work was Wise Owl's response.

He was not looking forward to having his camp out on the fringe of the valley.

Taelo let his eyes move slowly across the valley as he listened to the adults. His eyes traveled to the flat clearing on the other side of the river opposite the camp on the far side of the lake.

He, Golden Hawk, and their friends had often played on the far side of the lake.

They had wondered why none of the Clans ever chose to camp there.

Now Taelo spoke up and suggested the Elk Hide Clan camp on the other side of the lake.

Wise Owl pointed out that if they camped on the other side, they would have a long walk to get to where everyone else was camped and there would be the problem of crossing the river.

"Yes, but if we camp on the hillsides on this side of the river, we will need to carry our water from the river through the various camps. And you will need to walk just as far to go to all the activities. I think the hill side will be more work for the entire Elk Hide Clan," Taelo replied.

He and Golden Hawk would be two of the boys carrying water all the time.

Taelo pointed to the rapids just upstream of the lake and said that they could move a few large stones into place and create a walk across the rapids. The Clan could have a comfortable and easy to maintain location and the distance to the other Clans would be the same.

Wise Owl, Grey Fox Running, and Red Oak all looked at each other. It was rare for Taelo to talk so openly when the adults were talking. This made them pay attention.

He immediately liked the idea and already had visions of his sub-Clan marching grandly through the camps.

"It sounds like this may be a good idea. Before we commit to it lets send a team ahead. If they can get the stones in place and provide a solid crossing, they can light a fire on the other side and our Clan can come down the valley, through all the other Clan groups and cross the river. It would be a grand way to show our good standing this year," Wise Owl said with a twinkle in his eye and a new spirit in his voice.

He looked at Taelo and Golden Hawk and put them in charge of getting a bridge across the river and sending a signal when they had successfully done so.

He assigned four older and stronger young men to provide the muscle for the work and instructed them to travel around the camp on the ridge and do the work without being seen.

Wise Owl really wanted this idea to work.

Taelo and Golden Hawk looked at each other. They were to be in charge. They were both excited to have been assigned leadership roles for this venture.

This was a new experience!

Taelo immediately sensed some resistance from the older boys. They jogged along the ridge as they went around the rim of the valley. All six carried backpacks with various items needed to prepare a place for the Elk Horn Clan to cross.

Taelo and Golden Hawk set a fast pace keeping all of them from talking too much. They arrived undetected at the rapids a short time later. They were far enough upstream that they did not draw the attention of the nearest Clan group. The six of them studied the rapids.

Taelo used this period to get the opinions of the other four.

His approach was to get them to propose how the work could be done and then to let them go do it.

Leading to him did not mean controlling every action.

Golden Hawk shared the same feeling, so it was obvious to him what Taelo was doing by getting the other four to define the work.

Then it was as Taelo wanted, nothing was said, and the work proceeded. Taelo only commented when subtle adjustments needed to be made.

Taelo and the rest discussed how they could create a bridge across the gap. They decided to cut some small trees and make a walk to span the middle of the rapids. The remaining areas could be improved by moving stones to strategic positions.

They found a series of stones providing an almost continuous path across. Only in the middle was there a large gap.

The plans were made for the middle span. Taelo and Golden Hawk undertook the job of finding the main beams for the bridge while the older and stronger members moved the large river stones into place.

This arrangement had been reached among all of them in what seemed to be an open discussion, though Taelo had quietly guided it to achieve the outcome he desired.

Even at this young age Taelo already had the leadership skills needed to influence and guide the older boys.

Golden Hawk and Taelo found the trees they needed and after cutting them down began to prepare the bridge.

They used three small tree trunks for the bottom walk of the bridge and then lashed smaller willow branches across the three tree trunks. This made a strong three, foot wide section.

The four older members of the team carried and positioned the bridge across the center span of the rapids. Then a low railing was added to provide stability for those walking across.

When all was done, the group made the journey to the far side of the river. They collected enough wood for a good fire and cut some green limbs with leaves on them to make the smoke.

Once all was ready, they lit their signal fire and put some green wood and leaves to make a white smoke that could easily be seen.

The sun was now directly above them.

Wise Owl and the rest of the Elk Horn Clan had waited until the sun was at its zenith before starting down into the valley. If their young men were successful, they would proceed through the valley and across the river. Meanwhile, however, thcy would proceed toward the rest of the Clan and keep an eye out for the signal fire.

All the Elk Horn Clan members were now aware of the game they were playing. When the white smoke was spotted a small cheer went through the group.

It had been a very good year for them, and they wanted to show off a little and they did not want to do extra work because they were coming with generous gifts.

5 The Clan

There was always some competition going on between the various sub-Clans. They prized the chance to show off. Camping on the other side seemed like a great idea.

This walk through the camps would be a moment all the Elk Horn members would relish. They had changed into their best dress and had put some of their best work on display. All added a light swagger to their walk. Today they would show off their good fortune.

Silent Hawk watched as the Elk Horn Clan walked into the camp. It was clear to all the Elk Horn Clan had done very well. They were all healthy and were loaded down with their supplies and goods. It was good to see one of the Clans had done so well.

The rest of the Clan would seek to learn the secret of how this had been accomplished. Silent Hawk, eldest Clan leader and leader of the main Elk Clan, felt some pride for he had helped get the Elk Hide Clan started.

Several of his personal friends had gone with this sub clan.

The current leader, Wise Owl, was one of his best and brightest pupils who Silent Hawk had supported in getting the leaders role.

The lead hunter, Grey Fox Running, was the son of one of his best friends.

Silent Hawk felt a strong connection with this sub clan.

There was cheer and good tidings being shared but the Elk Horn Clan continued to move steadily toward the river. Several of the other Clan members kept telling them there was no room to set up camp in the direction of the lake.

But the Elk Horn Clan members paid no attention.

To everyone's surprise the Elk Horn Clan proceeded to the bank of the river and turned upstream and continued their march. There was a sudden puzzled hush in the main camp area.

It was then Silent Hawk saw the span of bridge across the center of the rapids.

When had the Elk Horn Clan built the bridge?

Now, he understood the smug look Wise Owl had when they greeted each other.

The Elk Horn Clan was showing off. They would have a place on the riverbank and a way across the river.

Silent Hawk let out a chuckle. It was good to see such spirit.

His pupil Wise Owl had become an exceptional leader. He would be someone to watch.

The Elk Horn Clan continued their march to set up their camp across the river from the rest of the other sub-clans. The crossing and the bridge set up by Taelo's and Golden Hawk's team worked perfectly.

The room they had available was more than they would have had if they had stayed on the other side of the river.

5 The Clan

The Elk Horn Clan was late and had been awaited, for several days.

The leaders from each of the other sub-clans came across the river and congratulated the Elk Horn Clan for being so ingenious. There were the general greetings among old friends but also the official ones. They shared the planned schedule of leadership meetings to take place starting the following day.

Without exception the leaders of the other clans all eyed the goods the Elk Horn Clan had on display. It was clear to all that this sub clan had exceeded all of them in the past year.

It was the custom of the Elk Clan to gather and have the elders meet to discuss the appropriate division of the surplus food, goods and even families. They were careful not to strip too much away from any successful group. There was sharing, but each sub clan was expected to feed their own.

This balancing allowed for the unforeseen accident of a key hunter. It allowed for a bad season in a specific part of the Clan's domain. It was also used to recognize the contributors and to encourage the less fortunate to try harder. If the same clan came up short more than once, the elders discussed the potential for a leadership change or the addition of a key hunter to the ailing clan.

This year the main Elk Clan was suffering from the loss of several key hunters. In the previous year, the establishment of the Elk Hide Clan had left the main Elk Clan weaker than desired.

However, at that time they thought they would be able to make do. They had been heavily loaded with older members but expected these members to still be productive. Events had not unfolded as had been expected. It seemed everything that could have gone wrong did go wrong.

Their main hunting party had been out running down a deer when they surprised a woolly rhino. The rhino reacted by attacking the group. Two members were gored, and the rhino broke the leg of a third before the brave hunters brought it down.

The lead hunter died from the goring he received as he defended the first injured hunter. Before dying he requested his funeral fire be out on the grassy plain where he died.

The other hunters had struggled to return to the main camp and those injured were still recovering.

Having three key hunters put out of commission was beyond what the Elk Clan could manage. The remaining older hunters had tried to help but had done poorly. The Elk Clan was living hand to mouth, hunt to hunt. Winter was close at hand, and the Elk Clan had no reserves of food.

Silent Hawk felt his age and felt the pressure of the dismal condition of the Elk Clan. The Elk Clan was at risk of not being able to survive the coming winter.

The hunter that died was to have been elevated to be the Elk leader at this gathering.

Silver Hawk would seek the counseling and help of Wise Owl.

6 The Meeting

*T*he composite Clan leadership was made up of three representatives from each of the sub clans.

One member was the overall leader.

Each sub clan was independent except for changes and agreements made during the meeting each autumn that won a majority of the vote.

Currently with six sub-clans there were eighteen representatives. The overall leader had one vote if there was a tie.

A talking staff controlled the flow of presentations and discussion. The speaker from each Clan stood in the center of the gathering and reported the condition of their Clan and identified any issues that needed to be addressed by the entire Clan leadership.

Silent Hawk, Leader of the Elk Clan, was the senior member and overall leader of the overall leadership team. He sat at the northern position on the circle.

In reverse order of their establishment, the Grazing Elk, the Shy Elk, the Swift Elk, the Elk Hide, and the Elk Horn Clan each reported on the events of the past year.

Wise Owl elaborated on the wealth the Elk Horn Clan had available to share with the all the rest. He reported on a new way of trapping fish that had led to this abundance. It was clear to all that the Elk Horn Clan had prospered and had out done the all the other clans.

Most sub-Clans would face the winter in a challenging but acceptable condition. The help that the Elk Horn Clan offered appeared to be the margin that would allow all of them to return in good stead the following year.

The sun was reaching its zenith by the time Silent Hawk stood to take his place in the center of the circle and report on the condition of the parent Elk Clan.

He shared the story of losing his main hunter and next in line for the Elk Clan leadership. He continued with the fact that the injured Elk Clan hunters were still in recovery. He painted a bleak picture of the condition of the main Elk Clan.

Silent Hawk admitted that the Elk Clan needed very specific and dramatic help. It needed a lead hunter and at least one additional experienced hunter. It needed a lot of food. He was sure it was more food than he thought the Elk Horn Clan would be able to share.

He let the other Clans know that the Elk Clan had nothing to pay with for this help that he was asking for.

He made the point that the Elk Clan was requesting all the help the other clans could extend.

Even as he made his request, he knew he was sharing only the minimum amount of information. It was even worse than he was reporting.

It was hard for him to stand before this group and show them that he had failed. He had no choice. He swallowed his pride to make the request and hoped the other sub clans would help in some way.

Having heard the condition of the other Clans, he knew most were not in position to give much help and he did not have much hope. The Elk Clan would have to look out for themselves. It would be a miracle if the Elk Clan could get the type of help it needed.

All the sub clans had been heard from and now it was time to see how they could help each other.

Silent Hawk's report and request had put a chill in the proceedings of the meeting.

One after another, the leaders of the various sub-clans made their excuse for not providing the manpower requested by the Elk Clan. Each did offer some small amount of food or some materials to help but backed away from giving up any key members. They had fared only a little better and were not able to give up any hunters nor could they provide much food.

Wise Owl listened and knew he would make an offer that would help. He had the resources and the reserves that would make the difference.

Wise Owl remembered how Silent Hawk had supported him in establishing the Elk Horn sub-clan. Silent Hawk had made sure the sub-clan had the necessary manpower to be successful. Wise Owl now watched as Silent Hawk sat stoically and listened to each subsequent sub-Clan reject the original Elk Clan's request for help.

It was hard for Wise Owl to watch his mentor in such distress. Silent Hawk was too good of a person and the main Clan too important to let it suffer a potentially hard winter without food.

Wise Owl concluded he could and would provide the support needed.

Finally, it was his turn.

Wise Owl stood to make his proposal for support.

"The Elk Horn Clan has had a very good year. We will generously share food, and we offer Gray Fox Running to take the position of lead hunter."

A hush fell across the circle of leaders. Everyone knew Gray Fox Running was the lead hunter in the Elk Horn Clan and next in line to become a Clan leader. He was in fact thought of as one of the best hunters in the whole of all the Clans.

Wise Owl continued, "He is my best hunter and leader. He has ambitions of being a Clan leader. The offer is to have his family join the Elk Clan and next year upon his successful contributions to your well-being, you Silent Hawk shall become an elder and let him lead."

The conditions of the offer surprised everyone.

Wise Owl was offering one of the best but stipulating a very tough condition in effect putting Silent Hawk to pasture. It was almost an insult, but all knew Wise Owl was a supporter of Silent Hawk.

What was at foot?

What was Wise Owl up to?

Wise Owl was trying to help Gray Fox Running achieve his own personal goal of becoming a Clan leader. Grey Fox Running would not be able to move into a leadership position for many years to come in his current position. This situation offered the opportunity, and Wise Owl saw a way to help two people at the same time.

Everyone in the meeting was quiet.

Gray Fox Running was known to all of them. His skill and ability to provide was known throughout the Clan. All the other Clans were amazed Wise Owl would offer him up.

Would Silent Hawk agree to such a condition?

Wise Owl figured the leaders around the fire thought him a little daft. However, Gray Fox Running and Red Oak were such good trainers, Wise Owl was confident even his youngest hunters could provide enough food to take them through the coming winter.

The Elk Horn Clan currently had enough food to take them through the hardest of winters without the need of any additional hunting. It was a small risk on his part and a way to solve two problems.

This was the only way he knew Gray Fox Running could quickly become a clan leader.

He also sensed his good friend Silent Hawk was about ready to step aside.

Silent Hawk thought about the offer. He knew it was a very good offer. He was tired. It would be a relief from the constant worry of ensuring the success of the Elk Clan.

When he stepped down from being the Elk Clan leader, Wise Owl would become a senior Clan leader and leader of the overall Clan assembly.

He would have the North seat.

He, Silent Hawk would become a junior elder. Still on the council but not its leader. He marveled at his protégé's cleverness as well as his generosity.

He understood and accepted the situation!!!.

Wise Owl was indeed true to his name, and he was truly generous in his offer.

It was a little hard for Silent Hawk to initially accept but he knew it was the thing to do.

"My friend, thank you for such a generous offer. I will certainly accept Gray Fox Running and the condition you stipulate," he replied in a strong, quiet voice.

There were tears of relief and hope in his eyes as he sat quietly down.

He hoped this would be enough. He had not told the whole story of just how desperate the Elk Clan was.

Later in the day, Wise Owl presented the opportunity to Gray Fox Running. The Elk Clan wished him to become the lead hunter. In the following season he would most likely ascend to be the leader of the Elk Clan.

"Think about this. It accelerates your rise to Clan Leader. Discuss it with White Swan and let me know tomorrow morning of your decision," Wise Owl said as the two approached the river.

He knew Gray Fox Running would accept the position. It was not an opportunity to be turned down.

Normally this would have been a great honor, immediately seized upon. However, Gray Fox Running was alarmed at the condition of the Elk Clan. Even if all the food was to be split up evenly, there would not be enough to carry the Elk Clan through even a mild winter.

If the coming winter were a hard one, many members of the Elk Clan would be lost.

He was honored for himself and bothered and fearful for the well-being of his own family. He indeed would need to talk this out with White Swan. He needed her consul, her support and most importantly he knew she would provide her observations from a very different perspective.

She had been his teacher in the way he now hunted.

He discussed this with White Swan long into the night. White Swan and Grey Fox Running, both knew he would accept the offer.

Taelo listened in, even though they thought him asleep. He was immediately alert to every word being spoken. He wanted to speak up, but he knew better.

Then his mother spoke the words he was thinking.

White Swan made a suggestion that seemed to pop into her mind from nowhere.

"You must become the Clan leader immediately and you must bring Red Oak with you as the lead hunter. Only then will you have the influence and power to save the Elk Clan.

She suggested that Silent Hawk become an elder now.

The injured hunters should come over to the Elk Horn Clan. This would immediately lighten the load of the Elk Clan," White Swan said confidently.

She was as surprised at the suggestion she was making and could see from the look on Grey Fox Running's face that he was too. White Swan continued to share her thinking and plan.

She recognized the danger of the situation of moving into the Elk Clan and like all mothers and wives, her protective instincts guided her thinking.

She was determined to ensure her family did not suffer from this situation.

White Swan was also thinking of the bond shared between Golden Hawk and their son Taelo. She wanted to ensure that bond remained intact and the only way to do that led to her suggestion.

Wide awake, Taelo listened to his parents discuss the situation late into the night. He did not remember falling asleep. However, the next morning he was immediately out and talking to Golden Hawk and sharing the situation as he understood it.

The two watched as Red Oak and Gray Fox Running went for a walk together. They quietly followed the two to a large boulder and hid behind it where they could overhear their two fathers talk.

"White Swan and I have talked all night. I have been offered to the Elk Clan as a lead hunter. Next year I will become the Elk Clan leader," Gray Fox Running began.

A feeling of loss and despair passed through Red Oak as he congratulated his best friend.

"There is more, the Elk Clan is in a very distressful situation. I believe it will take more than just me to save the Clan from devastation this coming winter.

I would like you to go with me," Gray Fox Running said as he watched the expression on his friend's face.

"I would be honored to go with you my old friend. However, will Wise Owl let this happen," Red Oak replied?

"He will certainly not be pleased but I believe he will. He knows the Elk Clan needs this help.

Silent Hawk is his mentor and dear friend. I will talk first with Silent Hawk and then with Wise Owl. I will ask Silent Hawk to send all the wounded hunters and their families to the Elk Horn Clan. The Elk Horn Clan has enough food. Additional hunting will not be needed until spring. By then the injured hunters will have healed. In this way the Elk Horn Clan will have a strong hunting group this coming spring," Grey Fox Running continued.

Taelo and Golden Hawk quietly left their hiding place and went out to roam the valley. They were excited about the new adventure they were about to embark on. Both were ecstatic they would remain together.

"There goes the other reason I am asking you to come with me," Gray Fox Running said as he pointed out the two boys disappearing into the forest.

"They would be lost without each other. They are more than friends, they are true kindred spirits meant to roam this world together," Gray Fox Running continued.

Red Oak grunted his agreement. He and Gray Fox Running shared very much the same relationship. They even had married sisters.

Grey Fox Running went to Silent Hawk and asked him to walk with him. He told him how honored he was to come to the Elk Clan and to learn how highly Silent Hawk thought of him. He shared that he and White Swan had discussed this for most of the night.

Then Grey Fox Running pointed out that very dramatic action would be needed to save the Elk Clan from starvation. This action would need to be carried out without question or resistance. To make this happen Grey Fox Running needed to be the Elk Clan leader and Red Oak his lead hunter.

Silent Hawk would serve as a coach and guide.

He stopped talking and looked directly at into Silent Hawk's eyes.

Silent Hawk was surprised and somewhat taken aback but immediately recognized the leadership abilities Grey Fox Running possessed. He recalled a similar trait in Gray Fox Running's father. He saw the same and perhaps sharper mind.

"Your father would be proud of you. You have his leadership skill. I appreciate the honesty and forthright way you have approached me." Silent Hawk replied.

Silent Hawk thought ahead to the situation the Elk Clan faced and decided what Gray Fox Running was proposing was indeed best for the Clan.

He knew the situation was even worse than he had so far shared, and the fact that Gray Fox Running had made such a clear assessment of the Elk Clan's situation did not escape Silent Hawk.

This knowledge and Gray Fox Running's clarity and strong leadership convinced Silent Hawk to accept the proposal.

"I see you have developed into a determined and forthright person. Your father and I were best friends. I was sorry to hear of his passing two seasons ago. If you agree to come over to the Elk Clan, I will do as you ask. I will step aside and let you lead. Sending the three wounded hunters to the Elk Horn Clan is an excellent suggestion. In this way they will not be a burden to us. Have you shared this with anyone else yet?" Silent Hawk asked.

"No, if you had not agreed with this proposal, I would have honored Wise Owl's proposal.

I have talked only to Red Oak to see if he would consider coming with me but to no one else.

I do not wish to hurt your position in the Clan, I am very aware of you great talent, but I am very concerned about this situation," Grey Fox Running said as he continued to look into Silent Hawks dark brown eyes.

As Silent Hawk thought about the power and leadership Gray Fox Running displayed, a confidence rose up inside of him.

It all felt right.

Here was the leader needed at this moment to ensure the Elk Clan survived through the winter. He felt relieved someone such as Grey Fox Running was available in this time of need.

Silent Hawk would help this young man as he took the mantle of leadership. He would hold his own pride in check and take the right action for the sake of the Elk Clan members.

Silent Hawk looked at Grey Fox Running and nodded his head. I will go with you to each of the Clan leaders and tell them that you and I have come to this agreement.

He realized Grey Fox Running was the only hope for the Elk Clan and without his open and public consent to this change, it would not happen.

Together the two made the rounds of the other Clan leaders and got their agreement and support. They began with Wise Owl who immediately felt the sting of this arrangement but agreed to it.

"Grey Fox Running, you drive a hard bargain. I hate to lose both you and Red Oak. However, I can see your logic. You have trained our other hunters well and the Elk Clan will give us their three recovering hunters who will be available when the next great hunting season begins.

I also see White Swan's hand in keeping Taelo and Golden Hawk together as well and I agree with her as well. Tell her that as always, she has great vision.

6 The Meeting

It must really have been a hard year if you, Silent Hawk, agree to step down," Wise Owl said as he looked into the eyes of his old mentor and nodded agreement to Gray Fox Running's request.

To Wise Owl, Grey Fox Running explained that the Elk Clan was in a desperate situation that needed immediate and drastic action. His respect for Silent Hawk was unquestionable, and he wanted his guidance, but he wanted the direct control that only by being the Elk Clan leader would give him. He was sure he and Red Oak together could save the Elk Clan from certain starvation.

Grey Fox Running end by saying that he looked to Wise Owl for support to make it happen and to Silent Hawk to make him a great clan leader.

Wise Owl put his hand on Grey Fox Running Running's shoulder and expressed his support.

Grey Fox Running was happy this meeting with Wise Owl had gone the way he had hoped. He would have to thank White Swan for sharing her insight on how to make this happen and let her know that Wise Owl had seen her design in keeping the two boys together.

That afternoon he and Silent Hawk visited with each of the other Clan leaders and let them know of the new situation.

All were surprised and shocked that Wise Owl had accepted the proposal but understood the logic of the change.

White Swan was proud of her husband's ability to negotiate the change in leadership.

She was also relieved he had been able to get agreement to include Red Oak as part of the trade.

Wise Owl's read on this confirmed her positive assessment of his keen mind and power of observation.

She was pleased that this would keep Taelo and Golden Hawk growing up together. This was as important to her as was Grey Fox Running's rise to leadership.

Taelo and Golden Hawk went running out of the camp to their favorite lookout across the valley. There they sat on the huge boulder with a view of the entire valley. They talked late into the afternoon about how they would contribute to the well-being of their new Clan, the Elk Clan. They were relieved to be going together into this new adventure.

The agreement to the leadership change was shared in a council meeting and the decision to make the change when the clans split to go their own ways was decided.

The clan celebrations could not lift the weight of concern from Gray Fox Running. He discussed the situation with Silent Hawk and Red Oak. Silent Hawk let them know that the situation of the Elk Clan was much worse than had been shared. The Elk Clan was celebrating with the last of its food stores. They did not have any food in reserve. Silent Hawk confirmed even with the generosity of the other Clans, there would not be sufficient stores for a mild winter.

Elk Clan mothers were already in fear for their youngest children. The young always suffered first when food was in short supply. The eldest members of the tribe would sacrifice themselves by not eating. This had been on the minds of all the Elk Clan members. They had not spoken of this with each other, and no one had shared this with the other sub-Clans.

They knew the basic survival was each individual clan's responsibility. They knew each sub clan would share what was possible without risking starvation. In their memory, there had never been a time when the Elk Clan had been in such a clear and dangerous situation. No one in the Elk Clan could conceive of anything but suffering and death in the coming winter.

Gray Fox Running and Red Oak came to understand how dire the situation was. They knew full well they would have to take extra ordinary action to ensure the survival of the Elk Clan.

Their days were spent discussing this with each other, with their mates, and with a few other leaders and hunters they respected. Together they were on a mission to create a plan leading the Elk Clan away from the edge of disaster and away from the precipice of death.

They knew they would have to do something different. They needed a miracle to save the Elk Clan, and they knew the ancestors had no way to send them real food. They would need to do something extra ordinary to get the Clan through the coming winter.

A week later the Clan gathering came to an end. The day of departure arrived, and the various Clans packed their belongings and departed to their wintering grounds.

The Elk Horn Clan broke camp and got ready to go back to their territory and their winter homes.

Red Oak and Grey Fox Running remained behind on the far side of the river as the Elk Horn Clan took leave. Red Oak and Gray Fox Running were rich in food and goods.

They would add much to the Elk Clan's stores. The food they brought with them was probably as much as the rest of the Elk Clan had in total.

As each family of the Elk Horn Clan was about to depart, they stopped by to wish Taelo's and Golden Hawk's family good fortune. Every family provided an extra gift of food. They too had seen the terrible condition of the Elk Clan.

The Elk Horn members all expressed their best wishes and that they would miss the two boys running around their camp.

The Weaver stopped by and gave his food directly to Taelo and Golden Hawk. He gave each a big hug and invited them to his campfire whenever they wished.

All the Elk Horn Clan wished the two well and that they would bring the same luck to the Elk Clan they had brought to the Elk Horn Clan.

"Well, my friends, I wish you well. We leave the best of the Elk Horn Clan behind. May you bring luck to the Elk Clan. I will miss all of you but especially Taelo and Golden Hawk.

They have been an inspiration and have brought good luck to the Elk Horn Clan. May they do the same for the Elk Clan," Wise Owl said as he departed.

Taelo and Golden Hawk waved as their friends both young and old proceeded across the river and up the valley back the way they had come.

Their departure had less swagger than their arrival, but they left in confidence as they returned to face the winter with a good reserve of food.

7 Survival Plans

*T*he grey cloud covered sky, a cool breeze, and the knowledge that they were in dire trouble dampened the spirits of the Elk Clan members as they waved to the last departing clan.

The valley seemed foreboding in the quiet of the grey morning and the threat of snow.

They were now alone. They had a new leader, but they faced the grim fact that many of them might not see the warmth of another spring.

The cool wind rose and with it the fear of hunger and starvation that winter would bring became more real.

The elder leaders of the Elk Clan gathered around in a circle with Gray Fox Running in the center.

The rest of the Clan surrounded them.

In a clear, loud confident voice, Gray Fox Running, asked that everyone, men, women, and children speak and suggest what each could do to ensure they all survived the winter.

There was silence.

The expectation had been that Grey Fox Running would tell them what they had to do to survive.

This behavior in a leader was new to the Elk Clan members. It was very different!!

A grumbling murmur could be heard as Grey Fox Running stood in silence.

Silent Hawk worried about how the Elk Clan would take to this new style of leadership, but he held back and did not interfere.

Taelo shouted out that he would hunt enough rabbits each day to feed five.

Golden Hawk joined in and said the two together would feed ten.

Next to him stood Floating Cloud and her granddaughter Quite Rabbit. They had asked to join the Elk Clan because they had just lost Quiet Rabbit's mother and father and did not want to return with the Elk Hide Clan.

Floating Cloud pointed to the large amount of food that they had accumulated and declared that she and Quiet Rabbit would share their personal food wealth with all Elk Clan members.

This broke the ice and soon the talking stick was being passed around to each person to control the flow of ideas.

As the talking stick was passed from member to member and each member shared what needed to be done, the general framework for survival began to take shape.

It had a natural and inclusive feel to it!

It was as Gray Fox Running had envisioned.

But rather than trying to force hard times upon the Elk Clan and be the person blamed for the suffering, the clan members themselves described the necessary survival actions. They prescribed the necessary medicine enabling the clan to survive through the coming winter. Each speaker in turn shared additional ideas and refinements in how the clan should govern and prepare for the hard times ahead.

The elders in the tribe immediately saw what was occurring and appreciated Gray Fox Running's respect for their situation. They saw he listened and his comments on the input showed confidence.

It became clear to them that he would lead them to overcome this dire situation. They also saw he allowed the clan members full voice and input.

As Silent Hawk watched Gray Fox Running in action, he knew he had made the right decision. This leadership style was different, but it allowed each person to voice their own opinion and that their opinion counted.

An eagle and a golden hawk circled silently overhead.

White Swan and Quiet Pheasant exchanged quiet words as they saw the totems of their sons.

This was an important sign for them!

White Swan wondered whether Gray Fox Running had seen the two birds high in the sky.

Though Taelo and Golden Hawk were young, Gray Fox Running and Red Oak had wanted them to understand the situation firsthand. They wanted the two young men to understand the serious nature of the situation. They knew the two would understand and would contribute greatly to the benefit of the Clan.

The two totems in the sky did not go unnoticed by Gray Fox Running and Red Oak.

It brought comfort to both, to know the totems of their sons were present on this serious occasion. They knew that somehow the two boys would play a key role in helping the Elk Clan.

Already the two had been the catalysts to get the clan talking. Grey Fox Running and Red Oak knew that somehow the two were as important as they themselves were to the survival of the clan.

Their totems were clearly on Taelo and Golden Hawk Hawk's minds. They commented that the two totems showing up at the same time was unusual. They were at full alert as they listened to their fathers.

Taelo pointed out to the lake. On the far side, near the yellowing cat tails swam a great white swan.

This was a surprise!

He walked over to his mother and turned her, so she could see her totem.

The swan on the lake surprised White Swam. Its presence made her realize that she too had been singled out as a person who would contribute to the recovery of the Elk Clan.

It signaled to her that she would take positive but forceful action.

After all the discussion had run its course and everyone who had wanted to say something had been given a chance, Gray Fox Running and Red Oak called for all the families to bring out their food supplies.

This was a surprise to all the Clan members, but they complied.

The two leaders went about examining the food supplies the Clan had. Grey Fox Running and Red Oak realized their two families and Floating Cloud had more food and supplies then the entire Clan put together.

Some of the families must already have been on short rations.

They talked quietly to White Swan and Quiet Pheasant and Floating Cloud and asked them to redistribute the food, so each family had about the same amount. The three warned each family this food would need to be rationed to ensure the clan would survive.

It was obvious to all that the new members from the Elk Hide Clan were being very generous with their own supplies and were sharing equally with all.

This increased the respect for Gray Fox Running and Red Oak. They and their family would face the same perils as the rest of the Elk Clan.

They were all one large family!

Gray Fox Running announced the clan would immediately go on short rations.

He spelled out specific actions for every member of the Clan. Everyone was to go out every day and gather anything that was eatable.

The older members were to fish and dry meat.

The youngsters were to go out to set snares and to use their slings to bring down birds and small game.

The younger women would gather nuts, berries, and edible roots. While the older women would prepare the food that was gathered.

One communal meal would be prepared each day.

Every member would be put to work to ensure the survival of the Clan. The care of youngest children was given over to the eldest Clan members.

Everyone would need to contribute if the Clan was to make it through the winter.

Gray Fox Running took another precaution. The entire clan would move southward toward the warmer climate by the sea.

This was outside of Elk Clan domain and held some risk but the area the Elk Clan had always occupied was stressed from years of hunting and the weather change had caused the animals to move southward.

Winter and starvation held the greater risk, so they would go to a new area and risk infringing on someone else's territory.

Grey Fox Running sent out runners to the each of the other sub clans to let them know of this change in territory.

The planning was detailed and meticulous.

Silent Hawk would lead the main body, made up of the women, children, and the elderly southward toward the sea.

Advance scouts, young men too young to go on the long hunt, would be sent out to find appropriate shelter several days ahead.

The elders would then move with the young children toward the new shelter. They would set up the new camp.

The older boys would move ahead with their slings gathering the game along the way. The women would explore in all directions for potentially fruitful areas to gather nuts, berries, and roots. Those fishing would stay in a good spot until another fishing spot was found.

Gray Fox Running then surprised the Clan once again by calling for additional long hunts.

This late of a hunt was unprecedented but both Gray Fox Running and Red Oak thought it necessary for the survival of the Elk Clan.

The long hunts were usually held at the end of the summer to prepare for the coming winter. It was during the long hunt this year when the Elk Clan had lost its lead hunter.

Gray Fox Running proposed a different approach to the long hunt. Instead of one large group going out together for the long hunt, three groups of six to eight hunters would go in different directions. Each would hunt long enough to accumulate every bit of meat they could drag back. Early kill of significant size would be brought back to sustain the travels of the clan.

One group led by Gray Fox Running would go to the south and would travel the longest distance, be the farthest away and return last.

The other led by Red Oak would go to the southwest. They would remain closer to the Clan since it was in the general direction of the Clans travel. Red Oaks group would return second.

The third group, led by the most experienced remaining Elk Clan hunter, Brave Deer, would go ahead of the Clan and leave the catch for the Clan to find. His return would be based on when his team hunted the area that ended at seaside.

The long hunters were to come back to the Clan at different times.

Brave Deer would be back first in time to help set up winter camp.

Red Oak would be back second just before the winter solstice.

Gray Fox Running would return last well into the heart of winter.

In this way Gray Fox Running hoped to guide the Clan to survive the winter. The hunters would fend for themselves thus lightening the burden on the Clan. They would send back extra food, and they would return at different and critical times into the long winter.

The mix of hunters also surprised the Clan. Each group would have a few of the older hunters, a few of the very young men and just a couple of hunters in their prime. This allowed for enough hunters to make up three teams.

Gray Fox Running and Red Oak had carefully plotted their hunting strategy. They anticipated the Clan would take some forty to sixty days to travel the long distance to the sea. They also knew the Clan had or would have enough food to make the trek if the short rations were maintained and the third hunting party, out in front were moderately successful.

They discussed the skill of each hunter with Silent Hawk and Brave Deer. Brave Deer would be given the more developed and seasoned hunters. The youngest and swiftest hunters were teamed up with Gray Fox Running. Red Oak took everyone else and had the largest team but the one that had the older and slower men among the hunters.

Silent Hawk voiced his concern on behalf of Red Oak.

"It seems Red Oak will have the weakest hunting team. Shouldn't we balance the teams a little better? Perhaps some of those young hunters with Gray Fox Running should be put with Red Oak," he said with some concern.

It seemed apparent to him that an imbalance existed.

He was surprised but somewhat relieved by Red Oak's amused response.

"This is the only way Gray Fox Running can hope to match my team's kill. Do not worry. My team will match the output of the other two teams. Grey Fox Running will be traveling at least twice as far as any of us. He will need to have the swiftest and the youngest. He will need to condition and train them to a new way of hunting, and he will need all his luck to out hunt us," was Red Oak's confident reply.

It was obvious these two had worked together before and they were following a strategy they had agreed upon. They both were confident in the design and the deployment of the hunters.

Silent Hawk looked at the two and said no more. He knew they had been very successful hunters for the Elk Horn Clan. He hoped they would continue this success now.

Grey Fox Running and Red Oak's plan was to gather enough meat to load a travois that two men could pull. The men chosen for this chore would be the strongest and youngest of each hunting party.

It would be up to them to move fast enough to catch up with the Clan. This would ensure the Clan had enough food to reach the sea and set up the winter quarters.

The primary burden for this initial supply of food was on Brave Deer and his forward team.

Grey Fox Running brought all the long hunters together in the presence of the Elders and Silent Hawk.

Gray Fox Running and Red Oak took turns describing what lay ahead. These two had hunted and traveled like this before. They were the reason the Elk Horn Clan ate well throughout the hardest winter.

"We will all jog throughout the hunt. We will jog to get into position and during all our travels," Grey Fox Running shared with the hunters.

"When a hunting party has enough for one travois, that travois will be pulled back to the Elk Clan," Red Oak continued.

"No matter how successful a hunting party has been, they will send back what they have after the passing of the first moon," Grey Fox Running resumed.

"We will go out with no food. It is up to us as we jog to kill the occasional rabbit or ground hog. If we are lucky, we will surprise a deer and eat very well," Red Oak continued the instruction to the hunting teams.

This caught the hunters and their families by surprise. Never in the memory of the Clan had a hunting party left with no food to carry them through the hunt.

All the hunters grumbled about this.

Red Oak ignored the grumbling and continued the explanations about how each major kill would be handled and how the meat would be processed.

The hunters would salt and dry enough meat for cold meals for the next several weeks. At other major kills, the meat would be salted and dried over fires.

If the short supply of salt ran out the meat was to be dried without salt. When winter became cold enough the meat would be left on the animal and brought back that way.

Red Oak and Gray Fox Running took Taelo and Golden Hawk aside and told them they expected the two of them to be the right and left hand for Silent Hawk. They were to obey and help Silent Hawk lead the Elk Clan to their new home.

"Silent Hawk is a very good leader. He has had some bad luck. He has much to teach you, and he has much to gain from you two. There will be a few older boys in the camp, but I am sure you two will be the best at hunting and finding food.

Red Oak and I are counting on you two to make a significant contribution to the well-being of this Clan," Gray Fox Running solemnly instructed the two of them.

Both fathers were still concerned for the well-being of their families. They would be gone for a long time. Any mishap no matter how small, could be the undoing of all they planned.

Taelo and Golden Hawk assured their fathers that they would listen and learn from Silent Hawk, and they would contribute significantly to the well-being of the Clan.

The next day, Taelo and Golden Hawk were up early. The grey morning sky was giving way to a clear blue cloudless day.

The two watched the white swan on the lake stretch its long neck straight as it awoke. Moments later it began a long flapping run across the water and slowly lifted itself off the water and began a long gentle rise. Their totems had departed the day before after broadcasting a series of cries. The departure of the white swan seemed to signal the beginning of their role in helping their new clan.

Golden Hawk commented that he already missed the Weaver's breakfast hearth. Taelo gave him a cold piece of rabbit they had captured and cooked the previous night.

The two had gone out hunting and had returned with a dozen rabbits that they had skinned and roasted.

They cut up the rabbits so that each of the long hunters would have one piece of meat for their morning meal before they departed.

The hunting parties each gathered together and prepared to depart the camp. They talked about leaving with no food.

Those remaining behind watched as the line of silent men, jogged out of the camp.

The Clan let their good-byes ring out. Wives, children, mothers, and fathers all wished them good hunting, the blessings of the spirits.

Everyone worried that the hunters were taking no food with them.

Taelo and Golden Hawk handed each hunter a piece of rabbit wrapped in a hide as they went past and wished the hunter's luck.

This surprised the hunters and pleased Grey Fox Running and Red Oak.

A cheer went up from the Clan members when they realized what Taelo and Golden Hawk were doing.

All knew the hunters would face many trials and dangers before their return and they knew the future of the clan lay in the success of these hunters.

So began the Clan's great journey for survival.

Taelo and Golden Hawk immediately began to meet their father's challenge.

They caught rabbits, squirrels ground hogs and a few wild boar.

They gathered nuts.

They found and brought in anything eatable.

Their actions and their success began to have a positive impact on the clan as it moved slowly westward.

Taelo and Golden Hawk stopped and admired the giant oak dominating the small dimple of a valley they were entering. Its leafless branches reached high up like thousands of tendrils floating to catch the white puffy clouds floating above in the crystal blue sky. Its trunk was as wide as Golden Hawk was tall.

A huge crack that ran the full length of the trunk drew them for a closer look. In some past lightning storm, the heavens had struck the tree and wrenched a giant crack down one side. Ants and termites had eaten much of the inner wood and created a hollow interior.

The buzzing of thousands of bees created a crescendo of sound that immediately peaked their interest. The tree was now filled with a giant beehive. They approached cautiously and looked up into the crack that extended at least a spear length above their head.

They were amazed to see the layers and rows of light and dark golden honeycombs covered with bees.

Taelo reached in and carefully brushed aside the bees, cut one section of honey cone, and slowly pulled it out. After each had enjoyed a small portion of the honeycomb, Golden Hawk wrapped the remaining cone in a piece of leather. They knew they had found a priceless treasure.

They returned to the Elk Clan and displayed the honeycomb. Silver Hawk immediately called a halt to the travel when he learned of the size of the hive. This was a treasure the Elk Clan needed to leverage.

Taelo and Golden Hawk led the way to the huge knurled old Oak tree.

The older Clan members marveled at the size of the hive.

The find reaffirmed to the Elk Clan the stories shared by the Elk Horn Clan members about the strong positive omen Taelo and Golden Hawk represented.

The honey was a treasure of unmentionable value!

The Clan stopped for an extra day to weave containers and to gather the honey. It was a stop all welcomed. They had been on the trail for nine days.

The amount of honey was a great fortune for the Clan. The quantity put up by the bees also told of a hard winter ahead.

The Clan left enough honey to ensure the hive would survive. This would be a place the Elk Clan planned to come every year. It was one of the few sources of sweetening and it provided a healing balm used to heal wounds.

Honey was one of the most valuable commodities the Clan could have access to!

Clan members now looked upon Taelo and Golden Hawk with new respect. The two had provided the first sign of hope to a Clan down on its luck and low on its emotional stock.

The Clan's luck seemed to be changing for the better.

And luck continued to improve. Four young warriors chanting the pull song that Red Oak had taught them were heard as they approached the Clan. They were pulling a travois loaded with the meat of one buffalo, two boar, a deer and four elk. This did not count the numerous small game, rabbits and ground hogs that was mixed in.

The Clan heard the chanting and looked back to see the approaching young men. A cheer rose up and the four pulling the travois increased their pace and the volume of their chant.

That evening after a meal of honey coated grilled buffalo the four told the story of Red Oak and his uncanny strategy of moving the game into a center area to maximize the kill. They talked in awe about Red Oak's speed and ability to take down the buffalo. They talked about the dusk to dawn jogging hunting style.

They thanked the cooks of their honey coated dinner but told of how well all the hunters were eating.

They were eager to return to their hunting team and the following morning they took up their jogging chant and went back the way they had come.

Taelo and Golden Hawk had listened intently. They knew how their fathers hunted and were surprised at the awe that the Elk Clan hunters expressed.

From these stories and the load of meat, the Elk Clan gained even more hope. Silent Hawk noted this encouragement came from the hunting party with the weakest, slowest and oldest set of hunters. He shared this with the remaining elders in the camp.

Silent Hawk and the Clan now began to believe survival was possible.

Now the advance scouts each carried large honey containers on their backs and pulled a travois with dry or drying meat.

Several of the older men pulled a travois loaded with honey and the remainder of the meat wrapped in the scraped and salted hides. Later, the hides would be properly treated or eaten if the food supply ran low.

Periodically they came upon the game left behind by the hunting party out ahead of them. The going became slower as the Clan gathered more and more sustenance. Soon half the Clan was employed pulling food laden travois.

They all welcomed this burden of hope!

Though now the travel was slower than before, Silent Hawk was pleased the food problem was becoming less of a concern.

Now the matter of good shelter was becoming the primary issue.

Taelo and Golden Hawk now had new visions and hunting games to keep them busy. They began to practice the jogging and hunting on the run.

To their amazement and more so to the Clan's they became the source of most of the daily food gathered by the Clan. Every day they provided the food for at least half of the camp.

Silent Hawk took note and praised them for their contribution. He also made sure each Clan family recognized the contribution the two were making.

7 Survival Plans

8 Dire Wolves

*D*ay after day the Clan slowly moved west and southwest. Their course took them through the mighty mountains and through the passes laden with snow. One narrow passage had the Clan proceeding single file. Silent Hawk, now less worried about food, worried about the Clan's ability to make the coast as planned. The mountains were a much greater challenge than anticipated.

He had also noticed that the wolves and other prey animals were beginning to follow the Clan. It was the lions and dire wolves that worried him most.

Taelo and Golden Hawk ranged wider and wider in their hunting. They began carrying their spears and stone headed clubs to supplement their slings. They did this quietly so as not to worry their mothers.

The two made excellent hunting partners. They operated together with a harmony developed from years of running and playing together.

White Swan and Quiet Pheasant of course noticed that the two were now going out with spears and stone headed clubs. They wondered why but the two agreed they felt better about them going out with more protection. Like all mothers, they worried about the well-being of their offspring.

One morning, the two boys left after a hearty breakfast and set out to make the rounds. They set out jogging and looking for sign of any game. About an hour out of camp they spotted the tracks of an elk and followed it up the valley breaking away to the right. Neither thought they would find the elk, but they planned to follow the tracks a short distance up the valley cross over and then come back on the other side. They were expecting to find rabbits and other small game.

They were jogging along enjoying the scenery when they both spotted what looked like a wonderful tree to climb. It was a grand old leafless maple tree with horizontal limbs growing out parallel to the ground.

This tree commanded a small clearing between the valley sides. It was similar in size to the old oak honeybee tree they had discovered a few days before, but this tree was enticing and calling versus the bee tree that had been towering and imposing.

It stood out by itself in the middle of a snow-covered valley that surrounded it like the white feathers of a swan. Its leafless branches reached out like a mother's fingers reaching for her young. Its appeal was like the lovers look making you want to take them in your arms.

They jogged over to it jumped up on the first low limb and swung up into the second limb. They did this several times for fun. As they played and frolicked, they could have easily been mistaken for their cousins the ape. They were able to swing up between their arms and pull themselves into a sitting position on the first limb and then pull themselves up and into the second limb. They did this several times in pure enjoyment of having found the perfect climbing tree.

Taelo commented that it was too bad the Clan was just passing through and they would never be able to see this tree with its leaves gracing the valley.

After enjoying themselves, they decided to continue up the valley for a few more miles.

Together they set off once again.

Just as they crested the hill beyond "their" tree, they surprised three huge dire wolves. These were the largest wolves that either of two had ever seen.

The wolves stood almost a spear high at the shoulders and were almost a half spear wide and as long as the length of the elk on the ground. The elk looked more like a small deer as it lay dead.

There was mutual surprise for both the dire wolves and the two young hunters.

Time froze as the two adversaries and competitors looked at each other in surprise!!

Taelo knew immediately that he and Golden Hawk were in mortal danger. The dark black eyes, more likened to pools of deep fury, of the largest wolf, burned into Taelo's mind as he shouted, "back to the tree."

In unison Taelo and Golden Hawk turned and at top speed sprinted back to the tree.

The wolves took up the chase.

Taelo's quick decision and action put the two far enough ahead of the three wolves to give them time to scramble up into the tree. This time they scrambled up with all their gear. They were standing on the second limb when the wolves arrived at the base of the tree.

The growling wolves circled the base of the tree and looked up to where the two stood.

Taelo looked down at what he thought of as three giant wolf hides and wondered how he might take them as trophies back to the Clan.

He pointed out to Golden Hawk that if they could kill the three wolves, they would be able to have a whole elk and some trophy wolf hides.

Golden Hawk looked down at the three growling wolves that were prowling around and trying to figure out how to get up to them, gave a small laugh and asked about the crazy idea Taelo had in mind.

"I wonder if they can jump as high as the first branch," Taelo conjectured.

"What are you thinking," Golden Hawk asked?

"If we tie ourselves by the waist to this top limb and have just enough length to stand on the next limb down, we may be able to tease the wolves to jump up at us. As they jump up, we could spear them and club them," Taelo explained.

"Sounds exciting, will we be able to get all three," Golden Hawk inquired as he got his length of hide rope ready?

"Well, it's worth a try," Taelo said as he tied his leather rope to the top limb.

They tied their back packs to the limb above them and then got everything ready.

When the two were prepared, they lowered themselves down at the same time to the limb below. Immediately the wolves reacted, and the largest one jumped up to attack Taelo.

The speed of his reaction surprised Taelo and he almost lost his concentration.

High overhead, the cry off an eagle pierced the morning quiet.

Taelo's attention was on the leaping wolf, and he did not hear it but out at the mouth of the valley where the Elk Clan had just arrived, White Swan heard the cry.

"We must stop. Some major event involving Taelo and Golden Hawk is taking place. We must be ready to help if help is needed," she informed Silent Hawk.

This pressure from White Swan, Quiet Pheasant and Floating Cloud was new to Silent Hawk. Confidence and leadership seemed to run in these two families, and he noted that they always had support from those that knew the two.

Silent Hawk was surprised by the insistence of both White Swan and Quiet Pheasant. He knew the eagle was Taelo's sign. He hesitated for a few moments but then called a halt.

High overhead the eagle cried out again.

Taelo and Golden Hawk were on the first limb when the first of the wolves charged and jumped up at Taelo. The height he achieved surprised both Taelo and Golden Hawk. The wolf was going to clear the limb they were standing on!

Taelo had his spear up and drove the spear into the open mouth of the wolf. The weight and the velocity of the wolf caused the spear to go in almost the length of the wolf's body.

He hit Taelo and then the two spun around. Taelo held on to his spear with both hands and as they spun, the wolf cleared the limb and fell on the other side. Taelo lost his balance for a moment but the leather rope, up to the next limb allowed him to regain his footing and he pulled himself back upright on the limb.

The second wolf attacked Golden Hawk almost simultaneously. He too had driven his spear down into the wolf's mouth. This wolf did not clear the limb but instead hit it full force and fell to a crumpled heap below.

The impact knocked both Taelo and Golden Hawk off the branch.

The remaining wolf made several snarling, snapping jumps as the two regained their perch on the limb. It seemed confused about what had just taken place. He checked out his two dead companions.

Both Taelo and Golden Hawk jumped down and pelted him with rocks from their sling. The rocks were not enough to inflict any major damage, but they did hurt. The wolf backed away and then turned and went trotting up the valley away from them.

Taelo and Golden Hawk took stock of the situation. The event from beginning to end had only taken a few minutes. They decided to first ensure both dire wolves were dead. Then they went cautiously to the crest of the hill to verify the three wolves had indeed been the only ones at the elk kill and they wanted to make sure the third wolf had left the area.

They were now the proud owners of the dead elk and two large dire wolves.

Taelo and Golden Hawk now heard the cry of the eagle overhead and watched as it flew out of sight.

White Swan looked at Quiet Pheasant, "Well whatever those two were up to, it must be done. Taelo's totem has departed. I wish I could be sure all was well. In the past the eagle has always left after one of Taelo's successes. I hope that this is the case now."

Taelo and Golden Hawk looked at each other as the eagle's cry reached them.

"I think this was a test and we passed it," Taelo said looking at Golden Hawk.

"However now we must sweat at getting the prize back to the Clan," he continued.

The wolves measured almost seven feet long and three feet high at the shoulders. They were larger than either Taelo or Golden Hawk had expected and certainly larger than they had ever heard about.

They then gutted the Elk and kept the heart, liver, and kidneys.

They skinned the wolves and kept the heads.

They carried the bodies of the wolves up the valley away from the elk. And then took the entrails to another location. They wanted this decoy spread out in case other wolves returned.

As quickly as they could they cut down two tall slender trees and used them to make a travois. They made the poles extralong. This gave them the leverage to pull the extra heavy load. They put the weight of the elk as far to the back on the travois as possible. The elk's large rack was tied to the travois poles, and several cross poles supported the body. The legs stuck up into the air.

The two wolf hides and heads were put across the body of the elk. The travois poles went a good six feet beyond the elk's head. Even with this extra leverage the two could barely pull the load.

Luckily, the journey back out of the valley was slightly downhill.

For the remaining part of the day and well into dusk, the two pulled their load slowly back to the main trail.

They were almost exhausted and had talked about spending the night away from the camp, when up ahead they saw the campfires. Their energy level picked up and they continued to drag their large load.

Had the Clan not stopped when White Swan had asked, the boys would never have been able to catch up that day.

White Swan and Quiet Pheasant had been on the lookout for them. At first, they thought it was one of the hunting parties bringing in more food. Then they realized how small the two individuals pulling the large load looked.

Both let out a yell and the whole camp came to life. Several people ran out to help the two.

White Swan was in the lead. She first saw the elk and then she saw the dire wolf skins.

She hugged both Taelo and Golden Hawk.

Quiet Pheasant duplicated her hugs.

Then the two mothers once again took in the sight of the two dire wolf hides and the large elk.

"Why don't we go to the central campfire? You can tell the story of your great hunt, while I prepare you some dinner," White Swan suggested.

She was overwhelmed with relief.

A combination of the older boys and a few of the elders pulled the heavy travois into the camp.

Taelo and Golden Hawk enjoyed the attention. They told of the events of the day. How they had first found and played on the tree they found so interesting.

How their play on the limbs had prepared them for their later use of the tree. How they had surprised the three large dire wolves and had bolted like lightening back to their tree.

They told of their stand and defeat of the very aggressive wolves.

The elders knew how dangerous dire wolves could be and were amazed at how the two boys had decided to kill them. Their success could not be denied, and the danger had been overwhelming.

The size of the wolves put them among the largest the Clan elders had ever seen. There was no doubt that these two young men had faced and defeated an enemy often a challenge for the most developed hunting parties.

This was a story to be told many times during the coming cold winter nights.

White Swan and Quiet Pheasant wanted to put limits on the hunting of the two boys. The elders joked the two women were protecting the wolves, but they knew a pack of dire wolves could devastate even a party of many hunters. The fact the two boys had gotten the better of three of the giant dire wolves amazed everyone.

Silent Hawk took the boys aside and cautioned them about going too far from the rest of the Clan or tangling with dire wolves.

"You must be careful. As the winter takes hold these animals become more aggressive. Their hunger drives them to do what normally they would be afraid of.

You have shown you are smarter than they are. You must use their hunger to make them fight each other and forget about you," Silent Hawk shared the hunting stories of old and how hunters had been able to outwit large packs of wolves.

His stories would later prove very valuable to Taelo in his own actions.

Silent Hawk, however, did not put any restraints on the two boys.

How could he?

When they left the protection of the camp, they were the ones out on their own. They had shown they could protect themselves as well as any of his other hunters.

He would give them advice and teach them, but he would not put any limits on what they should or should not do.

On the twentieth day, two hunters from Gray Fox Running's party were spotted ahead of the Clan. They brought with them a travois heavily loaded with some fresh but mostly dried meat.

They told of the new way of hunting they were learning, how they never walked but jogged from morning to night, of Gray Fox Running's great skill and his ability to find game. He was described as the greatest person they had ever known. They described his kill of a bull elk and cow with awe. How single handily Gray Fox Running had brought down both animals while over taking them from behind. They now knew why he was called Gray Fox Running.

He was the fastest runner among all the hunters. The stay of these two hunters was as short as the previous four.

The hunters heard of the success of the other hunters.

They learned of Taelo and Golden Hawk's triumph against the dire wolves.

It was clear to all the Clan members that they were going to survive. The hunters were eager to get back to the hunt with their new leader and share with him the improving status of the Clan.

The wisdom of Gray Fox Runing's leadership was already being lauded.

Taelo and Golden Hawk sat among the elders to listen. These two were now accepted as one of them. The two had an aura and intensity about them and after they brought in the elk and wolf hides, they were treated more like warriors then young boys.

When these two played, those watching always learned something new. These two were indeed good luck for the Clan. Their fathers were out working to save the Clan. These two should listen and learn.

Silent Hawk was reaffirmed about his decision to step down to allow Gray Fox Running to lead. Even in absence, this new leader was inspiring the Clan. His decisions were already having positive impacts.

Hope was on the rise.

Survival was now all but assured.

The food supply was now enough to last to the winter solstice. However, all members except for the younger children maintained their short rations. Though now once every other day a full meal was prepared and enjoyed by all.

This treat was complements of Taelo and Golden Hawk. Their elk was used for these feasts.

The journey and the food gathering continued. Taelo and Golden Hawk continued their hunting and bringing in of small game. The Clan was entertained many times as the boys ran down a rabbit with only a stick.

This technique was used when the boys would spot the tracks of a rabbit. If it had stopped at a point where a tuft of grass formed a shelter the two would approach the hiding spot from the downwind side. When they were within jumping distance of the hiding spot they would jump forward and as the rabbit finally bolted, they would hit it on the head with their club.

The other boys in the Clan began to use this technique to catch rabbits as well.

One late evening the Clan watched in amazement as the two boys ran down a deer. The two sprinted along each side of the deer and knocked it off its feet. Once down the deer was quickly dispatched. The entire Clan again enjoyed a feast.

The going was now more routine, less stressful. But the food expected from the third hunting party was no longer found.

Something had gone seriously wrong.

It would not do for the poorly defended Clan to be surprised. Silent Hawk discussed defense with the Clan Elders and quietly established sentries to closely watch the surrounding territory. He recruited some of the women to stand guard.

He put his two young runners up to a new task. Taelo and Golden Hawk were to go out away from the Clan as far as they could but still see the main body. Then they were to circle around and look for anything strange or signs of someone watching them. They were not to be seen or heard by anyone.

Taelo and Golden Hawk were excited. After each meal of the day, they would go out for their mission. They imagined themselves full warriors in defense of their Clan and so they were. Even with this added responsibility, the game they brought in from these jaunts was enough to feed their families and several others.

9 First Kill

Grey Fox Running and his team were the lead team when they departed the Elk Clan. He traveled westward for a day before turning and leading his team in a path that the sun would cross almost directly from his left.

This was new territory for him and all his team members. The snow-covered mountains, dark green sentinel pines and bare oak and maple tree covering their sides, rose to meet the sky on both sides of the wide broad valley he and his team entered.

Pine, willow and many old oak and elm trees grew along the banks of a river flowing lazily down the middle of the Valley.

The team made their first camp on its snowy banks. The evening meal was light because Grey Fox Running was the main contributor of small game.

The rest of the team had observed his skill at killing small game but had yet to learn be as successful.

He and Red Oak had put the fastest, lightest and the youngest Elk Clan hunters on his team.

9 First Kill

The pace Gray Fox Running set was grueling but the men in the hunting parties were in good spirits. They quickly learned to kill small game as they jogged. They began to eat and drink well.

Grey Fox Running knew they needed to eat well to accomplish the nearly impossible task of being successful at this long hunt held in the dead of winter.

They needed to hunt well enough to get the quantity of food needed by the thirty families of the Clan. His team needed to deliver the food that would take the Clan from the solstice through to spring.

Early each morning the hunting team would rise before the sun, eat a cold morning meal prepared the day before and then set out for a day of hunting. As they traveled, they would scout around in search of game. Small game was killed using a sling. The small game was cleaned as the men jogged. This was the food for the next meal.

Smaller valleys periodically breaking off roughly ninety degrees to each side were explored and often yielded substantial kills. Once a small side valley was explored the team would once again proceed down the main valley.

When the sun was at its zenith, they stopped and prepared a meal larger than they would need.

The extra food was packed and would serve as the evening meal and the breakfast for the following morning. This allowed them to hunt right up until the sun sank below the mountains rising high to their left.

After the hunt they ate a hearty but cold meal. They prepared any small game needed for breakfast and then fell asleep.

On the third day after leaving the Clan, as the line of hunters came over a rise leading to a shallow side valley, Gray Fox Running spotted a bull elk and two cows.

This was the first test of his hunting team. He barked out his single command of "Hunt" and took off after the three animals.

The team's reaction speed was mixed but they all dropped their packs and carrying two spears they followed Grey Fox Running.

They fanned out in a line behind him. One cow broke off and scrambled up a rocky slope and escaped. The bull and one cow began a run down the valley.

Grey Fox Running surged forward and moved ahead of the cow and placed the butt of his spear onto the ground and the tip of the spear on her chest. The cow was immediately skewered on the spear and dropped as Grey Fox Running surged forward to catch up to the bull and drive his second spear deep into the bull, behind the left front leg.

Grey Fox Running stopped and one of the younger hunters continued on to help bring down the mortally wounded beast.

The team gathered around the two elk and thanked the spirits of the elk for providing this abundance to the Clan. They then cut open the animals. The liver was symbolically offered to the spirits of the departed clan members. It was then sliced up and eaten raw as they continued to clean the animals.

The hunters were excited about such a good outcome. They had only been gone a few days and already they had enough meat to take back to the clan.

Grey Fox Running's speed and skill strengthened his position as their new Elk Clan leader. It was an absolute demonstration of the meaning of his name.

The next morning Grey Fox Running left two of the hunters behind to prepare the meat that would go to the Clan. He and four others went out to hunt for additional game.

He sent three team members jogging ahead for several miles along the side of the valley. He and the remaining member proceeded to move up the valley. The part of the team jogging out ahead, fanned out across the valley and then proceeded back toward Grey Fox Running and the other hunter. This created an area with hunters coming together from two directions.

The team killed a buffalo, two elk, a deer, and a young boar.

This extremely successful hunt meant the team spend the remainder of the day building a travois and then pulling the travois back to the processing area.

Grey Fox Running carried the young boar back to the camp while the rest of the team worked at bringing the remainder of the hunt back. He skinned and salted the boar and put it on a spit. He stuffed the inside with tubers and other greens he found near the riverbanks and then put it to roast over the open fire.

He assigned one of the hunters to periodically turn the roasting boar.

He was following White Swan's instructions on how to best cook over a fire.

He periodically brushed salt and water as the meat began to bake, and the smell of the cooking meat drew every hunter over to look at the feast they would soon enjoy.

They gathered together for their first of many celebration dinners. The young boar would provide an evening feast and tasty meals for the next few days.

Gray Fox Running took this time to let his men talk about the hunt and any other topics on their minds. Up until this time he had kept the talk to a minimum. He knew his men were wary and had many questions about his leadership.

They had never experienced this kind of travel and hunting. In two days, they had traveled almost eighty miles and had their first load of meat to be sent back to the Clan!

It was time for Grey Fox Running to have his team foster the mind set of success.

The men discussed their initial concerns about leaving the camp with no food supply. They were surprised at how much small game they had learned to catch on the run.

Though their muscles were still sore from the pace they were setting, they were amazed at how good they felt.

To a man they praised Grey Fox Running for leading them and promised to follow him in whatever lay ahead.

Grey Fox Running was pleased but he knew they didn't know what their promise might mean in the coming winter and the days beyond.

The next day Grey Fox Running left two additional men to prepare the meat for travel.

He and the two remaining hunters went out for the hunt. He would continue in this fashion until all the hunters were needed to process the kill. He knew he had several days before he needed to send his catch back. This re-supply of the Elk Clan would need to carry them until the solstice.

The location they had chosen to process the meat was near a small clear stream coming down from one of the mountains into the main river that ran down between the two ranges. Each morning the part of the team assigned to hunt would leave in the direction of the next side valley to be hunted. They used their travois to bring back their kill to the location by the stream.

The hunt and meat processing continued successfully for ten days.

Much of the meat was dried using a fire drying technique. The team did not have enough salt to properly season the drying meat. This meant the meat dried with little flavor.

The hunters would long be teased by their wives, mothers, and spouses to be, about the lack of quality of their drying technique.

They in turn would recall their own growth in confidence that the Clan would survive because of their efforts.

Grey Fox Running Running's team had the longest distance to travel to take the meat. He wanted to keep as many hunters as possible hunting versus pulling the load of frozen meat back to the Clan. His drying approach was effective in quickly reducing tons of meat into what could be brought back by two strong hunters using a travois.

Finally, all the meat was ready and properly bundled. These bundles were arranged on a large travois and two of the youngest and strongest men were selected to pull it back to the Clan.

Gray Fox Running and the remaining hunters continued on. The two young hunters were told the general direction the hunting party would travel and how to proceed back from the Clan.

He also gave them directions on how to cross the valley and the mountains to intersect the path the Elk Clan was traveling.

Gray Fox Running and the remaining hunters would leave a trail of stone piles marking their trail and they would light a smoking fire each morning and evening to aid the returning hunters.

He instructed the two pulling the travois to mark their trail frequently to ensure they would not get lost.

Navigation in the vast expanse of the mountains and valleys they were traveling was a huge challenge. The hunters all had practical travel capabilities, but it was very easy to get disoriented. Such a mistake could be a deadly one this late into the winter season. The mountain nights were very cold.

Getting lost meant death.

Grey Fox Running made a point of impressing this on the younger hunters and on coaching them on how to navigate using the sun, key mountain peaks and the evening stars and moon. His teachings were greatly increasing the survival capabilities of his team.

Earlier, Red Oak had waved to Grey Fox Running as he led his team past the first team's turn off point. His team would travel in a more westerly direction than Grey Fox Running. His team did not have as natural of a path as Grey Fox Running's team. They were crossing the foothills to the west of the mountain range Grey Fox Running was in and they would cross the mountains to the west.

This meant Red Oak was traveling up and down from one valley to the next. His team would exert much more effort during their travels.

Red Oak paced his team allowing them to acclimate to the strenuous travel they would experience.

He set a pace and kept a routine similar to Grey Fox Running and his team. He used a different but as successful hunting technique. At each promising valley in his direction of travel, he would stop and send two-thirds of his party on ahead along the ridge. Two and three hours out, two hunters would stop and position themselves on each side of the valley. Four hours out, the remaining hunters spread themselves in a semicircle across the valley and proceeded to march back up the valley.

The group left behind also spread themselves in a semicircle across the valley. They proceeded slowly up the valley. Small game was brought down using slings and processed as the group marched on. A deer or elk was quickly gutted and hung up away from predators. It was left as close to the kill point as possible. Once the hunters gutted and hung up an animal, they would run back to join the remaining group.

The net of hunters slowly and continuously closed in toward each other. Each kill being handled by a few while the rest maintained the hunting line across the valley.

A good valley would yield several elk and deer. Occasionally the team also bagged a buffalo.

9 First Kill

The kill from the first valley was so large, four hunters were needed to pull back the load to the Elk Clan.

The scene at the campfire the evening of the first major valley harvest was filled with excited hunters sharing their adventures. They sat by a small river around the fire and discussed the hunting they were doing and the fact they now felt the Elk Clan would survive the winter.

Red Oak had instructed the hunters to only kill the male deer, or elk. Yearling males and females were also fair game. This approach allowed the valley to stay fertile while ensuring an abundant take for the hunters. This approach was discussed in length among the group.

Some thought they should take all the animals, but the rest sided with Red Oak especially since they were already taking a record amount.

The entire group was impressed with Red Oak's hunting ability. He was the fastest among them. His keen insight seemed to make the difference in the outcome of the hunt. He was always at the right spot at the right time.

His men began to watch and to respond to Red Oak's leadership.

The processing of the meat took all of them almost a week. Since his team was closer to the Clan, his team was taking much of the meat back fresh. Red Oak picked four of his strongest young men and sent them on their way back to the Clan with the kill that they had taken.

He and Grey Fox Running had strategically loaded his team with the slower but stronger men. This allowed Red Oak to send back heavier loads to the Clan and allowed Red Oak's group to send back fresh meat. Fresh meat weighed significantly more than dried.

It would be delivered earlier to the Clan and ensure their intermediate food needs.

This approach maximized the contribution of the slower and stronger members without slowing down or hampering the hunting of the fastest group. By working together in this fashion, the kill was maximized and the energy to make the kill dramatically reduced.

Red Oak and Grey Fox Running had discussed and agreed on this approach.

Red Oak's group would travel half the distance of Grey Fox Running's group. They could travel more slowly, hunt very effectively and compete with the faster moving team Grey Fox Running led. By fitting the speed profile in this manner each team was designed to make the maximum hunting contribution.

The men on Red Oak's team were as inspired by him as those with Grey Fox Running were of their leader. They had never been led on a hunt by better leaders, and they had never enjoyed the hunting success they were currently experiencing.

Grey Fox Running and Red Oak knew they had the right survival strategy. The hunting success of their teams assured the success of the strategy.

Their only remaining worry was about the winter quarters the Elk Clan needed to survive the coming winter months. They had left this in the hands of Silent Hawk, White Swan, and Quiet Pheasant.

10 Fight for Survival

rave Deer watched as Grey Fox Running and then Red Oak led their team in the south and southwest directions. He and his team traveled almost directly westward on the path the Elk Clan would follow. He led the group of older seasoned hunters.

They had all been instructed on how to travel and gather food as they jogged but they lacked the confidence and hands on capability that Red Oak and Grey Fox Running provided to the other two hunting teams, and they did not fare as well.

They did succeed in killing several elk that they hung up in a tree and left for the Elk Clan that would follow their tracks. This also gave them enough meat to carry with them for their daily food needs.

They left a trail of food for the Clan and felt very good about their performance. On the tenth cycle of the sun, they came to a promising valley, and they turned and followed its northwest direction.

They hoped to take down some elk or deer and return to the main valley they had been following.

They surprised a large rhinoceros and were chased by it farther up into the valley in the opposite direction they wanted to travel.

After their escape Brave Deer called a halt and the team set up camp for the night in an out cropping of rock that gave them a defensive position.

Several of them had been members of the team that had faced a similar surprise by a rhino. Their leader had been gored and died. They did not want to go directly back down the valley and face this rhino again.

The next morning the hunting party continued to travel up through the valley.

They were hunting both for game and for a way out toward the west.

The hunting was strangely sparse and the forest ominously silent. It seemed this valley had already been hunted out. They wondered if some other group was ahead of them.

On the third day into the valley, they ran into their competition.

A large dire wolf pack had hunted this territory clean. The dire wolves were hungry and were fighting with each other. The lead wolf was ready to lead the group from the valley.

He had brought his growing pack down from the cold northern territories. His success and the overpowering of the packs whose territories he invaded had continuously grown his pack.

The only problem facing this very large pack was finding enough food. The leader of the pack was ready to move on when a fresh and new scent worth following came to him.

The pack spotted their quarry ahead of them. This was a new animal to this dire wolf leader. The quarry was large but seemed defenseless.

The pack would eat well this day!

Brave Deer had been following a game trail when the rear scout shouted a warning. Quickly, the hunting party formed a circle ready for defense. This surprised their oncoming enemy and bought the time needed for Brave Deer to move his men to a more defendable location. Ahead along the trail he spotted a large boulder. There was abundant dead wood all around.

Brave Deer deployed the men to gather wood and to move some stones up closer to the large boulder.

He made sure there was no other way to the top of the boulder.

The gathered wood was placed in a semi-circle around in front of the boulder. Additional wood was taken to the top of the boulder.

He continued to have the men gather wood.

He counted more than fifty dire wolves. This was the largest pack he had ever heard of, and they seemed unusually brave. The wolf pack surrounded the boulder and sat on their haunches watching the hunters.

"They must be desperately hungry to stalk us," Brave Deer shared with his team.

"Did you see the size of these wolves? Their leader seems to be twice the normal size," one of the hunters replied.

There was much discussion and concern about the bold action on the part of this pack of wolves.

They did not seem to know the humans as a threat.

"Let's get ready for the night. We will take turns keeping the fire going. We will keep watch in pairs. Be careful when you put the wood on the fire. They may be brave enough to rush you when you go to the edge of the camp.

The leader of the wolf pack circled the camp. The smell of food had him drooling. These creatures were different from any other game he had led his very successful pack in hunting. They were able to defend themselves with a power he did not know how to overcome. All night long he continued to circle the camp. He tested the perimeter but there was no way in.

Brave Deer awoke the next morning to find the wolves still gathered around the camp. He led a small group out to gather additional wood.

They had not gone far before they were challenged and had to fight their way back to the camp. They had gotten enough wood for the next day, but the hunters knew they could not stay in their present location and survive.

From the vantage of the large boulder, a cliff could be seen about a half a mile away. It appeared there was a crack running up the cliff.

"See that crack going up the cliff? We are going to make a break and run for our lives. Once there we will climb into the crack and move up and defend ourselves against this pack of wolves," Brave Deer shared his plan with his men.

"When it gets dark, we will light a fire on the valley floor. The moon will provide us enough light to run through the forest. We will need to jump through the fire and get out ahead of it," Brave Deer continued to coach his team.

The wind was blowing in the right direction. The moon rose and when it was at its height, they lit the underbrush and watched as the flames began to travel in the direction they needed to go. Carefully the hunting party followed behind the flames. They knew as soon as the wolves got behind the flames, they would quickly follow the scent of the group.

The leader of the dire wolves was caught by surprise. The flames posed a serious threat. His pack moved away from the flame. He led them back around the flame to where he expected his prey to be.

They were gone!

Quickly he followed their scent.

It led to the ashes where the fire had been started. Faintly he caught their scent among the ashes. They were following the flames!

He would trap them between his pack and the flames. He let out a howl of anticipation.

The howl was what Brave Deer had been waiting for.

"Now let's move through the flames and get out ahead of it. We will need to run for our lives. It will either be the flames or the wolves if we are not fast enough," he shouted as he dashed through a low point in the flames ahead of him.

No one wanted to be left behind and all quickly followed Brave Deer through the flames. Everyone experienced a few burns but all of them were quickly out in front of the fire and running for their lives toward the cliff ahead and the crack in its face.

The pack caught up with the flames just in time to see the last of their prey leap into the flames and disappear.

This was more than the leader could handle. He turned away from the flames and led his pack to the stream they had been using as their base.

Brave Deer was the first to reach the crack in the cliff. He turned to look behind and was relieved to see the dire wolves were not following. The trick with the fire had worked. He checked all his hunters and other then a few minor burns and cuts all seemed to be in good condition.

They took a few minutes to scan the cliff and decided to take a trail leading up the face.

"As we go up this cliff trail let's put some brush barriers to prevent the wolves from following us," Brave Deer instructed as he led the team up the trail.

They hiked slowly up the steep trail throughout the night. By early morning they were at the top of the cliff. They decided to jog along the ridge in what they thought was a westerly direction.

By late afternoon they realized the ridge had taken them more north then west.

An elk was spotted, and the team surrounded it and then closed in to take it down. The elk's reaction was too late, and it met two spears as it tried to make an escape.

They pulled the elk over to a series of boulders that provided a place to set up a defensible camp.

They had just completed skinning the elk and sectioning it so they could transport it when the wolf pack was spotted by one of the team who shouted a warning.

The wolf pack had followed the scent of their quarry and then they had picked up the scent of the blood of the elk.

Brave Deer had his men throw out the entrails and scrap pieces of the elk. The pack found the entrails, fought over the scraps, and discarded parts. This delayed the pack long enough for Brave Deer and his team to prepare to defend themselves.

The leader of the dire wolf pack could smell the blood of the recently killed elk as he circled the camp. He could smell the remainder of the carcass inside the ring of the camp. He moved in toward the camp. This time he ignored the fires and attacked immediately.

Brave Deer shouted a warning as the wolf leader ignored the fire ring around the camp and led the wolf pack directly at his quarry.

Brave Deer called for a tight fighting ring and for the team to fight for their lives.

He led the team in a loud vocal roar that slowed the wolves down a little.

He shouted for his men to kill as many as they could with their spears. Then using clubs and hand knifes they continued following his instruction as the wolves charged the team. They stood in a ring and fought the wolves from all sides.

The battle was unbelievably fierce. The majority of the first wave of wolves died as the flint pointed spears pierced through their chest and cut through their hearts. But the second wave made it past the spears, and it was a hand to wolf fight.

The fact the wolves would dare to attack a group of hunters was unthinkable.

There were wolves laying stunned, wounded and dead all around the circle of hunters.

The growling and snarling, the howling and grunting came from both groups.

Several of the hunters had been severely wounded. They retreated into the center of their fighting circle. They cared for their wounds as quickly as possible and then rejoined the fight.

The leader of the wolf pack watched to see which one was the leader of these strange creatures. He finally made his move and attacked Brave Deer. The timing of his attack came as Brave Deer delivered a fatal blow to another wolf.

Brave Deer's swift reaction of deflecting the wolf's leap with his left arm saved his life. Instead of the targeted throat, the wolf clamped down on Brave Deer's shoulder. As Brave Deer fell backwards, he drove his spear into the huge body above him. He could hear the bone in his arm crack.

Sharp Beaver, the warrior standing next to Brave Deer clubbed the wolf with his war club. A third hunter drove a second spear in from above and through the wolf's body.

The giant dire wolf leader collapsed on top of Brave Deer but did not let go of his prey.

The fight went on with Brave Deer trapped below the dying wolf. He could see the light going out in the eyes of the giant wolf.

The remainder of the pack backed away from the fight. Their leader was missing and most of their pack was dead. Their leader was dead. They backed away from the circle of fighters and away from the circle of fire. Several of the wolves were carrying the burns they had received during the fight.

The remaining wolves stayed in the forest surrounding the camp.

Brave Deer instructed the team to feed a quarter of the elk to the remaining wolves.

He had the wolf hides and what was left of the elk distributed among the team as he had them prepare to retreat southwest toward the coast.

Brave Deer had a deep cut on his face, a bite on his left forearm where he had protected himself and his right collar bone was broken where the wolf had clamped down with his first bite.

Brave Deer could not use his left arm. He had his shoulders strapped to a two-finger thick limb to hold his shoulders square so it would give the broken collar bone that he personally set for himself, a chance to heal.

Sharp Beaver stitched the gash on Brave Deer's face and cleaned and closed the wound on his forearm.

Another hunter had his left leg broken just below his knee. Brave Deer supervised the setting and splinting of the hunter with the broken leg bones. A travois was made for him to ride on. He would ride with the wolf hides and elk meat.

Everyone had suffered bites on their arms or legs. They all carried the marks of the fierce battle that was fought.

Brave Deer knew their only hope was to escape the wolves.

There were twenty-seven dead wolves including the giant leader.

The able team members skinned the dead wolves and threw the carcasses out around the camp as instructed.

Brave Deer thanked the team for saving his life and made the point he could not have killed the wolf pack leader by himself, but he was claiming the giant hide.

"I will wear his hide with pleasure. This wolf cost us all our hunting success, and he led this pack in a way that threatened all of us," Brave Deer said as he watched the hide put on the travois he would be pulling.

He would not be able to carry his belongings on his shoulders and would need to pull a small travois with his belongings and the hide behind him. He had this travois strapped to his waist.

When everyone was ready to travel, several of the team threw parts of the elk as far away as they could and in the opposite direction they planned to travel.

Once this was done and the remainder of the wolf pack began to fight over the meat, the hunting party hurried westward toward the coast.

Brave Deer led the way and moved as fast as he could. He put the three healthiest hunters behind the hunting party as their rear guard in case the wolves continued the chase.

The travel was down the mountain, through a long valley toward the sea. The team could not move very fast. They continued to worry about the wolves, but they did not encounter them again.

Brave Deer and his team took almost two weeks to make it to the coast. The team was exhausted, and he called a halt to their travels, and they spent several days camped in recovery by the seashore.

They would have a difficult story to tell the elders, but they felt lucky that they were all returning.

Brave Deer and the rest of his team knew they had been lucky and were happy to begin the travel southward down the coast in search of the Elk Clan.

11 Winter Camp

*T*he continuing winter snows and the challenging terrain as they crossed through the thick pine forest that towered over them often blocking the little sun the day offered made their travel frustratingly slow.

Silent Hawk was growing more concerned as the days became increasingly colder. He made sure everyone had protection from the cold and the snow. The Clan needed to find a good winter home.

The Elk Clan members knew their fate, whatever it would be was quickly descending upon them. They had traveled for fifty-eight cycles of the sun.

The mountains were finally growing shorter on the horizon behind them, but the snow-covered hills and thick brush and trees slowed their progress.

Taelo and Golden Hawk ranged far and wide. They out distanced the lead scouts and were first to reach the ocean. They arrived as a storm rolled in from the sea.

They marveled at the thunder of the waves sweeping into shore. They waded in waist deep and experienced the strong surge and freezing cold of the saltwater waves. The water was cold but warmer than the air. They wanted to feel the power that accompanied the thunderous sound.

They left as the advance scouts reached the beach and were back in time to receive these same scouts back to camp.

When the scouts reported they had reached the sea, Silver Hawk called the council of elders together to discuss how to go about finding the winter quarters for the Clan.

He suggested that two scouting groups would go in search of suitable winter quarters for the Clan. There would be at least three persons in each group. They would travel along the coast until suitable quarters were found or for three days. Then each group would return.

The Clan would move immediately to the first suitable quarters found. If a pair returned to find the Clan gone, they knew to follow to the area where suitable quarters had been found.

Silver Hawk was worried about the fact that Brave Deer and his party had not returned. He was afraid the clan might face an enemy and did not want to leave the Elk Clan unguarded.

To ensure he would have enough able warriors to protect the camp, he took the unusual action of asking White Swan to take the lead of one of the scouting groups.

She confidently accepted and asked Soft Down, a young woman in the Clan, to accompany her and Quiet Pheasant. White Swan watched Soft Down on their trip to the coast and wanted to give her recognition if front of the Clan.

Silent Hawk would lead a second group toward the northwest.

Taelo and Golden Hawk were two of the young men he was leaving behind. He instructed them on keeping watch while he was gone.

Taelo and Golden Hawk were to continue their surveillance of the surroundings, and they were to report any suspicious activity to the Clan elders.

Taelo and Golden Hawk was proud that their mothers had been selected to lead the search for the Clan winter home. He and Golden Hawk watched as the two and Soft Down left the beach camp toward the south jogging alone the water's edge.

He and Golden Hawk followed their progress as they traveled parallel through the forest on their surveillance route. They stopped when they reached their limit and watched the three continue on their way.

Then they dutifully turned into the forest on their route around the camp.

White Swan, Quiet Pheasant, and Soft Down jogged mile after mile along the beach looking for the Clan's winter home.

The dark green tops of the towering pines touching the blue sky on their left blocked the view of the white snow-covered mountains that lay beyond them. Ahead they could see the cliffs that might offer a coveted cave or out cropping that could serve as the shelter the Clan would need.

They jogged all day until almost sundown and then found a place up in the woods where they could shelter for the night. They shared their warmth as they huddled in a single buffalo hide for the night.

The next day seagulls flying inland gave them hope. They continued and found a small cove protected from the sea by a long finger like spit of high rocky cliffs running out to sea and then hooking back around the beach. This formed a protected cove with rocks on the beach to break up any waves making their way in around the finger.

They carefully searched along the cliff lining the shore on the land side of the cove. A small tumbling stream of fresh water falling down a large crack in the cliff formed a short freshwater canal that ran into the cove.

The broad area below the cliff running out to the shore provided the space needed for a lodge and individual habitats needed for the Clan. There were enough stones of various sizes that White Swan knew a clan lodge and the individual homes for families could be built.

There was no cave, so they would need to exert their labor to make this into a suitable place to winter.

They all gave a prayer to the good mother. With some hard work, this would be a good home for the Elk Clan.

The three talked through what needed to get done as they set a swift pace back that brought them back on their third day.

The journey, of the two search parties, was a contrast in speed and style.

Silent Hawk moved cautiously west and along the forest line. Fearing the sea and its storms, he was looking for a place in among the trees.

His team traveled out for three days and found nothing.

Taelo and Golden Hawk had explored a fair distance in both directions along the coast. They were sure White Swan, and her team would find the best winter quarters.

They were the first to see White Swan returning along the beach and ran back to alert those waiting in camp.

White Swan, Quiet Pheasant and Soft Down shared the description of the cove and beach area.

White Swan then requested that everyone follow her down to the Clan's winter home.

A significant part of the Clan wanted to wait until Silent Hawk returned, or the missing hunters returned before committing to the area White Swan had described.

White Swan quietly but firmly pointed out it could be several days before Silent Hawk's return.

The appropriate action for the Clan to take had already been agreed upon before he had left. The time could best be used to set up the winter camp and gather wood and water.

White Swan signaled Quiet Pheasant and Soft Down, and they gathered their belongings.

"We will lead you to your new winter homes. It is a beautiful place. You must be brave, and you must act if you wish to survive this winter. We have little time for arguments. They keep us from building our winter homes. Follow me now," White Swan spoke calmly but forcefully.

Taelo called loudly to Golden Hawk to follow Silent Hawk's directive and to follow White Swan down the beach.

Floating Cloud and Quiet Rabbit stood up and declared they were going to go to their new home.

White Swan turned and set off. She did not look back. Slowly, grudgingly, one after another, the Clan members began to follow.

White Swan, Quiet Pheasant and Soft Down exchanged a look of pride and gave each other a hug as they continued down the beach to their new winter home.

"I am amazed the Elk Clan elders have granted you so much respect," Soft Down said as she followed the two and saw the rest of the Clan was doing the same.

"Leadership is something you must demonstrate. When you do it properly, then few can stand in its way and most will follow," White Swan replied over the thunder of the breaking waves.

Taelo and Golden Hawk exchanged looks with each other. They were extremely proud of their mothers and openly showed it.

The Clan set out along the beach. White Swan and Quiet Pheasant were in the lead. Soft Down and her family quickly caught up.

Taelo and Golden Hawk explored the forest sides of the beach as the Clan proceeded.

White Swan was discussing with Quiet Pheasant, Soft Down and Floating Cloud the work required in setting up the winter camp.

In her mind she divided up the work.

White Swan was in a continuous dialogue with her three supporters. They evaluated everyone's capability and organized the work assignments.

They planned to have the camp functional and be able to provide the minimum survival shelter needed by the Elk Clan in a seven-sun cycle.

Then weather permitting, the comfort features and additional individual shelters could be built.

As the Clan proceeded eastward along the beach, White Swan spent the time moving among the older men and women discussing what needed to be done. She was establishing the relationships that would allow everyone to work together with as little friction as possible.

She did not want any head on conflicts with the Elders!

By the time they arrived at the inlet to the cove, everyone knew what to do and all were anxiously looking forward to getting their winter quarters built.

The cove presented itself like a person leaning forward and holding its arm above its face to ward off the worst of a rain or a blowing wind. The Clan stopped and took in the towering cliffs, the stone arch extending out to sea to form the cove and the stream falling down the waterfall to the stream below.

They now appreciated what White Swan had said.

The sea would provide a way to get salt and fish. The cliffs and the hooked spit of land would shield the site from the worst of the winter storms.

Quickly and efficiently the Clan went to work.

There was general agreement that White Swan had been right to push them to follow her.

White Swan was now recognized and listened to as a leader in her own right. She quietly went about ensuring the work proceeded smoothly, harmoniously, and efficiently. The first order of business would be to build the main lodge.

The cove area was heaven, to Taelo and Golden Hawk. They climbed the cliffs. They followed the small stream above the waterfall and found the spring where it vigorously ran out below a section of the cliff.

They went above the camp and rolled down stones from the top to help in building the lodge.

This action quickly led the planners to move the camp away from the base of the cliff beyond where a person could throw a large stone. They did not want to put themselves at the mercy of attackers coming in from the cliffs.

Taelo and Golden Hawk became the primary explores of the area surrounding the camp.

White Swan became the supervisor directing the building of the main lodge. This building was designed so half to two thirds was built into the ground. Several of the older men knowledgeable on the procedure to properly build and drain this structure supervised the selection and layout of the site.

The Clan members, supervised by these elders, then set out to excavate the dirt and rocks. A thirty-foot wide and fifty-foot-long area situated on high ground was marked off. A trench about three feet wide and four feet deep was dug around the perimeter of the area that would hold the building structure.

The dirt was carefully laid up along the outside of the trench. Stones of the size of a head or larger were put to the inside area of the building for use in building the lower part of the walls.

The smaller stones were piled in one area and would be used as fill between the larger stones.

The digging was hard, cumbersome work. Building the main lodge was usually the responsibility of the men of the Clan. Since most of the able-bodied men were hunting, it was now being done mostly by the women with the help of a couple of older men and many of the children. This main building would be the pride of the women both young and old, of the old men rejuvenated by the need of the clan, and of the young boys inspired by being needed.

The trench was dug in three cycles of the sun. This was a record, but everyone was working as hard as they could, so they would have a warm place to escape the cold.

The stones required to build a retaining wall around the entire compound were gathered up from the beach, the campsite area and from the cliffs.

Everyone carried, dragged, and rolled the stones needed to build the wall.

The retaining wall came up and the digging continued. Basket-after-basket was passed down the line toward the outside perimeter. The dirt piled up on the outside would be pushed up against the wall that would extend above the ground. The lower wall would be stone, and the top third would be made of woven small branches covered with the dirt being piled up. The dirt would provide insulation from the winter cold.

The materials to make the roof and interior were obtained from the surrounding forest and Clan supplies.

The roof structure was made up of logs anchored on the stone wall and tied together with raw hide. It was first covered with a series of mats made of small branches woven into larger long slender branches. This was then covered with several layers of hide.

Strategic vents to control the comfort of the interior were positioned along the circular wall and in the roof structure.

All the hides of the Clan were gathered. Unless the long hunters brought back additional hides to replace the ones being used, the Clan would spend the winter as a group inside of the gathering house because there were no additional materials for the individual huts.

All usable hides were needed to make the covering of the large central lodge.

The Clan had been at the site for about three cycles of the sun when Silent Fox returned from his search. He had not found any acceptable place. He was surprised that the main lodge structure was up and already provided significant protection from the weather.

He was pleased with the progress of the Clan and openly thanked White Swan for her excellent leadership.

"It is good we have made so much progress in getting ready for winter. The signs are for a storm at any moment. We will need the long hunters to bring in more hides and meat," the medicine man informed the group.

He was openly voicing what everyone had already realized.

The final touches were just being made to the great lodge when a lookout at the top of the cliff spotted a hunting party returning.

Brave Deer, still pulling his personal travois was leading his ragtag group of hunters.

The local game and fishing had increased the Clan's food supply to the point White Swan had suggested it was time to celebrate so the Clan prepared a welcome home dinner in anticipation of the first returning hunting team.

As Silent Hawk led the long hunters up to the lodge, a hush went through the Clan.

Brave Deer, limping as he came in, now had a long scar on the side of his face, and had one arm still in a sling. He was greeted by his partner and Busy Bee his daughter. The three hugged and tears could be seen in the eyes of all three.

The hunters looked grim. Each had a visible wound or scar.

Wives with tears in their eyes approached their husbands. Children at first afraid of their long absent fathers were quickly held in hugs.

This was not the triumphant return Brave Deer had wanted but he was relieved to be back and that all his hunters were back with him.

The Clan's medicine man quickly began to examine and treat the wounded hunters.

White Swan organized the women, and the Great Lodge was prepared for its first use.

It would hold all the Clan members as they celebrated the return of the first of the long hunters.

Tonight, the story of Brave Deer and his men would be heard.

A well bandaged but clearly severely wounded Brave Deer stood before the Clan to tell the story of his group of hunters.

"Our hunting went well when we first began. As you know we left the game from these first successes for you to find. Then we turned up a promising valley.

We traveled north just beyond a huge old maple tree commanding an area just up from the entrance of the valley. There we surprised a woolly rhino. We were in his territory. He chased us farther up into the valley. The valley seemed to have been thoroughly hunted out. We wondered if we had encroached on another Clan's hunting grounds. Then to our surprise we became the hunted. A pack of very aggressive and surprisingly aggressive dire wolves attacked us," Brave Deer began his story.

Taelo and Golden Hawk looked at each other as they heard Brave Deer describe "their" tree and the place the two of them had confronted the dire wolves. They commented that they had been lucky not to have run into the wooly rhinoceros.

"Brave Deer's knowledge and wisdom saved all of us from the most aggressive pack of wolves I have ever experienced or heard about. The pack was at least sixty strong. The leader of the pack, the skin which is now being held up was the largest wolf that I have ever seen.

White Swan commented to Quite Pheasant, "Taelo and Golden Hawk have the same size hides. It indeed was a miracle the two did not end up like Brave Deer's team."

"After being surrounded for two days by this large pack of wolves, Brave Deer had us light a ground fire. The wind was blowing toward a cliff about a mile away. Brave Deer had us follow the flames. When the wolves began their attack, Brave Deer led us through the fire, and we all ran for our lives toward the cliffs. We thought we had lost the wolf pack," Sharp Beaver continued the story.

"The next day we cornered and killed an elk and were just getting it butchered when the wolf pack showed up again.

Even though we were inside a ring of fires, the pack leader did not hesitate but attacked immediately. The battle was intense and we almost lost," Wild Raven picked up the story.

"Then the giant wolf leader directly lunged at and caught Brave Deer by the shoulder. Brave Deer survived only by his quick reaction and the act of driving his spear through the wolf. The wolf died on top of Brave Deer and even in death would not let go. We had to pry his mouth loose to get Brave Deer free.

We killed two thirds of the pack. When the leader was killed the remainder of the pack backed away," Wild Raven stood and silently looked around at those listening before sitting down.

"Even though he was sorely wounded, Brave Deer organized us to move out and come home. Many of us were wounded. Standing Buffalo, who bravely fought and killed many of wolves was bitten several times in the leg and could not walk. We thought his leg was broken but found out later that it was not. We are thinking of changing his name for making us pull him while he sat comfortably on the travois.

His new name is Sitting Buffalo one of the team said quietly and got a laugh from the listening Clan members.

Brave Deer pulled a small travois attached to his waist with his possessions and the dire wolf leaders hide on it. We made a ragtag group coming down from the mountains to the sea. We fed the remaining wolves more than half of the elk. Luckily, they no longer followed us. I do not think we could have fought them off again," Sharp Beaver continued the story.

"I apologize for our poor performance. We are pleased to be here and happy that even though we failed in our long hunt, the others have been successful, and you have found such a good winter camp. As we recover, we will do all we can to contribute to the clan," Brave Deer finished the story.

"Brave Deer, the food you first left us made a big difference. It came at just the right time. It gave the Elk Clan hope. Your return is a gift in itself. We all recognize your accomplishment. We understand your disappointment in the hunt.

Your clan has been doing its share and together we will survive the winter. You will be able to help us catch the fish in the cove and finish building our winter homes.

Do not dwell on your hunt but at being here with your families," Silent Fox spoke elegantly.

The Clan gave a loud cheer.

All the Clan members vigorously pounded the lodge floor and gave a loud hurrah.

The Elk Clan now had two more long hunt teams to welcome home in the near future.

12 Long Hunt Success

The drying rack fires were burning low, and he watched two hunters go out to gather wood. The camp had been busy drying meat since they had arrived. Burley Bear had been watching them for several cycles of the sun. He wondered how they had accumulated so much meat.

The bitter cold reached into his sleeping hide and rudely poked its cold fingers to awaken a weary Red Oak. An inner sense urged him awake. He had dreamed of a raid on his team. Without moving or indicating he was awake; he silently studied the area around the campsite.

The fires were burning low. This immediately alerted him and brought him fully awake.

He could not locate any of the night watch. He quietly prodded awake the hunter in front of him with the tip of his spear. He left the tip of his spear on the base of the hunter's neck. As expected, the hunter was quickly alert and did not move.

Red Oak signaled the hunter to do the same to the next in line. Quickly the entire party was awake and alert. Silently they withdrew into the woods and began to circle around toward the stream.

The quiet morning air seemed especially unfriendly. A disturbing silence hung in the cold gray morning.

He and his hunters had now been out for almost two months. Winter had launched its army of freezing winds, extremely cold nights, and blustery snow.

The successful hunting team was now headed back to the Clan. Red Oak and his hunters had camped at this place for the past week. A small stream provided water, and the surrounding forest yielded an abundance of firewood.

With relief, Red Oak surprised the two sentries who had the early morning watch. They were returning with more wood.

Most leaders would have assumed the fires had run low because of the lack of wood and gone back to the camp. However, for the last several days Red Oak had felt someone watching. Red Oak's senses were still on edge.

He told his men to prepare for a fight and that something or someone was close at hand and was watching them. He sent three of his hunters to look around the edge of the camp to see if they could find any sign of someone watching the camp.

High on the hill on a rocky outcropping, Burley Bear quietly backed away from the edge of the boulder he was lying on. He did not know how the leader sensed his presence, but it was obvious he knew he was being watched.

Burley Bear had found this camp of new ones a few sun cycles before and had decided to quietly observe them.

His Clan was on short rations and on the verge of running out of food. He was on the way back after an unsuccessful hunt. He would now go and inform his Clan members these hunters seemed to have enough food to feed them for the entire winter.

Since it meant survival, a raid on these hunters was worth the risk.

He made sure he left no tracks as he departed the area. It would not do to alert the group below. They looked quite capable, and they must be good with their weapons to have killed so much game.

When Red Oak's hunters passed by the place Burley Bear had been, he was already gone. He had used his skill well and his sign was not detected.

The hunters returned to Red Oak and reported there was no one around.

Red Oak's team had been very successful. Success meant the team had slowly become more pack mules then hunters. The load was heavy enough that he decided to dry as much of their meat that they could salt. This would lighten their load and allow them to make better time on the trek home.

The men were now getting restless. They were ready to get home to their families. The respect the team had gained for Red Oak over the last several grueling weeks kept the team from revolting.

Red Oak in his thoroughness carefully processed all the game killed. He made sure the meat was well salted and dried slowly over the fires. This meant around the clock watches.

The huge supply of meat they were now carrying proved to be as trying as if they had been unsuccessful.

Red Fox had announced the day before that they would load up and move out on the following day. By Red Oak's reckoning the hunters were no more than a seven sun cycles from the Clan's location.

He had led the hunt south, southwest. He should be no more than a two sun cycles march from the sea. The team should be able to go southward along the coast at a good pace and locate the Clan's winter quarters.

Red Oak had his men prepared the travois in a special manner. Two travois were set up in the woods out of sight. All the meat would be loaded on them. Two empty travois were put on top of the heavily loaded ones. Four men were assigned to pull the two travois slowly through the forest.

In the camp four additional travois were loaded with wood and stones with some minor amount of meat placed on the top layer to cover the wood. Someone watching their progress would see four travois set out for the last leg to the sea.

The travois heading to the beach would be the ones loaded with the wood.

Red Oak anticipated an attack either as the group was approaching the beach or when they were on the beach.

He sent the strongest four men he had with the meat loaded travois up over the ridge to the south. He told them to protect the load of meat with their lives and to immediately send someone for help if they were attacked.

Red Oak and the remaining eight hunters pulled their decoy loads toward the sea.

Red Oak's actions put his hunters on edge. Only their successful hunting experience with Red Oak made them do as he asked. No one had seen or heard anything warranting the precautions Red Oak was suddenly taking.

Never-the-less they did as he asked. After all, he had worked miracles on the hunt. His leadership was not to be questioned easily.

His hunters had decided to humor him as far as the beach.

When the stream finally approached the sea, Red Oak began to go southward. The team had gone about a mile down the beach, when a group of about thirty warriors of the Others burst out from the forest just ahead of them and began to run toward them.

Red Oak and his men burst into a high-speed run. This caught the advancing group of Others by surprise.

Red Oak and his men were able to run past the group and leave them behind. The months of running was now paying off. The load however slowed Red Oak and his men down enough to allow the oncoming group to close the gap.

When spears began to fly, Red Oak gave the signal to cut and run.

A few of the group pursued Red Oak and his men for a short distance but it was obvious they would not catch up to the men running away.

The hurrah from those converging around the four travois quickly drew back those chasing Red Oak back.

As Red Oak and his men ran into the forest, he looked back to see the travois being hauled off up the beach to the North. The warriors were clearly members of the people the Elk Clan called the old ones or the Others. He hoped they would not inspect the whole load until they reached their camp. He also hoped their camp was several days away.

He was laughing so hard he could barely run. His ruse had worked. He hoped to be back to the Elk Clan before his attackers found out they had been duped. He was glad he had acted on his premonition even though his hunters thought him a little touched.

They caught up with the other four hunters.

They quickly redistributed the load into four travois and then attached themselves like sled dogs and began a forced jog home.

They came out of the forest some five miles down from where they had been attacked.

Red Oak made sure all tracks made coming down onto the beach were erased. He knew that anyone seriously tracking them would quickly figure out the direction they were going but Red Oak wanted to make it hard on anyone following him.

Then he and his men jogged along the water line pulling the four travois. Each travois followed directly behind the other. The rising tide would erase all traces of their having gone this way.

Except for brief rests to drink and eat, Red Oak kept the men in harness the remainder of the day, throughout the night and throughout the following two days.

There were no complaints. The men now had total confidence in Red Oak.

How he had known they were being watched and would be attacked was a mystery to all of them. None of the members of this team would ever doubt or question his leadership again.

After three days of moving south Red Oak was beginning to question whether they might have missed the camp and jogged by it. He did not think so.

On the third day just after sunset and just before he was going to halt, an armed party emerged out in front on them.

Under his breath, Red Oak made some disparaging remarks to the spirits. He then turned his men in among the rocks and prepared to fight. He went out alone to meet the oncoming group of warriors.

At twenty paces, Red Oak's war cry stopped the oncoming group.

"If you are of the Elk Clan or friend you are welcome," Silent Hawk replied.

Red Oaks heart soared. Yet he needed to make sure.

"I am Red Oak of the Elk Clan. Who is the Elk Clan leader's wife," Red Oak inquired?

"None other than me, White Swan," White Swan replied.

The tension broke and Golden Hawk followed by Taelo ran out to greet the returning hunters. After a quick greeting out on the beach, the returning hunters were escorted into the camp.

The travois loaded with meat were pulled over to the edge of the great lodge and left.

Once again wives, children and parents greeted the returning men. When the villagers saw Red Oak and his men up close, they knew they had used all their strength to bring back the bounty that would tide the Clan over a few more months. The load now in front of the Clan's main building provided another boost to the moral of the Clan.

The memory of starvation was now replaced with hope and a growing confidence that the Elk Clan would survive the winter.

The men were exhausted and needed a good night's rest. Everyone was still staying in the great lodge since there were not enough hides to cover the individual shelters.

After a good meal, Red Oak declared it was time for his team to get a good night's rest. His men followed their leader and without exception retired for the night.

Silver Hawk was somewhat amazed and commented to White Swan and Swift Deer as they watched the hunters leave the central fire, "It seems Red Oak's men have the ultimate respect for him. They are not going to allow us to get information from them until they are all together to share their tale."

The next day was spent preparing for an evening feast. The great lodge would now hear the stories of the second group of long hunters. Clan members tried to get the hunters to talk. None of the hunters would divulge their story until they were all together around the evening meeting fire.

Quiet Pheasant spent the day preparing Red Oak's favorite dishes.

Golden Hawk and Taelo followed Red Oak around as he surveyed the camp and the surrounding area.

"This is a very nice winter's quarter. It is well situated and will provide for early fishing. The Clan has done well in getting the main building up.

We must use the additional hides my team just brought back and cover additional living quarters. Then we can build more living quarters and plan to use the hides Grey Fox Running will bring," Red Oak commented to the two boys.

He listened to the two tell of their journey to the winter quarter, of White Swan having led them to this location, of having helped in digging and getting rocks and timbers.

"You two have done well. You each have grown a good hand in height. I am proud of your contribution to the Clan," Red Oak reaffirmed them as he gave them a hug.

He was impressed with the way the two acted and carried themselves. He was a proud father and uncle.

The evening was spent in the telling of the travels and hunting of Red Oak's team. Each team member spontaneously contributed to the telling, and all were especially vocal about crediting Red Oak on his hunting and leadership abilities.

Silver Hawk was impressed with the camaraderie this team had established.

Red Oak finally got to the part of the story when the team was being watched.

He had the team make eight travois. They loaded four travois with wood and stone covered with a thin layer of meat. These travois were left in plain sight in the middle of the camp.

Two travois loaded with all the meat were out of sight.

He then told of being attacked by a group of about thirty warriors of the Others as they began their trek down the beach and how they had abandoned the four decoys, travois and saved the main load of the kill from their long hunt.

The last part of the tale was the best, but it was also the one that most concerned everyone. There was great laughter about the trick the hunters had pulled on their attackers.

He shared his concern that the Others might pose a threat to their winter camp.

Two days later, after his team had enjoyed the triumph of their return and he had time to rest from the grueling days preceding. He voiced is concern that somewhere to the north the Others needed food and were desperate enough to attack them. It was very likely the need for food would cause a fight between the two groups.

The threat of the Others finding and attacking the Elk Clan's winter quarters greatly concerned Red Oak. He felt he needed to send out a runner to warn Gray Fox Running and to get him to return as soon as possible.

Since Grey Fox Running was not due back for another two months, Red Oak decided he would go out and replace him as hunt leader. He discussed this with Silver Hawk and the elders and after much discussion they agreed with him.

Red Oak stayed a few more days to allow for a thorough recovery and to prepare to once again go out for a few months.

"I really hate to go out again but Grey Fox Running needs to return and take up leading the Elk Clan," Red Oak commented quietly to Quiet Pheasant.

Then with one other warrior he set out to find Grey Fox Running.

13 Battle for the Beach

White Swan held a different view of what needed to be done to address the presence of the Others. She had listened to the stories that Grey Fox Running had told of friendly interactions he and his family had with the Others.

The Elk Clan was struggling for survival and had feared starvation. The Clan of Others might be in the same situation. A hungry desperate Clan would be a danger to them. Perhaps help given early would prevent a later battle with desperately hungry people.

White Swan had kept quite when Red Oak talked of the coming battle. She had a very different idea in mind. She had her own plan she wanted to try.

She talked to Quiet Pheasant about her idea. She wanted to try friendship and aid as a way to approach and find out what the Others needed.

The two decided in the absence of their two best warriors, their husbands, they should take the initiative and try a non-threatening approach. If it did not work, then when Grey Fox Running returned, he would know what action to take.

She convinced Silent Hawk the worst that could come from trying her approach was rejection on the part of the Others. Such information would be invaluable for the Elk Clan to have.

White Swan asked Silent Hawk to call the council of elders together to convince them of the appropriateness of the action.

White Swan took the council talking spear, with the Elk teeth and a variety of decorative feathers, from Silent Hawk and turned slowly to look at each of the old warriors who served on the council. She understood she had to overcome Elk Clan culture and biases. She had carefully thought through the argument she faced and the points she would need to win to get her way.

Her approach was to reach out to the Others with the offer of help and friendship. A small amount of food and small gifts would provide a way for the Elk Clan to better understand the situation faced by the Others and the risk to the Elk Clan. The worst outcome would be that they found out the Others were hostile and Grey Fox Running would know he needed to lead a war party when he returned.

After much discussion and the quiet supportive guidance of Silent Hawk the council reluctantly agreed to the plan. They were hesitant to deny the wife of the new leader of the Clan.

White Swan thanked the council for their approval and assured them they would be positively rewarded for this important decision.

She openly praised Silent Hawk for his continued leadership of the Elk Clan.

Taelo approached his mother and informed her that she was not going to go see the Others by herself.

White Swan was on the verge of telling him that he would stay in the Elk Camp when an eagle scream from high overhead stopped her in midsentence.

Instead, she smiled, gave Taelo a hug and told him he and Golden Hawk would be welcome.

She looked to see Quiet Pheasant smile and nod in agreement.

Two days after Red Oak left, White Swan, Quiet Pheasant, Taelo and Golden Hawk waved to Silent Hawk as they set off up the wintry beach.

The tumultuous waves crashing violently up onto the beach and the gusting wind blowing in from the ocean created a white haze of freezing salt spray sweeping across the beach like a miniature snowstorm.

The four of them proceeded as close to the tree line as possible in an attempt to skirt the worst of it. Even then their hair was soon encrusted in a coating of ice, and they laughed at how wild they looked.

Taelo and Golden Hawk pulled a travois with some fresh fish, dried meat, some frozen meat, some honey, and some salt. It was a substantial amount and would probably feed thirty people for several sun cycles. They also had a few freshly worked leather pieces, some headbands, some gloves, and some shoes.

Taelo and Golden Hawk had contributed some delicate seashell necklaces.

The idea had been half accepted and half rejected but White Swan had insisted they try a peaceful way before they tried a more forceful way.

This was a matter of principle to her.

She was not going to accept a battle until she was sure all other means had been exhausted.

White Swan had been raised to believe goodness given was always rewarded.

"Taelo, Golden Hawk, if anything goes wrong or the people are unfriendly, you and Golden Hawk run as fast as you can," White Swan instructed as they continued their walk northward up the coast.

She was sure the two boys could outrun any of the Others. She was not worried about herself but as she thought about the situation, she worried about Taelo. Perhaps she should have insisted he stay home.

Silent Hawk had insisted Taelo, and Golden Hawk accompany them.

Taelo and Golden Hawk looked at each other as if their mothers were a little daft. They both knew without speaking neither one would ever leave their mothers behind. If anything were to happen, they would all leave together.

"Mother, if anything goes wrong you had better be running ahead of me or we will both be standing together," Taelo replied.

"Yes," was all that Golden Hawk added.

White Swan looked over at Quiet Pheasant who just smiled back at her and raised her right eyebrow to show her support of Taelo's response.

Quiet Pheasant looked back and commented that such a plan would work because both she and White Swan could outrun the two them.

After walking all day, they all sat down and had their dinner and arranged a small camp for the night. They had moved into the woods and found a small depression to protect them from the ocean winds. Taelo and Golden Hawk scouted around and came back with some fresh water.

On the evening of the third day, Taelo climbed a tall pine tree on the edge of the beach. To the north he could see some campfires. The fires were off the beach and back at the edge of the forest. The camp was probably a day's walk.

He came down and shared what he had seen with the rest of the group. They settled down for a small dinner.

13 Battle for the Beach

Taelo and Golden Hawk cleared the snow from an area large enough for all four of them to lie down on and got some pine needles from under one of the pines.

Then they lay out one large bear skin for all four of them. They each had a smaller one to cover up with. They set up an elk hide lean to over their heads.

Once everyone had crawled into sleep, the edges of the larger lower hide were folded over them all the way around. This made for a very warm bed, and it provided cover over their heads.

The next morning after a breakfast of hot fish soup the four set out once again.

After walking most of the day, they saw the tendrils of smoke rising above the camp site of the Others.

Several of the camp's warriors came toward them as they slowly made their way up the beach.

The Others were rather short but powerfully built broad shouldered, hairy men. Several of them walked toward White Swan. It was clear to her that they were being very cautious but did not seem to be too concerned.

The initial interaction was awkward since they did not speak the same language. However, White Swan spoke softly and indicated they had come as friends and had gifts for the camp.

The men were suspicious, but they could see no other people back along the trail.

They were not worried about two women and two young boys. The ones standing before them seemed weak.

It was clear to White Swan that they were being accepted. She had counted on just this attitude.

One of the Others took the lead and two followed behind as they all went into the camp and were quickly surrounded by the entire camp membership.

A huge burly young man came out and spoke loud and roughly to White Swan and Quiet Pheasant.

Taelo immediately moved around to the giant's side. Golden Hawk saw Taelo's move and put himself in front of Quiet Pheasant.

White Swan indicated they came in friendship, and they had gifts of food and other items for the women. She picked up a headband and gave it to the burly man. She then picked up some fish and gave it to a woman standing close by.

Immediately the camp members crowded in close.

White Swan was surprised when the burly man grabbed her roughly by the arm and began speaking loudly to her. He seemed to be exceedingly rude and rough. He was unaware of the movement around him.

Taelo had been watching this situation and decided to act. Suddenly, he let out a loud cry, ran forward, used the man's body to launch himself into the air and hit him across the head with his oak club.

The man grunted, sank down on his knees, and fell flat on his face.

Taelo stood over him as the camp stopped in a stunned silence.

Taelo held his club in the air and pointed it to the surrounding members of the Others.

"Be kind and gentle to my mother." Taelo said as he pointed to his mother.

"We come to give you gifts, but we are warriors of the Elk Clan. We harbor no ill will to any person who treats us well. We eliminate those who do us harm," Taelo spoke evenly as he stood over the large warrior at least three times his size and let his hand swing smoothly in an arc and take in the people around him.

The silence was suddenly filled with a loud whooping from several of the older warriors as they came forward and raised Taelo high into the air just as an eagle swooped down from the mountains and let its cry be heard over the camp.

All eyes looked upward. The members of the Elk Clan knew this was Taelo's totem. Now the members of the old ones saw his totem and reacted as well.

"It is as the omen said. A young eagle will overcome the bear. This young boy is a future leader of men. See even the eagle sends him congratulations at his victory.

Let's celebrate this visit and enjoy the food being shared with us.

Move Burly Bear into his tent and keep him calm for the rest of the day. We will have enough problems this winter without antagonizing a group of well fed and well clothed new ones," one of the older warriors said.

"What is your name," the leader of the camp asked Taelo and used sign language to make his request clear.

Taelo explained his name was the claw of the eagle. He drew the eagle in the sand and pointed to the sky. He then drew the claw.

A hush descended on the camp.

The mood of the camp changed and Taelo was seated at the right side of the leader.

Golden Hawk had stood ready to defend himself, his mother, and his aunt. The three of them watched as Taelo became the center of attention.

White Swan recovered from her initial alarm and proceeded as if nothing had happened.

She was somewhat amazed by what Taelo had just done but she had long ago learned he was full of surprises. She was not sure what had caused the sudden change in the camps atmosphere.

She presented the leader's wife with a shell necklace Taelo had made.

"This is from my young warrior, Taelo," White Swan indicated as she presented the necklace.

The necklace was made of tiny shells strung on fine elk gut cord. In the front center was a blue crystal woven skillfully into a holder.

"I call it the Eye of the Sea," Taelo said quietly as he drew the picture into the sand.

"I am Little Doe, thank you Taelo, for this wonderful necklace. I will proudly wear this "Eye of the Sea," the leader's wife said quietly.

Everyone came around to look at the necklace.

They all looked at it and then to Taelo. He was the center of attention of the camp.

"They are of the old people we call the Others. They are a large Clan, but they are running low on supplies. They do not seem to have good hunters though they have many men," White Swan said in a low voice to Quiet Pheasant.

"Yes, they need help if they are to survive the winter. It will be difficult to keep them from attacking us when they get desperately hungry," Quiet Pheasant replied.

Taelo listened to the exchange between the two and looked around at the Clan of Others.

"Why do your men not fish the food from the sea," Taelo suddenly asked as he looked around the camp.

He drew his question out in the sand. A hush again fell on the camp. This boy was talking to the leader and the elders and was asking why the camp seemed to need food.

"Boys can fish, girls and women can fish, and everyone can eat. Hunters can go to the mountains for meat. There is no reason to go hungry," Taelo said as he drew out his words in the sand.

"Golden Hawk and I can teach you to fish, to hunt rabbits and to find herbs. I am sure my mother, the mate of the Elk Clan's leader can let us stay and teach you," Taelo said as he continued to draw his message.

"Taelo, where did you get such an idea, and how do you know I will agree to let you stay," White Swan said in shocked surprise?

Taelo looked calmly at his mother and asked if she had a better idea.

She saw the wisdom in his approach, and she did not have any other ideas on how to resolve the problem.

"There is little choice. Either we show them how to get food or in a short time they will be attacking us for our food supply," Taelo replied astutely.

Suddenly, there was a roar in the camp and Burley Bear came roaring out of one of the huts.

"Where is the warrior who attacked me without warning?" Burley Bear shouted looking around for his attacker.

He was expecting a grown man.

"Burly Bear, I am Taelo. The scream of the eagle, the claw that strikes," Taelo said as he stood up and extended his hand to Burly Bear.

Just then everyone heard the eagle scream as it again flew back across the camp. Even Burly Bear looked up into the sky.

"It is an omen, the sign we have been awaiting," the leader, Quiet Fox, said to Burley Bear.

Burley Bear looked around, "Are you telling me this stump of a lad was the one that put out my lights?"

"Yes, he is the one and he is holding out his hand in friendship. You made the mistake of handling his mother too roughly," Quiet Fox continued.

Burley Bear let out a loud laugh.

"This is great. I have fought and beaten every warrior in this camp. Now I come face to face with, Taelo, "The scream of the eagle, the claw that strikes," and I have my lights put out.

Well done my small friend," Burley Bear said as he took Taelo's small hand and shook it.

"I am at your service, and I apologize to you mother," he continued.

"Burley Bear, I am glad you feel that way. Taelo has agreed to stay here to teach us how to fish and to find small game. I believe his young friend will stay with him. I am putting them both in your care. See nothing happens to them." Quiet Fox said with a smile.

He was glad to have this out of the way. He had wondered how he would handle the mountain sized, over strengthened, burley young man.

White Swan and Quiet Pheasant talked quietly and decided Taelo really had provided the best option.

"We will send a few Elk Clan members to teach you how to set the sea traps and how to efficiently make salt, is there anything that you need immediately," White Swan asked?

"Thank you for the offer of help. However, do not send anyone else. We have all the people we need. We know how to do all these things. We were waiting for a signal prophesied by our seer. A young eagle was to come and show us the way. Taelo, I believe is the person we have been waiting for," Quiet Fox replied.

"Mother, before you leave, I need to ask you for some advice," Taelo said after the gifts had all been given and the food distributed.

"Well, now my young man needs advice. And what advice do you need," White Swan said as she held him by the shoulders and looked into his eyes?

"Well, I have been looking around this camp. It seems to me they are so vulnerable to the weather here. Shouldn't they be farther up the beach into the woods and away from the surge of the sea?" Taelo asked.

"Yes, this place is very vulnerable to a large sea storm. It would be good to scout out a better location farther away from the beach. However, it will be difficult in this weather for them to move.

The day came to a close and after a grilled meat dinner, they all spent the night in one of the huts.

The next morning White Swan and Quiet Pheasant walked back down the beach toward the south toward their own camp. They were uncomfortable leaving their sons at this camp. However, they knew this was the best course of action.

They also saw Taelo, and Golden Hawk were being treated like royalty. The clan of Others looked to Taelo to guide them. The two mothers waved back to Taelo and Golden Hawk who were standing on the edge of the camp.

It was clear the camp needed a lot of help.

"Let us hope Taelo and Golden Hawk can inspire the camp to self-survival. These are the old ones. They know how to survive but for some reason they have not chosen to do so. The boys can learn as much from this Clan as they will teach them," White Swan said as she and Quite Pheasant marched south to the Elk Clan's winter quarters.

So, the battle for the beach ended peacefully. If all went well, there would be no bloodshed. More than likely there would be harmony and friendship.

Later, White Swan would see her actions reaffirmed over and over.

14 Taelo's Guidance

Burley Bear had stayed with them on the beach. He was impressed with the two young men.

"These two are as one. They have strength and yet they have much passion. They are young but fearless and brave. These are leaders of men," Burley Bear observed to himself.

Taelo and Golden Hawk waved goodbye as they watched their mothers fade in the distance.

The sea was calm.

The rays of the morning sun was burning away a light haze that lay over the camp.

The two turned toward the camp and slowly took in the situation.

It was poorly arranged and very susceptible to the wind and an ocean surge.

They stood quietly talking and agreed that their first task was to find a better location for the Clan of Others.

They would need to act immediately to change the situation. They slowly walked back up from the beach exchanging ideas about what to do.

Burley Bear listened to the two exchange ideas. It was clear to him they were discussing the situation they were in. He was impressed at their focus and earnestness.

Taelo made the point to Golden Hawk that the Elk Clan had just finished its march for survival and a search for a winter home. They should do what the Elk Clan had done and see if it would work for the Others.

"The first thing we should do is to see if we can find a winter worthy place to make camp. We will send one group back into the mountains toward the east, another group toward the north. You and I will search up the coast in hope we can find another spot similar to what was found for the Elk Clan," Taelo said to Golden Hawk.

Taelo and Golden Hawk walked back to the group of elders standing awaiting their return. The two looked around at the grizzled group of worn veterans.

"They must know ten times what we know. Why have they not taken better care of themselves," Taelo quietly asked Golden Hawk?

"I feel a little out of my league but let's get the action going," he continued.

"These two young men seem to be very self-confident and self-reliant. Let's see what they are thinking," the oldest of the group of Others said to those around him.

Taelo began talking and drawing his thoughts about the vulnerability of the camp.

He sketched out the three groups going out for three days and then returning. Each group would do two things; first they were to look for a better camp for the clan, second, they would hunt and bring back all the food they could.

The group of elders talked among themselves.

"This young one is the one sent to show us the way. We were to wait on the beach until we received guidance. Even though it comes from someone so young from the new ones, we are being given direction," Quiet Fox expressed his thoughts.

"Broken Spear says he is the one. He wants to see what this young man does before meeting with him. He did not realize from his visions he would be from the new ones and be so young. Many years ago, Broken Spear watched through the eyes of the eagle as it took the claw from his small hand," another of the elders shared.

"It is a reasonable and well thought out plan. We will act on this and organize the three groups to go out in the morning," another of the elders summarized.

Taelo and Golden Hawk listened to the exchange even though they could not understand any of the guttural language the old ones used.

"We need to learn some of their words so we can communicate more clearly with them," Golden Hawk said as he listened to the conversation of the leaders.

"Well, they seem to be agreeing to the search for a better camp and food. Let's hope we are as successful in finding them winter quarters as good as our Clan has found," Taelo observed.

Several of the women brought food to the group and took the new information back to the rest of the clan. They were buoyed by the fact better quarters would be sought.

"Let's walk around the camp and see what the situation is in more detail," Taelo suggested to Golden Hawk.

Burly Bear followed the two around during the inspection tour. He observed the two as they walked around taking in the living conditions. It became obvious to him the two were concerned about the condition of the camp. Burly Bear became concerned as well. How had he missed the poor condition the camp was in? He felt a degree of shame for having been so preoccupied with himself and to have missed what now was becoming so obvious.

Taelo and Golden Hawk noticed a disturbing fact they had not noticed before.

There were no young children. The youngest were almost young adults. What had happened to this Clan?

After dinner one of the women approached them and motioned for them to follow. The two were shown into one of the shelters and pointed to their beds. They were in the shelter next to Burly Bear's.

Darkness was quickly drawing over the camp and preparations were being made for everyone to sleep.

"We may as well get a good nights' sleep. We will have a full day tomorrow," Golden Hawk suggested to Taelo.

The two walked down to the beach, stripped their clothes off and waded knee keep into the cold water. They used a piece of leather hide to wash themselves off.

They turned and waved for Burley Bear to join them, but he shook his head and sat down.

Afterwards the two took in the camp one more time before retiring to their beds.

In the morning, Taelo was up early and had gone around the camp once again to see its condition.

"It is as if they have stopped growing, stopped having children. They seem so cowed and remorseful. They have lost their survival will. We will have to find out what is happening in this Clan," Taelo said to Golden Hawk.

After a light breakfast, Taelo went to the center of the camp. He found the group of elders organizing the three groups.

Quiet Fox was organizing each team. Burly Bear and one other warrior would accompany Taelo and Golden Hawk. The two other groups were each made up of three young warriors.

Taelo quietly inspected the packs of each search team member. He took out two thirds of the food and put it aside on a separate pile. He made a point of giving the now much smaller packs to each of the hunters.

"You will all hunt as you go. Any large find of food will be brought back to the camp by one of the team members. This is a search for better shelter and a search for more food.

As you travel, you will kill any rabbits, squirrels, groundhogs, fox, or deer you encounter. The small game will be your daily food, the larger game will be brought back to the camp," Taelo explained as he drew pictures of what he was saying.

"This young man is a tough leader. He expects you to find food as you go. The food from here is only for emergencies. Now we know why his Clan was able to give us so much food as a gift," Quiet Fox said to the group as he looked at Taelo and Golden Hawk with new respect.

If these young men represented the new ones, he could see why they were doing so well.

Taelo saw each of the two groups off as they set out.

"Look carefully for a home with water, shelter, and access to food. Hunt carefully, feed yourselves well, send much food back to the Clan," Taelo said to each of the members of the search party.

Golden Hawk and Taelo made a point of looking each member in their eyes as they put their hand on the shoulder of each and wished them good luck on their quest.

The leadership these two young men displayed impressed the elders of the Clan. Never had such direct contact between the new ones and themselves occurred.

Quiet Fox immediately saw the impact Taelo, and Golden Hawk's manner and actions had in challenging each team to do their best. He was impressed with these young men of the new people. They had high expectations of those around them, and they communicated these expectations well even with a language barrier.

After the second team left the camp, Taelo engaged Quiet Fox and the leadership team. He wanted those staying at the camp to hunt for small game around the immediate area. He also wanted the beach combed for any food that might have washed up. His final request was that some fishing be done.

Quiet Fox smiled and agreed to organize the Clan members to do what Taelo was requesting.

Golden Hawk and he were ready to depart. Taelo looked at Burley Bear and another warrior called Rolling Stone. Taelo had prepared their packs in public so all could see that his team had no more food than those who had already left.

He and Golden Hawk set off on a brisk jogging pace. Taelo knew the beach was not going to be a very good place to hunt. He hoped they would be lucky and find a small stream for fresh water and maybe some fish.

On their second day Taelo saw what looked like a huge boulder in the waves. As the team drew nearer the size of the boulder grew and he realized it was a small, beached whale.

It appeared to be a very recent event because there was no damage to the whale. The cold weather had kept it in good shape, and the wild animals had not yet found it.

This was a huge treasure for the Clan of Others. They would be able to live off this for the rest of the winter. The team needed to get this whale anchored and then processed.

Taelo led the way into the woods to find some stakes with which to anchor the whale.

Burley Bear carried a stone the size of his head and used it to pound the three stakes brought back to the beach.

Taelo realized they had no rope to tie the whale to their stakes. Golden Hawk suggested they drive the stakes through the jaw of the whale into the sand below it. This worked well, and Burley Bear put a stake through each side fin as well.

"Tonight, we will eat well. Early in the morning Rolling Stone will return to the Clan. The Clan must send a team, so we can immediately process the whale. Burley Bear, you will stay here and guard the whale carcass.

Golden Hawk and I will go on to look for shelter. I see high cliffs up ahead along the beach. Perhaps we can find a cave big enough for the Clan.

We will spend the rest of the day to gather wood for fires to ward off the animals. We will need enough to last for the next several days," Taelo explained to the other three.

They gathered and brought wood out to the beach, set up a camp for Burley Bear.

They drove some additional stakes where the fins met the body and another two in the whale's mouth. Taelo was worried about losing the whale to the sea or to scavengers from the land.

Taelo hoped the Clan would arrive in time to recover most of the meat and fat from the whale.

The temperature was dropping and the sky to the west looked as if a storm might be approaching.

The next morning after a hearty breakfast of whale tongue soup, Rolling Stone started out on a brisk trot back to the camp of Others. He was excited by the find. He knew it was another sign Taelo was the one chosen to show them the way. He would use all his energy to return rapidly to the Clan.

Taelo and Golden Hawk went the opposite direction.

Burley Bear watched as Taelo disappeared along the coast.

"He is the omen we have waited for. The gods have sent up a whale to keep us fed for the winter. He is of the new ones, but he has a good heart and a sharp mind.

I am sure he is being led by the ancients," Burley Bear thought as he watched Taelo and Golden Hawk running swiftly up the beach.

He began to set up the drying racks and continued to gather wood and bring it to the edge of the beach. He would begin the preparation for the processing while he awaited the arrival of the Clan.

Taelo and Golden Hawk were now able to travel faster. The Others were much more powerful than Taelo and Golden Hawk, but they were much slower.

The cliffs Taelo had seen were a good two days away and much larger than he had imagined them. As they approached it became clear they would need to find shelter before they got there, or they would run out of beach. The cliffs ran right out to the edge of the sea.

They could see the end of the beach when they came to a small stream cutting through the beach to the sea.

"Let's follow this upstream and see if there are any likely camps and any good fishing holes," Taelo commented to Golden Hawk as they continued up the creek away from the beach.

They had gone about a mile when the stream ended at the base of a high cliff.

"Well, why don't we set up camp here? This looks like a good place to try to catch some fish. I will look around and see what I can find," Taelo suggested.

"I will set up our camp and try my hand at fishing. Don't get lost out there. Try to make it back for the fish dinner," Golden Hawk replied as he started to set up camp.

Taelo left the camp with only his bow and quiver of arrows and a flask of water. He approached an extremely high and solid cliff with no indication of any caves.

His eyes traveled up the dark, almost brown, smooth stone to the point where the light blue of the sky made it appear someone had etched a jagged line outlining the cliffs top.

He began to follow a game trail to the right, away from the stream. He had not gone more than a quarter mile when he spotted a huge Elk stag and his three cows. Taelo had his arrow in his bow and was moving silently toward them. Suddenly the group ran and to Taelo's surprise disappeared in front of his eyes.

Taelo went forward to the spot where the Elk had disappeared. There he found an opening in the cliff. Had it not been for the Elk he would very likely have walked by without seeing it.

From high above, Taelo heard the cry of the eagle.

The cry let Taelo know the path taken by the elk would lead to the shelter the Others needed for the winter.

The elk was his tribal sign, and the eagle was his totem. Both were letting him know the way. He was being guided. He knew that he did not walk alone.

Carefully, Taelo went through the fracture in the face of the cliff.

As he came out the other side, he saw a gentle slope leading to a wide-open valley surrounded by dark green tree covered white capped mountains.

The overhang he was standing under ran to his right for several hundred yards. The overhang to the left tapered in to where a waterfall was tumbling down into a steaming pool. Water from this pool went down to another pool at the base of the cliff and disappeared into the ground.

With a little work, this area would make an excellent shelter for the Clan.

The overhang to the right was ideally arranged to allow for the building of a wall, a full spear high, to protect the cave from the valley outside.

The cooler lower pool of water kept the surrounding area warm enough prevent any snow from accumulating.

Taelo returned as the sunset and the evening darkness set over the small camp Golden Hawk had set up. Long before he arrived at the camp the smell of cooking fish made him hungry.

Golden Hawk had been successful in his quest.

"I heard the cry of the eagle. Has it been guiding you again?" Golden Hawk asked as Taelo came into camp.

"Yes, the eagle and our friend the elk guided me to a place I wish the Elk Clan could winter.

However, this Clan of Others needs it worse than we do. Perhaps the richness of their new home and the valley it overlooks will spill over into the fertility and growth for their number," Taelo replied.

"From what I understand, this Clan is made up of all that is left of several Clans. It seems they have not had children in several years," Golden Hawk shared.

At about the same time they were enjoying the trout, Rolling Stone arrived at the camp of the Others and delivered the good news about the beached whale.

This news energized the Clan.

It was noted the team led by Taelo along the beach was the one finding the food needed by the Clan.

This was taken as confirmation of the omen.

The elders acted immediately and prepared to send a crew out at the break of dawn. The camp would be packed, and the rest would follow with all their belongings by evening.

The eagle had visited Burley Bear, during the late afternoon. Its screams had inspired the large, powerful young warrior.

"Are you letting me know Taelo has found us a home?" Burley Bear said as he looked up into the crisp blue sky and watched the graceful flight of the eagle.

He knew in his heart his young friend had succeeded.

Burley Bear worked tirelessly throughout that day and the next. He made a dozen drying racks and gathered enough wood to dry most of the meat.

He checked the stakes holding the whale and added several more. He did not want high tide to take this from his clan.

His last act was to wrap himself in his large sleeping hide, put his back to one of the stakes holding the small whale and fall asleep.

The next morning, Taelo and Golden Hawk came swiftly down the coast. They were not hunting or looking for anything. They were running at a constant pace along the very edge of the sea. It had taken them two days to reach the point where they had found the shelter.

They were determined to make it back in one.

As the sun was setting on the third day, Burley Bear was sitting and watching the ocean when he spotted the two runners. He marveled at their sleekness and grace. None of his kind could run like those two. The two looked as if their feet were not touching the ground but were instead flying along the edge of the sea.

He went down to the beach to greet the two young runners.

They ran up to him and gave him a bear hug in greeting.

This surprised Burley Bear. He was taken aback by their exuberance and friendliness.

"We have found the ideal place for the Clan or Others. With this food and the shelter, we have found, your clan will enjoy many seasons of comfort and prosperity," Golden Hawk shared.

"Well, my bear of a friend, you have really been busy," Taelo said as he looked at all the wood and the drying racks.

"Tomorrow we will begin to process the whale. We will begin to move the meat up the shore. I hope your clan will arrive soon," Taelo said.

The next morning Taelo tied a cutting flint on the end of a long pole and went up to the whale and made a cut down from the backbone to the ground.

He moved half the length of the pole and made another cut. Then he went up on the whale and made a cut along the backbone connecting the two vertical cuts. Soon he had the skin and about four inches of fat rolling down the side toward the ground.

Golden Hawk knew what Taelo was doing. The two had listened to the stories of the Weaver about how to process a whale.

Burley Bear watched in puzzlement but when he saw the skin and fat rolling down toward the ground, he got the idea. When the skin and fat was about halfway down, he and Golden Hawk were able to reach it and guide it.

Taelo had instructed them in setting up a grid of logs to lay the slab of fat and skin on to keep it off the sand. Cross members had been laid and lashed down with strips of willow bark.

Now as the slab of fat came down toward them, Burley Bear and Golden Hawk pulled it across the platform. After the first slab had been cut off the three pulled the sled across the beach and up to the edge of the woods.

They set up another sled and cut the piece off the opposite side of the whale. By the end of the day, they had stripped the carcass of its fat layer.

After each trip they gathered around a large fire and to thaw out. Taelo had never been so cold.

"If we are not careful, we will all turn into chunks of ice," Golden Hawk commented.

They went to sleep totally exhausted. They had eaten some of their food from their backpacks and collapsed into their sleeping hides.

Burley Bear made sure all the fires were lit and then he too fell asleep.

Just before dawn, Taelo awoke to the grunting of a giant brown bear. He watched as the bear helped herself to a portion of the whale fat laid out at the edge of the woods.

He noticed a pack of wolves sitting on their haunches just beyond the giant bear. He was glad they were not dire wolves. It was clear they were waiting for the bear to leave before they came in for their share.

"Well, mighty bear. It seems you are hungry. Please help yourself but earn your meal by staying long enough to keep the wolves away," Taelo said quietly to the giant.

The bear looked at him and grunted and continued to eat her helping. She was out between sleeps and was extremely hungry. She did not know what had roused her, but the fat was a luxury that she could not pass up.

Taelo went quietly about putting wood on the fires. All the while he carried on a quiet conversation with the giant female bear.

The bear seemed to answer with grunts and low growls as she went about helping herself to a full stomach of whale blubber.

Taelo went out to the beach and started the fires around the whale. He knew the wolves would soon find the carcass on the beach and he wanted to be ready to defend it.

Golden Hawk had quietly gotten up and gone out to where Taelo was lighting the beach fires.

"Are we going to be able to defend this carcass against the wolves," he asked Taelo?

"Not tonight. You must run down the beach and bring a troop of warriors on the run. Come back immediately. You must be here by sundown, or we will be in big trouble. Our bear protector will not be out to help us tonight," Taelo replied.

Burley Bear quietly watched the entire interaction between the bear and Taelo. He was in awe at the bravery of the young man who talked to a grown female cave bear and walked confidently around and stoked the fires to keep the wolves out.

He crawled out to the beach so as not to aggravate the feasting bear. He was not sure she would be as kind to him as she was to Taelo.

Once out on the beach he saw Taelo was lighting the fires to prevent the wolves from making an early morning raid on the meat of the whale carcass. He also saw the dim form of Golden Hawk running swiftly down the beach toward the direction of the Clan.

The bear took her time eating. Taelo and Burley Bear agreed she was welcome to whatever she wanted. The bear, as much as the two of them, was keeping the wolves at bay.

Taelo cut some flesh off the whale and was putting it on sticks. He remembered the advice of the Weaver about how to distract wolves.

He planned to toss pieces of the meat out among the wolves to keep them back and fighting among themselves. He showed Burley Bear what he had in mind. Burley Bear was impressed with Taelo's thinking.

The giant bear gave a grunt and stood up and gave a roar and seemed to wave at Taelo and Burley Bear.

Taelo immediately advanced back into the camp and threw more wood on the fires around the camp.

The wolves were making ready to rush in, but Taelo strategically threw out some pieces of meat to scatter and break up the pack. Instead of coming forward they were fighting among themselves for the pieces of meat Taelo was throwing out.

"I will share the bounty with you my wolf brothers. But you must retreat after you have had your breakfast," Taelo instructed them as he went about tossing out the food.

He made sure every wolf got some meat, but he always threw the stick, so the wolf pack was scattered and moved away from the area.

Burley Bear went back out to the carcass and made some more of the throwing sticks. He was amazed at Taelo's approach to managing the crisis. He talked to the bear and fed the wolves. Both chose to mind him.

Finally, the sun broke through and the day began to warm. The wolves seemed to be satisfied with the meal they had been given, and they retreated from the humans.

By late afternoon, the two had brought in more wood and had established a perimeter of small fires spots around the camp. They would be lit to keep the wolves away. What they needed was some help. It would be impossible for them to keep the wolves away on their own.

A splendid red, yellow, and purple sunset was painting the sky to the west when the chanting of running warriors came to them. This immediately cheered them. Taelo gave Burley Bear a big hug.

Sharp Blade led the jogging warriors in. He surveyed the scene and saw all the preparation and defensive work.

"Well, Burley Bear, we thought we might find your carcass, instead we see you have protected this whale very well," Sharp Blade said in greeting.

"You speak to the wrong person. Young Taelo awoke this morning to talk with a giant female brown bear. He greeted her and thanked her for helping keep the wolves at bay. When she had eaten her fill and the sun was just rising, she thanked him and waved goodbye, so Taelo had time to get the campfires burning.

Taelo fed the wolves and told them they could have what they needed but they were not to come into the camp.

He has found us enough food for the entire winter and has also located our winter quarters. He indeed is the messenger sent to guide us," Burley Bear replied in greeting.

Everyone was amazed at such a long speech from Burley Bear. He was known not to speak more than a few words in multiple cycles of the sun.

Sharp Blade conversed with Taelo and Burley Bear for a few more minutes and then took charge of the camp. He assigned warriors around the perimeter and set up a rotation to cover the entire night. He could see Taelo, Burley Bear and Golden Hawk were asleep on their feet. He thanked all three and told them to get a good night's sleep.

Taelo was asleep as soon as his head hit his sleeping pad.

The next morning went without incident. Taelo instructed the warriors in how to strip the carcass of its meat. This he knew from listening to the Weaver's stories.

He also knew most of the entrails should be washed and used to encase the meat and to use as storage for the rendered fat.

The warriors were making good progress when up the beach came a group of the younger women. They were jogging along singing some ancient song. All the warriors sang back in unison.

Taelo took in the scene and marveled at the camaraderie taking place. It was good to see the hopes of these people rise.

Taelo went about telling the women what they should be doing.

Golden Hawk had gone out with a few of the warriors and collected some flat stones to be used to melt the fat. Several melting stations were set up to melt and catch the fat in bags made from the entrails of the whale.

The bags of oil were hung in the trees well away from the wolves and out of the reach of the bear.

The merriment and happy chatter could be heard everywhere. The story of Taelo talking to the bear and feeding the wolves was added to the other stories of the tribe. It would be repeated for years to come as the Clan sat around the fire and marveled about the young boy sent to guide them.

Quickly the great whale was reduced to bone. Even these would be kept and used for a variety of purposes. The Ivory of the teeth would be carved into figures and bartered for various other products from Clans all around them.

The remainder of the day was used to continue the processing of the whale. First to arrive were the younger half of the Clan, finally late in the afternoon the remainder of the Clan came up the beach dragging all their belongings on travois. Everyone ran down the beach and helped the elders bring their belongings into the camp.

In the evening Taelo sat with the elders and told them of the fine camp he had found. In the morning, he would lead the elders to this place, so they could begin to prepare it.

Burley Bear sat with the Elders and in their tongue again shared the tale of Taelo and the Bear. The Bear continued to grow in size and the number of wolves was now in the hundreds.

Everyone enjoyed the story, and they all were amazed at the change in Burley Bear. He was starting to be fun to be around.

They joked that this change in Burley Bear was the best present Taelo had given the camp.

15 New Home, New Hope, New Beginning

As the sun rose, the morning shadow receded up the beach to where Taelo was sitting. Today, for the first time, he would meet the Others Clan medicine man. He was not sure why he had not met with him before, and he was curious about the man they called Broken Spear. Broken Spear had been carried up the beach the night before by four of the younger warriors.

Taelo knew that it was he who had predicted an eagle would come to show the clan the way.

"This is Broken Spear. He was our leading warrior and hunter until he was injured and almost died when his group surprised a mother brown bear. She killed two other hunters and left our proud Sure Spear, broken. Since then, he has had visions and has guided our Clan," Quiet Fox introduced Taelo to the medicine man.

There was a twinkle in the eyes of this old warrior as he shook Taelo's hand, and his eyes seemed to penetrate the very being of what Taelo thought was his inner self.

"I have heard much about you. I expected a giant and here standing in front of my eyes is a normal young man of the new ones. You must indeed have strong magic guiding you to have done so much. In only two weeks you have brought more hope to our clan then we have had for years.

Burley Bear has told us about you talking to the giant brown bear. I wonder did the bear have a notch cut from her left ear," Broken Spear asked?

It took Taelo several moments and some drawing in the sand by Broken Spear until he understood the question.

"Yes, this bear did have a notch missing in her left ear. Is she a bear you know?" Taelo replied in surprise.

"Yes, it was she who almost killed me. I see the ancients have used her again, this time to help us," Broken Spear replied.

"Let us proceed to the new home you have found for us. Tell me did the eagle scream when you found this new home," Broken Spear asked Taelo?

"Yes, the ancients showed me the place by using the Elk, the sign of my clan. Once I had found the opening, the eagle screamed. I took it as a sign this was the place I was seeking," Taelo responded.

Just before they were ready to leave, one of the other two groups out seeking better shelter returned. They were in good health and had an abundance of small game but had not found any shelter for the clan.

216

The three were in awe at all the food and looked at Taelo with new respect when they heard the stories of the last few days.

The elders, the older women and a selected group of warriors and younger women were to be part of the journey to the new home. They would bring every bit of food they could carry. About two thirds of the Clan of Others was left on the beach to process the remainder of the whale and melt the fat into oil.

Golden Hawk and Burly Bear stayed behind at the beach to help in completing the processing of the whale. Taelo led the remainder of the group up the beach toward the Clan's new home.

It took three additional days to guide this larger and slower group to the opening in the cliff. Like before, the opening was unnoticed until Taelo took the group around an outcrop of stone.

Quiet Fox stopped the procession and told them to wait until Broken Spear and Taelo went ahead and blessed their new home.

Broken Spear and Taelo walked in together. Broken Spear used Taelo like a crutch and the two, one from the past and one for the future, hobbled in together.

Tears were in the old man's eyes as he beheld the pool of hot water, the valley below and the living area to the right. After years of suffering and decline, here was a place where the Clan should prosper. The weight on Taelo's shoulder lightened ever so lightly. Broken Spear's heart had soared and lifted him to new hope.

They had been mistreated by many of the new ones, but it was something else that had been causing the Clans decline.

Broken Spear was sure the ancients and spirits were ending the time of the Others.

He chanted thanks to the ancestors and blessed this as their new home. Broken Spear sat down and sent Taelo back to lead the rest of the Clan in.

There was an immediate hush as the group beheld their new home. This was an unbelievably rich and comfortable place. The Clan members spread out and began to examine the layout of the cave. There was excited talking and pointing as they grasped the richness of their surroundings.

Quite Fox took charge. He and the group of elders walked around the entire overhang area. They quietly discussed how to lay the place out.

Taelo guided them to a place he had selected to be the latrine and another where he indicated waste should be collected during the winter and then moved out for the summer. Taelo was focused on improving the hygiene of the Clan. He had been a little appalled at their current practices.

Taelo was hoping to add a couple of new habits. In his home each day they would sit by a steaming pot and wash. Bathing was one thing he had not seen this Clan do. In the evening, he invited the group of elders to the hot pool.

He went to the edge and sat to one side of where the water ran out. Here the water was pleasingly warm. He took off all his clothes and stepped into the pool. He lowered himself into and under the luxuriously hot water.

He came back to the surface and washed his hair. He washed his entire body and then rubbed it down with some crushed pine needles he had prepared before getting in. He also rubbed some whale oil scented with pine needles into his hair. He then rinsed his hair one last time and stepped out of the hot water and dried himself off with a leather drying cloth.

The Elders watched in wonder. They were afraid to sit in the water.

Taelo indicated that they should do the same. Broken Spear knew it was up to him to overcome this fear. Bathing had been a Clan custom until the last great illness. He took off his clothes and joined Taelo.

Taelo helped Broken Spear into the hot water and helped him to sit on a large stone. This provided a convenient place to sit and wash. Taelo helped Broken Spear wash off. The rest of the elders slowly followed and soon they were enjoying the warmth of the hot pool.

Taelo left the group for a few moments and returned with a large skin full of whale oil. He poured some of the oil into a cooking skin and put in some cooking rocks. He added the crushed pine needles to the oil and let it cook for a while. The oil from the pine needles mixed with the whale oil and provided a lightly scented concoction.

Taelo again rubbed some of this hot scented oil on his skin and put a small amount in his hair. Finally, he dried himself off with one of his leather drying clothes. Everyone watching got the idea and copied what Taelo had done.

For the first time in days Taelo felt clean and comfortable.

Taelo noticed the lice and fleas floating away in the hot water. He and Golden Hawk had talked about this problem and the fact they were getting infested.

Taelo pointed to the dead lice, and fleas and commented to Quiet Fox and Broken Spear, "You must bathe each day and keep doing so until there are no more small animals living on you. Then you must do this at least once every two or three days. Then the Clan will be healthy, and all will feel better."

"He speaks like the medicine men of old. They taught us how to prepare various oils with the smell of flowers, and other plants. This lost favor many moons ago because people thought the water and the oils were causing members to get sick and die. He is telling us to do what the elders told us. It is as if they are using Taelo to awaken the memory of the Clan," Broken Spear spoke to the rest of the elders.

The rest of the Clan had watched in silence and awe as the elders all shed their clothes and got into the water with Taelo. Then came the bigger surprise, they were instructed to get into the water and wash as Broken Spear instructed. Soon they were enjoying themselves in the warm water and the new feeling of being clean.

Everyone in the camp enjoyed the hot water and the chatter indicated that they were enjoying the feeling of getting clean and of the luxurious scented oil on their skin.

Taelo stood back and watched as the entire group took a communal bath. He sat down on his rabbit skin blanket and enjoyed the festive nature of the communal bath. For the first time in several weeks, he was clean, comfortable, and warm. He fell asleep sitting on his rabbit skin blanket as he watched the group in the pool.

The Clan left him by the warm pool and proceeded to make dinner. One of the women brought him some whale meat cooked in salt water and gently woke him up.

Taelo took a few bites and then walked over to where he had put his things and climbed onto his sleeping hide. He was very tired and fell asleep immediately.

He dreamed of the Clan. They were to prosper here. They would live in this valley for years to come. He would visit them often, yet they would slowly decline in number. They would have children, and they would be around until he was an old man. He had tears in his eyes when he awoke.

He felt someone's hand and looked into the eyes of Broken Spear.

"Now you know the fate of this Clan. We are of the old way. You are of the new. We will soon be gone. I have told no one of our future but you should know so you will know we are of no threat to you," Broken Spear said quietly as he sat by Taelo's side.

Taelo immediately realized it had not been a dream. Not in the sense of other dreams. He was sure Broken Spear had in some fashion spoken directly to his mind. He was surprised at this feat.

"Can all old ones do what you just did," Taelo asked.

"No, not all, all can hear the ancient ones. All have visions but they do not understand them. When the bear injured me, she caused much damage to my head and body. Whatever she broke caused me to be more sensitive to the ancient ones and to the other spirits surrounding us.

There are many animal spirits I can feel. I can feel and sense the spirit of your totem, the eagle. I know when it is coming. I have seen through its eyes," Broken Spear shared with Taelo.

"Your mind has many places I cannot see. I sense your general spirit but can't see details. I can send it my thoughts, and you receive it well, but you block any other probing I do. Your mind is quite interesting," Broke Spear confessed.

Taelo was not sure what to make of this exchange other than the fact he often wished he and Golden Hawk could exchange thoughts. The fact the old ones had such power did not surprise him and it confirmed the stories his father had told him.

The work in the camp went quickly. Stones were gathered, and walls built and held together with mud mixed with grass. The outer wall went up first.

This insured the Clan would be able to defend themselves from any predators. The individual quarters were decided next and communal fires and cooking areas allocated.

Taelo had little to do with the majority of what was now going on. He had all the tribal clothes and sleeping blankets washed and processed. There was an immediate change in the energy of everyone in camp. Unknown to any of them including Taelo, the camp had been suffering a continuous fever due to the lice and fleas.

The entire smell of the camp became more favorable.

On the fifth day Golden Hawk brought another group loaded with dried meat, fresh meat, bags of oil and processed whale skin, ivory, bone, and gut. The group was welcomed, and the food put into the communal pantry area prepared for it.

The final search group had found them on the beach, and they were back helping the processing of the food.

Amazingly the first group took the new arrivals to the hot pool and had them take a bath before letting them into the camp.

This caught Golden Hawk by surprise. "What have you done to this Clan," he shouted to Taelo as he plunged into the warm pool and showed the others how to bathe.

Afterwards, Taelo talked to Golden Hawk, and they agreed on how many trips it would take to bring in all the food. They discussed this with the Elders and plans were put into place to bring in the remainder of the food.

Taelo interjected a sense of urgency. He told them his Clan was preparing for a very long and cold winter. They would need to get all their goods in and be prepared for the cold.

Taelo thought how lucky this group was to have a hot spring to provide them with a warm cave and hot bathes. He knew his mother was bathing using water carried in from the stream and then heated by stones.

Thinking of his mother made Taelo decide it was time for him to return to the Elk Clan. In the evening, he sat with the elders and let them know as soon as the rest of the food was brought in, he and Golden Hawk would return to their own Clan.

It was close to the Winter Solstice. The Elk Clan always celebrated the solstice with a night of eating telling stories and drinking a special brew the women prepared.

Taelo discovered the Others also celebrated the Winter Solstice with a similar ceremony. The Elders decided to hold the celebration a few days early so they could host and honor their new friend and young leader. The event was planned and when the last of the food was brought in the party was to be held.

A few days later the last of the whale was brought to the cave.

The remaining members of the Clan were indoctrinated into the new bathing ritual and then allowed into the camp.

In the evening, a celebration was held. All night the elders told stories of days past and the feats of heroes of old. Taelo and Golden Hawk felt the presence of these old ones, and it seemed they walked among them.

It was surprising how many of the stories about heroes were similar to the ones told by his people.

Toward the morning the elders added the stories of Taelo and Golden Hawk and the scream of the eagle in with the rest of the Clan's history. This embarrassed Taelo and Golden Hawk, but the Clan considered them their honorary new ones.

The two told the elders they were not worthy but honored that they were included in the Other's history.

The elders all invited Taelo and Golden Hawk to stay longer, though they understood their wish to return to their own Clan. They, however, decided the two should be escorted back by Burly Bear and at least three other warriors. It would not do for the messenger sent by the ancients and ancestors to befall any harm.

The next morning a well provisioned Taelo and Golden Hawk jogged down the beach. They ran just ahead of the four young warriors of the old ones. Someone watching might have mistaken the scene for two slender people being chased by four burly, rough-looking attackers.

16 Return Home

The fire warmed Gray Fox Running as he sat by the coals of the night fire and quietly discussed the progress of the hunt with his team of hunters.

Their harvest was abundant.

Most of the meat was dried.

They were now fully loaded.

Grey Fox Running was ready to return to the Clan earlier than planned. The team had performed beyond expectations and had sent back two previous loads. There was enough dry meat to sustain the Clan until spring. They were finishing drying the huge amount of meat from the large mastodon they had taken down.

This last excursion had been a great success but one of the warriors had his leg broken when the mastodon fell on him at the end.

Grey Fox Running had set the warrior's broken leg, and he was doing well. To the injured hunter's chagrin, the other hunters had renamed him Falling Mastodon.

This tale would grow in its telling and Falling Mastodon knew his new name was his and would always be so.

This injury put the team short of people to pull all the travois of meat and the tusks of the mastodon.

Grey Fox Running was deep in thought when one of the warriors called in a warning.

Two people were coming across the valley toward them. This was empty territory, so Grey Fox Running went out to see who was coming. Looking out across the wide, snow covered plain below, Grey Fox Running, recognized Red Oak's red feather flying from the top of his spear.

The sight of Red Oak brought immediate apprehension to Grey Fox Running. Something was wrong otherwise Red Oak would not have come. He went out to meet him. The two were the best of friends and were always happy to see each other.

After their initial greetings Grey Fox Running asked, "What brings you out to find us?"

"When I returned from my long hunt, I was attacked by a large group of Others. I tricked them and gave them mostly stones and wood, though they got about ten percent of what I had hunted. We lured them with a decoy and then ran away ahead of them to where four of our strongest hunters were pulling two very heavily loaded travois. This allowed us to get most of the food to our Clan.

The Clan has found a very good place to spend the winter, but I am afraid the Others will attack. They are a much larger group than our Clan and you know how strong and fierce they are.

I came as soon as I could. It has taken me ten days to find you. I think we should return as soon as possible. Perhaps you should go ahead, and I will bring the hunters back as soon as possible," Red Oak hurriedly told his story.

"No, we will all go back together. We have enough food and the two of you are exactly what we need. Now we have enough muscle to pull our load home.

The Others usually do not attack us. It is usually we who attack the Others.

Yes, they are very strong, and they are unusually hairy and fierce looking, but I have lived with them, and they are reasonable. They are unusually wise and seem to be able to do things with their minds of which we have no knowledge.

I will heed your warning, and we shall proceed back quickly. However, I will be surprised if they have attacked," Grey Fox Running replied.

Grey Fox Running recalled how his father had befriended a group of old ones and had lived with them for several years. This was before they had joined the Elk Clan.

"Let's get the others ready to return home," Red Oak replied not feeling as confident as Grey Fox Running.

He wanted to return as soon as possible.

It took the hunters two days to pack up all the food and position it on a travois each would pull. Falling Mastodon had a crutch, but he would ride one of the travois along with some of the food. It was too soon for him to travel on his bad leg.

It would take them a good fifteen to twenty sun cycles to make the journey home. Red Oak had marked the trail on his way out and knew if any danger was to befall the Clan's winter quarters a runner could quickly find them.

The fact no runner came was somewhat reassuring.

The hunting on the way home was only for their daily meals. It consisted of a few unlucky rabbits or deer surprised by the slowly moving procession of heavily weight travois each pulled by two warriors.

Now with the hunt over, Grey Fox Running and Red Oak were eager to return to the Elk Clan. They set a grueling pace and marched for at least ten hours a day. This was a dawn to dusk march.

They only had one small, heated meal prepared hastily in the evening. No one had time to enjoy the beautiful but cold vista of mountain valley's and streams. They were now into the heart of winter and eager to get back to the Clan.

The cold was deep and bit through their clothing and coats.

This was truly breath-taking country. The long valleys held abundant game. The various thickets showed signs of blackberries and dewberries.

Red Oak and Grey Fox Running shared what they had learned about the country around them with each other and agreed this land offered the Clan a bountiful territory in which to take up their residence. Hopefully, they would not run into any other people claiming this area.

They hoped to enjoy this abundance and keep the Elk Clan well fed.

After almost two weeks of travel, they finally were headed down the valley leading to the sea. Red Oak figured they would make the main camp in about three sun cycles.

They had targeted to make it home by the winter solstice, so they could all celebrate the shortest sun cycle and the lengthening of sunlight afterwards. They looked forward to the feasting and the celebration which would take place.

They moved out onto the beach at about the same place Red Oak had before. Red Oak was wary but there did not seem to be anyone about. He wondered where the Others were, but he was pleased not to have to deal with them.

On the third day they were moving down the beach as the sun set far out to sea. A far away golden glow, with gray and purple shining from the clouds greeted them to the beach.

The loud crashing of the waves made casual talk almost impossible. The sight of the sun's rays painting the clouds a pink, grey and golden yellow, caused Grey Fox Running to call a rest halt so all of them could enjoy the beauty.

The winter quarters are just about a mile down the coast from here," Red Oak informed the group as they were enjoying the sunset.

Not far down the beach Taelo, Golden Hawk, Burley Bear and the other three warriors accompanying them were sitting down enjoying the same sunset.

"There are other people on the beach just north of here," Burly Bear said as he drew his message in the sand.

"Now how does he know such a thing," wondered Taelo out loud to Golden Hawk?

"Let's move over to that log and see who it is," Golden Hawk said as he looked around for some shelter.

The six of them moved to a large log located on the beach and lay down behind it.

As the sun dipped rapidly below the horizon, Grey Fox Running Running's group set out with new energy. Their legs were strengthened by the fact they were close to their new home. All were looking forward to seeing their families and loved ones.

Suddenly an eagle cried out and the cry of the hawk followed.

Red Oak and Grey Fox Running looked at each other. They knew these calls. Grey Fox Running returned the call of the eagle and Red Oak did the same for the cry of the hawk.

Up ahead they saw two bodies stand up from behind a large log. The two ran out toward the oncoming group. It was Taelo and Golden Hawk.

Behind them came four strangers. As they drew closer, Grey Fox Running recognized them as some of the Others. He wondered if they had indeed attacked. The Others stopped a good distance away and were not making any moves to come any closer.

The two boys rushed to their fathers.

"It's very nice of you two to come out to greet us," Grey Fox Running said as he hugged Taelo. He noticed Taelo had grown a good hand in height.

"No, it is you who are greeting us. We are just returning from several weeks at the camp of the Others. We would have made it to our Clan's winter camp if we had not stopped to enjoy the beauty of the sunset," Taelo replied.

Just then, from down the beach came the cry on the eagle. Taelo eagerly replied since he recognized his mother's version of his cry.

"Well, this is a great home coming. I don't know who is greeting whom, but it is nice to be back," Red Oak said.

White Swan, Quiet Pheasant and three of the Elk Clans warriors met the group. There were hugs and quiet rejoicing.

White Swan was a little overwhelmed to have the two men in her life back home at the same time.

Quiet Pheasant had the same feelings as she greeted Red Oak and Golden Hawk.

Burley Bear sat down cross-legged on the beach as he watched the two groups. He talked quietly to the three other three warriors.

"Look at the amount of food this hunting party is bringing home. This Clan will eat as well as ours. It seems that these new ones have a gift for gathering food," Burley Bear said to the three younger warriors.

"Look at how they care for each other. They are just like us in so many ways. I wonder why we have not been friends," Burly Bear asked but he was not addressing anyone?

"Who are your new friends? And what are their names," Grey Fox Running asked?

He walked toward the Others, and the rest of the Elk warriors followed him.

The two groups came together.

Burly Bear knew that though Taelo had helped his Clan, most of the new ones were usually afraid of the Others. The new ones looked very frail, but they were very fast and agile.

The Others were much stronger and muscular but as Burly Bear knew they were slower.

Gray Fox Running approached, Burley Bear and extended his hand in friendship.

Burley Bear stood up and returned the handshake. This was the first time one of the new ones other than Taelo and Golden Hawk had approached him in a friendly manner.

"You must be the father of the great one we call, Taelo the scream of the eagle," Burley Bear said to Grey Fox Running.

To his surprise, Grey Fox Running replied in rough but understandable language of the Others.

"Yes, Taelo is my son. I hope he has provided your people the help he promised," Gray Fox Running replied as both groups looked at him in amazement.

Only White Swan knew Grey Fox Running had this talent. It was because of the stories he had told her that she had been so certain her actions were the right ones to take in trying friendship first.

"We were sent to escort Taelo and Golden Hawk home to ensure their safety," Burley Bear explained his presence and of the other three warriors.

"Well let's get to the camp and see if there is a decent meal for all of us," Grey Fox Running continued speaking in Burley Bear's language.

16 Return Home

Taelo was surprised by Grey Fox Running's ability to speak Burley Bear's language. He and Golden Hawk had been practicing and had picked up quite a few words, but neither could fully understand what Grey Fox Running had just said.

After repeating himself in the language of the Clan, Grey Fox Running with White Swan, at his side, led the way toward the village.

The group proceeded back to the camp.

Gray Fox Running took in the work done in making the camp winter worthy. The main shelter had been finished. Down near where the water fell from the cliff, he could see a fire pit that he would later learn was the one personal lodge put up by Floating Cloud the mother of his good friend who he had lost during his last long hunt.

Several cooking areas had been set up outside of the main lodge. A few separate quarters had been completed and the frames for most of the other quarters had been erected but remained uncovered.

Grey Fox Running figured the shortage of hides was the reason. His return would solve most of this problem.

Silent Hawk greeted both Grey Fox Running and Red Oak.

They all listened to the account Taelo brought back to them about finding food and relocating the old ones to the cave with hot springs. Everyone commented the perhaps they should have sent Taelo out to find them winter quarters with a hot spring.

White Swan moaned and acted hurt about such a comment, but she smiled as she did so. She complemented Taelo and Golden Hawk for having done so well.

Taelo and Golden Hawk thanked White Swan for the kind comments and in turn introduced their friend Burley Bear and the three other warriors.

Burley Bear stood as he was introduced. He was a good head taller than Grey Fox Running and at least twice as wide. His smile looked like that of a snarling wolf to many in the Clan.

Even though there was a language barrier, it was Burley Bear who told the story of Taelo and the whale. He told his account of Taelo finding the whale, of talking to the huge female brown bear, of feeding the wolves and finally of finding the new dwelling with a heated spring. The surprise for everyone was that Grey Fox Running translated this account to the entire Elk Clan as Burley Bear told it. The Clan in turn sat quietly taking in every word of the story.

Taelo became even more mysterious and symbolic to the Clan than before.

Taelo sat quietly by White Swan. Golden Hawk sat next to him with Quiet Pheasant and Red Oak.

It was clear to both he and Golden Hawk that they needed to get away from all the attention they were getting from both Clans.

16 Return Home

17 Winter Takes Hold

*T*he days got progressively colder and the storms coming in from the sea more powerful. Even with the protection shielding of the spit of land, the camp was buffeted by powerful storms and became coated with a salty ice. It was good the camp had been built up away from the beach, for the beach disappeared under the surging sea.

The main shelter stood the weather well. Its construction had been thorough and solid. The earth bank on the outside kept the cold winds at bay. The movable sections of the roof allowed for easy temperature control.

Only a few families were now without their own family shelter. The Clan was still short on the materials to make all of them individual family shelters. Grey Fox Running had made all the additional family shelters in the same way as the main building. This provided each with good insulation against the cold. A small fire in the center of each building provided all the warmth needed.

During these brutally cold days, everyone busied themselves inside with the preparation of the few leather hides not used for shelter, carving on the ivory of the elk or the teeth of the black rhino.

Taelo had brought back several ivory teeth from the beached whale he had found. He was intricately carving the scene of the beach on one tooth and on the other he was carving a picture of the Clan's camp. He would work on his pieces for a while and then do something else for a while before continuing. He figured it would take him most of the winter to finish his two pieces.

Burley Bear had chosen to stay with Taelo and had sent the other warriors back north to their new home. Burley Bear felt a kindred spirit in this young man called Taelo and felt it was his role to protect him. He would accompany Taelo and talk with him wherever they went.

Taelo and Golden Hawk were quickly picking up the language of the Others. They would sit around and practice with Burley Bear and then try their new learning on Grey Fox Running.

The camp members soon accepted this burley young warrior from the Others as just another Elk Clan member. He looked much different, and it was clear he was covered with enough hair to make his name appropriate. He worked hard and he seemed always at Taelo's side.

Even if they had wanted to, none of the other boys Taelo's age would have dared confront him. His own bodyguard looking like a wild bear usually shadowed him.

After a few weeks of fixing his clothes, his shoes, his weapons, and anything else seeming to need repair, Taelo grew restless. He and Golden Hawk decided to climb the cliff behind the camp and see what was on the other side and beyond. They talked it over and decided not to say anything to anyone. They prepared everything in secret.

Early one morning they left.

They prepared themselves for the extreme cold they expected to face and carried plenty of warm clothes. They were not sure hunting would provide enough food at this time of year, so they carried a supply of dried foods.

Long before dawn, Taelo and Golden Hawk quietly left the comfort of their beds and started up the cliff. They were climbing the cliff just as dawn broke. It was slow going up the steep cliff face, but they made good progress.

Once on top they followed a trail they had found when they first arrived. By the time the camp began to stir, they were almost to the top of the cliff. By the time Burley Bear began to look for Taelo, the two boys were over the top of the cliff and on their way along the ridge leading eastward away from the beach. They took off trotting in their normal traveling gait.

The timing of the two could not have been worse. A cold front came in during the day and the temperature took a steep drop and the wind steadily increased. A severe winter storm was blowing in from the west.

On the backside of the cliff, away from the sea, the turn of the weather was not immediately noticeable to Taelo and Golden Hawk. The air was noticeably colder, but the wind had not yet started to blow. They were trotting along a ridge going inland away from the sea. The wind was at their back.

They had left a message for their parents not to worry and were quite satisfied they would not be missed. The self-confidence they had in themselves and each other shielded them from any concern they might have had.

The weather continued to get colder, and the wind picked up. This became noticeable to both Taelo and Golden Hawk and they began looking for a place to shelter. They had slowed to a walk along an old animal trail when they heard the sound of a waterfall. The trail went around a huge wall of stone and seemed to disappear down the mountain on the other side. It was a sheer drop down the narrowest of trails. The sun was making its final descent, and the trail would be impossible to follow.

Taelo turned back to where they had first heard the waterfall. He found a crack in the rocks and followed it.

He found himself looking into a large cave with a steaming pool of water inside. From a crack in the rocks on the other side, cold wind was blowing in and pushing the air through the crack where he was standing. There was a flat area all the way around the pool and what looked like benches around the edge of the pool area.

"Look at this place. If we can close the opening on the other side, we will have a warm winter home," Taelo exclaimed to Golden Hawk.

"Let's, find some timbers and get the opening closed. I think we are going to need a good place to escape from this cold winter storm," Golden Hawk replied as he looked around for the wood he wanted.

The two found the timber they needed in the forest they had been jogging through. They also found some stones they could use to help close the far gap as well as the entrance gap. They brought all the materials to the cave and set about closing the far opening. They determined the final closing could best be accomplished with the use of some of the hides they were carrying. Together they closed the opening with a thick buffalo hide. It would allow them to open it to let light in during the day.

Taelo closed the cracks on entrance to the cave in such a manner that he created a cold area to the left side of the entrance. This would be a great place to keep meat and other food.

This was separated by stone from the warm area surrounding the pool. They gathered enough stones to close the entrance opening.

This greatly reduced the airflow through the cave. Immediately the cave began to warm.

Using the hide, they had put across the top of the crack in the cave closest to the waterfall, they were able to control the air flow so a small fire could be placed on a flat stone. The smoke went up and out through the crack in the roof.

They did not need the fire for warmth, only for cooking. The heated pool provided all the warmth needed. This kept the air in the cave very fresh.

The two had spent most of the day working on making the cave fit for use and they had not spent much time worrying about the weather. By now the storm was beginning to be a serious raging storm. They, however, were in warm, comfortable quarters. The evening brought the storm, and the temperature outside took a steep dive.

Back at the Elk Clan camp White Swan worried about the two getting caught unprepared by the incoming bad weather. To her surprise it was Burly Bear who seemed the most worried. He had been caught off guard. He had not sensed or anticipated this event. He immediately prepared his belongings and was going to follow the two.

Grey Fox Running and Red Oak thought it would be a good idea for Burley Bear to find the two young adventurers. They figured he would find them and help keep them safe. They loaded the young warrior down with extra dried meat and other food that would travel well. Finally, they gave him a great bearskin to carry with him.

Even if caught outside Burley Bear and the two adventures would have a warm place to sleep. Burley Bear's pack was almost as large as he.

The camp watched somewhat amazed when Burley Bear climbed the cliff with the load he had on his back. All the Clan members found it strange to have this warrior from the Others so attached to Taelo and Golden Hawk.

"In his short time, Taelo has made strong friends who are willing to risk their lives for him. Let's hope our young man does not overextend himself in his adventures," Grey Fox Running said as he held White Swan to him.

Together they watched Burley Bear's progress up the steep cliff.

"I am not too worried about Taelo, but it is comforting to know he has such strong friends who will risk themselves to know he is alright. I am sure Taelo will again surprise us," White Swan said as she returned Gray Fox Running's hug.

She sensed this was another of Taelo and Golden Hawk's adventures where they would distinguish themselves.

Burly Bear struggled as he climbed up the cliff. He wondered how Taelo, and Golden Hawk had made this climb. The capability and resilience of the two were constantly surprising him. Their daring and capability seemed to overcome all obstacles put in front of them. He finally made the summit and after taking some time to recover from the climb he began a constant gait as he followed their trail.

Thank goodness they had followed the ridge and taken a fairly level, somewhat downhill path. Burley Bear figured he would catch up to them by noon. Noon came and passed. He continued at a constant jog as he chewed on some of the dried meat sent with him. He realized he had greatly underestimated the speed at which the two traveled. He had previously watched them seemingly and effortlessly glided across the ground as they jogged along. He now was personally experiencing just how fast the two moved.

Finally, as dusk was falling, Burley Bear came to the end of the trail he was following. The weather by now was biting through his clothes and he was worried he would have to stop and prepare a camp. Snow was falling heavily. Where had the two disappeared? For the third time Burley Bear read the tracks. The tracks all lead to a huge stone and disappeared.

"Could Taelo walk through stone," Burley Bear thought to himself?

246

"Taelo, Taelo, where are you," Burley Bear shouted repeatedly as loud as he could?

Inside the warm cave, both Taelo and Golden Hawk heard the bellowing of what they thought was a bear calling Taelo's name.

"Is our friend, Burley Bear shouting your name," Golden Hawk said in surprise?

"We had better go out and look otherwise if he is, he will freeze in such weather," Taelo replied.

The two carefully removed the stones they had put in the entrance fissure and stepped out to greet Burley Bear.

"On the spirits of the Ancients, you can walk through stone," Burley Bear stepped back in amazement, as it seemed to him the two literally stepped out of the stone!

"Now what is going on with you," Taelo said as he stepped forward and gave the much bigger warrior a hug and pulled him toward the opening in the stone.

The cold by this time was bitter and was immediately going through the light clothes the two had stripped down to.

Burley Bear at first hesitated but the bitter cold urged him to follow. Then he noticed the fissure he had previously missed and realized the two had closed it with a series of well-placed boulders to close the gap.

It was a tight squeeze for him to enter, and his height meant that he had to lower his head as he crossed to where they were sitting.

Once closed, the snow quickly covered the stones. From outside the face of the stones seemed solid. A few moments after they stepped inside, anyone approaching the fissure would not recognize it as an opening. This was a perfect hiding place.

Burley Bear took in the work the two young warriors had already put into the place. He was impressed with their capability. The place was very comfortable. He noticed the heated pool and marveled at Taelo's ability to find such places.

The big bearskin he was carrying was a perfect finish for the cave. It provided a sleeping area allowing all three to lie down in comfort and with their own lighter sleeping hides be comfortable in the warmth of the cave.

Back on the beach the storm raged and the waves from the sea crashed up against the base of the camp. It was by far the worst storm to have come at the camp up to this time.

"I hope Burley Bear has found Taelo and Golden Hawk. Now I am more worried about him than the other two," White Swan said quietly to Grey Fox Running as the two lay by each other enjoying the warmth they shared as they listened to the storm outside.

Not far away, Red Oak and Quite Pheasant were exchanging similar words.

"As long as Golden Hawk and Taelo are together, I do not worry too much. The two complement each other and together they seem able to accomplish anything they set their minds to. I believe this is their naming journey. It is early but these two do everything ahead of their time," Quite Pheasant shared with Red Oak.

"You are probably right. I will bring this up to the council tomorrow when we meet," Red Oak replied.

He hoped the two had found a good place to make camp and that Burley Bear had found them.

The winter seemed to take a dive into temperatures that made a bearskin coat seem to be made of thin grass. A person could only stay out a few moments and then be in peril.

Everyone gathered close to the campfires and tried to stay warm as the weather continued to stay cold. The storms seemed to come unabated. The cold literally crept through every crevice, came across the floor, and grabbed a person at the ankles or any part of the body close to the ground. The gathering of firewood became a dangerous effort. It was the only work to take anyone outside.

North, up the beach, where the Others were passing the winter in their warm and relatively comfortable cave, Broken Spear shared a vision with the Clan.

"Last night, I saw Taelo, Golden Hawk and our very own Burley Bear. They are on a journey together.

This is Taelo's journey into adulthood. He has gone out in the middle of winter on a call from his ancestors. He does not hear them as we do but he responds to their call none-the-less.

He will find the food to carry his Clan through the spring and a prosperous place for his Clan to live. He will return at the end of the winter with the food the Clan needs to make it through the final days of winter.

We will see him in the spring when he comes to greet us and invite us to live in the same valley as the Elk Clan," Broken Spear shared with the others sitting by the fire.

The Others all understood what Broken Spear had seen would come to pass, as had all his visions.

They began to discuss what it would be like to live with the new ones.

Taelo awakened to the constants roar of the waterfall and the light coming in from the opening nearest the waterfall. He walked to the opening and looked down into the valley below. The snow of the night before had stopped falling.

The morning was crisp.

The view was crystal clear.

He could see far into the distance.

Below the earth seem to move and undulate.

It took Taelo a moment to realize a huge herd of Bison stretching as far as the eye could see were digging through the snow and eating the grass bent below it.

"Golden Hawk, Burley Bear, come see a most spectacular sight," Taelo said in both languages.

As the three stood watching, a lone eagle soared over the valley and let out a long, lonely scream.

A shiver ran down Taelo's back.

Once again, he had been led to a place and been given a sign.

Once the storm subsided, he would go down into the valley and explore it.

17 Winter Takes Hold

18 Valley of Plenty

*T*aelo took one last look to the valley below and marveled at the dark brown sea of buffalo undulating like the waves of the ocean. He tied down the hide to securely close the opening and turned and looked around the shelter with its warm water pool and the small stream flowing by his feet out to join the rest of the water coming down the fall to the pool far below.

Golden Hawk and Burley Bear were waiting for him at the exit. They were ready to close the entrance once he was out. They had left some dried food hanging out over the warm water pool to keep it safe from the rodents. They had talked about coming back to their personal hot water pool when they wanted to get away from everyone.

The mountain snow was deep and the downward path treacherous. They made their way slowly and carefully down the trail to the valley below.

Working together they were able to descent the steep, icy dangerous path down the face of an almost vertical grade.

The valley floor seemed to move and crawl on its own. The sight of a sea of buffalo greeting them was overwhelming and astounding. Never had any of them seen so many buffalo in one place. The undulating mass of buffalo extended as far as the eye could see. The motion of this mass seemed scripted and harmonized as it slowly undulated with the movement of buffalo foraging for food.

The three kept just into the edge of the forest as they progressed down the valley. They did not want the herd to be frightened. The large number of buffalo would make it extremely dangerous to hunt them.

They traveled three days down the valley and still the herd had not broken. Had they wanted to cross the valley to the other side they would have had to risk going through the herd.

After traveling for four days, they came to the end of the valley and the end of the herd.

The small stream meandering down the valley from the waterfall ended at a bend of a medium sized river. The herd of Buffalo ended on the bank of the same small river.

Taelo, Golden Hawk and Burley Bear decided to travel down the river to see where it led.

Burley Bear pulled three dried wooden logs to the river where they made a raft on which they could float and keep dry. From this platform they were able to spear fish and catch the food they needed. Several rabbits met their fate as did a fat ground hog. All became a meal for the three.

They saved the dried meat Burley Bear had brought for the times when nothing presented itself to them.

The three had every intension of hunting the herd of Bison but they decided to wait until they were returning to the Clan. They figured to come back and harvest a few buffalo to take back to the Clan.

The trip down the river was uneventful. It led to a large harbor, and they followed the western shore until they came to the opening to the ocean. The three had followed the valley south and the river west. They had traced an arc leading them back to the ocean. Though the three did not know it exactly, the range of travel put them some twenty-one sun cycles travel south of where the Clan had its camp.

They finally decided to return to the valley of plenty, secure a sizeable amount of buffalo meat and then find a short cut to the ocean and return from the south along the seashore, back to the Clan.

Winter was still testing their tolerance of the cold. The large sleeping hide Burley Bear carried provided them ample warmth each night.

The three would sleep side by side with Burley Bear in the middle. Half the hide would be the bottom, and they would fold the other half over the top. They then used a lighter hide to cover their heads.

The snowfall was unusually heavy and fell steadily as they made their way back to the valley. The going became a test of their stamina. They reached the mouth of the river and found they could not effectively push upstream. They figured to use it again, so they beached their raft and pulled it up on the bank and into the forest where together they stood it on end to keep the logs from decaying.

Burley Bear surprised Taelo and Golden Hawk by stopping by a willow stand as they struggled to make their way back to the valley. He cut several small willow trees and bent them into teardrop shapes. He used the bark to tie them and then used the smaller branches to create a crisscrossed pattern. He then tied them to his feet and demonstrated his ability to walk more easily across the top of the snow.

Taelo and Golden Hawk immediately copied him and made a set for themselves. From then on, the three made better time as they proceeded back to the valley.

Burley Bear cut several more willows and carried a large bundle of them on his back.

"What are the willow branches for," Taelo inquired.

"You will find out later. It is a surprise," he replied in a smug secretive manner.

This time they stayed to the western side of the valley. About halfway up the valley, the three found what appeared to be a westward way out of valley. However, to reach the cut leading toward the sea they would have to climb about halfway up the mountainside.

It would be a challenge, but they decided it was probably the best way they would find. After some scouting and consideration, they decided they would have to make several trips up the mountain to haul up the meat they planned to take back to the village.

On the evening before their hunt, Taelo, Golden Hawk and Burley Bear sang their praises to the ancients and the ancestors. They asked for guidance and for accuracy in the use of their weapons. Using hot stones and their cooking pack they prepared and ate a hearty meal made from the dried meat cooked into a stew.

Burley Bear appreciated the cooking talent the two displayed.

They agreed Taelo and Golden Hawk would try and take down two young bulls. They would stay to the edge of the herd and separate their quarry from the rest of the herd. They desperately wanted to avoid a stampede.

The buffalo meat would be their return present to the Clan.

Early the next morning the two left Burley Bear at the edge of the forest and slowly approached the herd.

They each were covered with a buffalo skin and were moving very slowly toward the edge of the herd. It took them a full hour to get close to the herd.

Taelo slowly began to edge a young male yearling away from the herd.

Golden Hawk was doing the same with a second young bull.

The bulls nervously moved away from the herd toward the edge of the forest.

Suddenly, Taelo dropped the skin he was using as a cover. He dashed out toward the young bull. The bull immediately began to run toward the forest.

Taelo ran alongside of the bull until they were near the edge of the forest then he put on a burst of speed and dashed ahead of the young bull. He planted the butt of his spear in the ground as he had seen his father do and put the spear tip in the middle of the young bull's chest.

Immediately the spear was driven almost half of the way into the young bull. The young bull stopped and staggered a few steps and then collapsed. Taelo looked around and saw Golden Hawk had accomplished the same feat.

Burley Bear stood in amazement at the edge of the forest. He had never seen such a feat. His people could not run fast enough. They would guide their quarry into traps where the warriors would take down the buffalo.

This would be a story he was going to love to tell the Others. It would be hard for his listeners to believe, and they would probably think he was just embellishing the story.

But he would tell this story many times.

The rest of the herd continued grazing as if nothing had happened. This was exactly what Taelo had hoped. He had worried the herd would stampede. He wanted the herd to stay in place so the Clan members could come to the valley to hunt more of the buffalo.

Taelo, Golden Hawk and Burley Bear pulled the young bulls into the edge of the forest.

This was where Burley Bear's size made a huge difference. His strength made it possible for the bulls to be pulled up into the trees and there the three gutted and skinned them. When they were through with the skinning, they cut the bulls down into transportable sections and moved them about a quarter mile away from the point of the butchering and pulled the sections up into the trees.

They made their camp a few yards away.

In the afternoon, Burley Bear began to assemble a device neither Taelo nor Golden Hawk had seen before. Burley Bear patiently warmed the young willow saplings over the fire and then bent them into sled runners.

Then he tied a straight willow section between the two curved ends of the willow. Next, he began to link the two runners together with X braces and some straight braces. This made a floor for the sled. The device took shape as both Taelo and Golden Hawk finished their work of butchering and moving the meat into the trees where they could protect it.

They bundled the heart, tongue, liver, kidneys, and the tail into one section of hide. All of these were special gifts to be given to the elders. The hump of each young bull was carefully wrapped and would be a gift to each of their mothers.

It was not until they had finished their grueling work when Taelo and Golden Hawk finally had a chance to study what Burly Bear had been making. His device was about two spears long and had curled ends. The sled could be pulled in either direction. But the end with the largest curled end was definitely the front.

When Burley Bear demonstrated the sled by using it to slide down the slope away from the campfire, both Taelo and Golden Hawk let out a whoop and got excited.

"This is unbelievable. This device will let us transport the meat out in a much faster way," Taelo pointed out to Golden Hawk.

"Yes, it will also let us pull much more weight than we could with a travois," Golden Hawk replied as he pulled Burley Bear back into the camp.

The two stood looking at a smug Burley Bear.

"See, we of the Others, still can teach you something," Burley Bear said with a fair amount of pride.

Taelo took a slice of meat from each of the bison humps and presented it to Burley Bear.

"To our brother Burley Bear, thank you for sharing this new tool with us. It will allow us to transport the meat we have harvested," Taelo said as he put the meat on a spit.

He spread some of the precious salt on the meat and then held it over the fire. He presented the cooked meat to a proud Burley Bear.

They all sat around the fire talking, roasting pieces of fresh meat and sharing their vision of the future. It was hard for Burley Bear to remember he came from a tribe which was shrinking. His two brothers of the new people had so much enthusiasm and dreams of the future. Their enthusiasm carried over into his soul.

The next day was spent slowly moving the meat up the mountainside to the higher exit leading out of the valley and down to the sea. The sled was easy enough to carry up to the beginning of the valley. They used the hide of one young bull to cover the bottom of the sled.

They then carried, pulled, and generally manhandled each section up the steep mountainside to where the sled was positioned. They put the sections on the sled and used the second hide to cover the load from the top.

They tied the bundle securely to the sled.

Each of them tied on to the sled with a pull line and slowly began to pull the load along the valley floor. By this time, it was late afternoon. They immediately began looking for a defendable place to spend the fast-approaching night.

They had gone a little more than a mile when they found a huge tree that had blown over. The roots had pulled out and left a shallow depression. The roots themselves offered a backdrop and a defendable shelter. The same tree provided an abundance of wood for a fire.

The three of them worked the sled up against the tree roots and then made three small fires out around the periphery of the root depression. They hoped they would not need to fight off any hungry wolves.

They had another hearty evening meal of fresh roasted meat and a few boiled roots. Then they pulled out their giant bearskin and the three huddled in the middle with the skin pulled around them.

They took turns sleeping. One of them was always awake to feed the wood into the fire throughout the night. Their sled provided a backdrop to lean against. The night was uneventful, and no animals bothered them.

It took them two days to slowly descend to the sea. The sled Burley Bear constructed allowed them to make the journey in record time. They were all glad when they saw the ocean spread out before them.

The three turned and headed northward toward the Elk Clan's winter quarters. They found that by staying close to the forest, the snow on the ground allowed them to pull the sled.

Almost two months had passed. During this time, the supplies for the Clan was slowly depleted.

"I had hoped we would catch more fish, but the storms have kept us away from our fish traps," White Swan bemoaned her frustration at not being able to stretch her supplies.

"We will need to send out a hunting party to see if they can find some game to tide us over into late spring," Grey Fox Running replied as he thought how frustrated spring often made him feel.

The weather would improve but food was hard to find and many a Clan lost their members to hunger just as summer began to promise riches.

A lookout scout came in with the news three people were coming up the beach from the south. They were pulling a strange contraption behind them.

Grey Fox Running, Red Oak, and several of the younger men went out to see who was coming and what they were pulling. From the top of the peak of the rocky cliffs making up the spit out to sea, the two friends smiled when they saw the three figures pulling an unbelievably large load behind them.

"I am not sure what those three are bringing home but if it was not for the figure in the middle, I don't think that load would move," Grey Fox Running said with a chuckle to Red Oak.

"Truly that has to be Burley Bear in the middle. No other person we know looks so much like a bear," Red Oak replied.

"Let's get down there and see if we can help them bring in what I hope is a supply of food," Grey Fox Running instructed the group of young men around him.

The Elk Clan members descended and met a jubilant but very tired trio. They had pulled two thousand pounds of meat for more than fifty miles up the coast.

Now six fresh young men harnessed themselves to the sled and pulled it the rest of the way to the village.

It had been almost two moon cycles since the two had climbed up the cliff behind the village.

They had ventured out and made their own way across the mountains and had arrived with a load of meat just as the stores of the Clan was running low.

Taelo and Golden Hawk presented their gifts to the elders and finally they presented the richest gifts to their mothers.

To Grey Fox Running and Red Oak, the two presented the spears with which they had each killed their first bison.

Grey Fox Running accepted the spear and for the first time told the story of having learned to hunt the buffalo in this manner form his mate White Swan and Quiet Pheasant on the hunt they had gone on together and where White Swan had extracted his request that she be his mate.

In a joking manner, Red Oak added that not only did they show them how to hunt in a new manner. The two also captured the best-looking men of the Clan.

Taelo and Golden Hawk looked over at their mothers, raised their eyebrows, and winked.

During the evening Clan dinner, they told the story of Burley Bear teaching them to walk on the snow and showed them their snowshoes.

The sled was another story. Burley Bear now had his story intertwined with the Elk Clan's stories. He sat proudly as various members of the Clan thanked him and patted him on the back.

Two different peoples, despite their differences, were learning from one another.

Taelo had marked the way into the valley and hunters would be sent to gather more bison. The well-being of the Clan was ensured. Several trips would be made to harvest more meat and hides.

The weather seemed to take its cue from the return of the three adventures. It began to warm up and spring descended on the beach.

Fishing once again became feasible, and the Clan emerged renewed and reinvigorated after surviving what they had anticipated as the winter of their demise.

19 Spring on the Beach

*T*aelo and Golden Hawk stood on the top of the tooth spit that protruded out into the opening of the protected cove in front of the Clan village. The top of the cove's jaw was the rocky arm of the mountains running in a semicircle three quarters of the way around the beach on the seaward side. This protected the beach, and it attracted a variety of fish that fed on the seaweed growing abundantly in the cove. Large green turtles also frequented the cove to feed on the algae and seaweed.

Across from the tooth rock thousands of birds nested in the steep cliffs.

The two discussed how they would set up a way to guide fish into an area where they could easily be speared. Some fish would be guided to shallow pools where they could be picked up by hand.

They were reapplying the same idea that they had devised to catch salmon when they were in the Elk Hide Clan.

Building the fish trap in the cove was a huge undertaking as compared to the small trap they had built in the river a few years ago.

They located the position for a series of vertical poles to guide fish into a trap where they could more easily be speared.

Taelo and Golden Hawk tied large stones to the bottom of straight three-inch poles about twenty feet long or longer. The poles needed to stick out of the water, so a narrow walkway could be built along the top of the poles. The poles were positioned about six feet apart and formed a cone that narrowed to about a two-foot opening.

Some small, curved willow limbs were tied at a ninety-degree angle to the last two poles. They acted like whiskers allowing the fish to easily enter but were an obstruction for those fish trying to swim out. Woven mats of willow limbs filled in the six-foot sections between the main polls.

Taelo and Golden Hawk enrolled everyone in the camp in some fashion.

Red Oak and Grey Fox Running were impressed with the planning capability of the two. Several of the Elk elders had expressed some doubt about the value of such an effort.

Taelo and Golden Hawk managed the many different groups putting together the various parts of this huge fish trap. They hoped it would work as well as the trap the two had built in the river.

Taelo had pointed the end of the cone into a round shallow area about three feet deep.

Here, standing on the walkways built on vertical poles, it would be extremely easy to spear the fish once they had been guided into this area.

Opposite the entrance was one more opening were the water was only a foot deep. The fish going into this area were usually smaller, they could be scooped out with pronged sticks and thrown up on the beach.

There was some skepticism about doing all this work for a few fish. Grey Fox Running, however, continued to encourage the members to participate and help Taelo and Golden Hawk.

Once the mouth of the cone was opened and the fish began to come in, it became obvious the Clan would enjoy an abundance of fish, an abundance beyond what they could imagine.

The number of fish captured kept everyone busy throughout the spring and early summer. Thousands of fish were dried. The Clan prospered, and everyone was well fed and healthy.

Burley Bear made a trip back to his Clan to invite them to a fishing festival that he, Taelo and Golden Hawk had devised.

They knew this would be a way for the two Clans to learn about each other.

White Swan and Quiet Pheasant knew that salt was critical to processing all the fish and other meats. She recruited several of the women and a few of the older warriors and created a broad flat pool that could be repeatedly filled and sundried. It was on the far side of the cove's tooth stone where the sun beat down through the entire day.

The salt production could barely keep up with the demand. Many fish were dried with no salt on them.

Once the salt processing area was functioning, White Swan turned its operation over to several of the older hunters whose job became that of repeated filling of the evaporation pools until the salt was thick enough to scrape off the flat rocks where the salt accumulated.

The salt was used in drying the fish but also in processing hides and for the normal cooking of the Clan's meals.

Taelo and Golden Hawk explored the cliffs along the spit and were constantly bringing back a wide variety of berries, sea conches, and sea plants.

Taelo and Golden Hawk came home from one trip loaded with eggs they had gathered along the cliffs. They passed out the eggs to all the families.

Their generosity was one of the things which made the two stand out. It always seemed to take the Clan members by surprise.

White Swan and Quiet Pheasant led a band of young women to the area described by Taelo and gathered enough for a special dinner for the whole Clan.

One day there was shouting and a great deal of commotion from the cove. Taelo, Golden Hawk and Burley Bear found that a huge shark had become trapped. It was at least twenty-five feet long and seemed to take up the entire shallow area.

They speared the beast and the three fought with it for more than an hour as they worked to pull it ashore.

Burley Bear repeatedly hit the shark in the head with his stone headed war club until the shark finally died.

Taelo and Golden Hawk erected a tripod from which they hung the huge shark.

The sharkskin would be a rare and valuable item.

Taelo and Golden Hawk gutted the shark. Then they carefully skinned the shark and peeled the skin from the tail to the head.

The shark skin would be processed to make shark skin leather.

Taelo and Golden Hawk presented this very valuable leather to their mothers.

Burley Bear planned to do this as well.

Then they cut the meat off from each side. Two thirds of the meat was divided equally with all the families in the Elk Clan.

One third was for Burley Bear to take to the Clan of Others.

The shark teeth were carefully removed. There were at least fifty full size razor teeth and many smaller ones in the formation stage. These would make good spear tips and about one hundred more could be used for arrows and various cutting tools.

Taelo and Golden Hawk gave the best teeth to Grey Fox Running, Red Oak and to Silent Hawk.

Burley Bear became the keeper of one third of the shark teeth. He would share them with the Clan of Others.

Taelo, Golden Hawk and Burley Bear each kept a half a dozen teeth for themselves and then gave each of the other young men in the Elk Clan several teeth.

They made a special presentation to three of the young women who had been most active in guiding the construction of the fish trap.

These were Quiet Rabbit, Busy Bee, and Talking Wren.

Little did either Taelo or Golden Hawk realize the significant role these three would play in the near future.

The shark teeth were one of the most valuable items one could possess. Their sharp edges and piercing points made the best and sharpest spear tips. This treasure could make a young man rich in their society.

This unselfish sharing of such a valuable treasure again surprised the Elk Clan members. No one had expected such generosity.

Grey Fox Running, Red Oak, White Swan, and Quiet Pheasant took pride in the character of their young warriors.

Burley Bear also took note of the character of the two. Their equal recognition of the Others and their generosity toward them fused his spirit to theirs. He filed yet another story to tell his Clan upon his return. The tales of Taelo and Golden Hawk were beginning to add up.

Silent Hawk spoke to the elders of the Clan, "These young men have repeatedly shown they deserve to be considered as full adult members of the Clan. It is time we honored them as they have honored us. Let us give them their adult names and make them full members of the Clan."

There was little debate about the merits of the recommendation. There was considerable discussion about their age but in the end everyone agreed. They would be the youngest members of the Clan adult council.

Most of the discussion had been about what the other Clan leaders would say when the entire Clan met in the fall. However, the Elk Clan figured they could face any of those concerns at the time of the Clan gathering. There might be a few questions, but no one would be able to refute the contribution the two had made to the well-being of the Elk Clan. It was the right of the elders of the Elk Clan to decide.

The council picked a date about a full moon away to induct the two as full adult Clan members.

Taelo and Golden Eagle spoke about this to White Swan and Quiet Pheasant. They always approached their mothers when it concerned the politics of the Clan.

"We would like to invite the old ones to this ceremony. They are part of our story, part of who we are and who we will be. We would like them to attend," both confided in their mothers.

They knew if these two were supportive, then their fathers would also be supportive. Then they could face the rest of the Clan with full confidence in their request.

"That is an excellent idea. It will be a good way to bring the two people together. I will speak with Grey Fox Running about it," White Swan replied.

The fishing get-together had worked very well, and this would extend the interaction between the two Clan's.

The discussion on the topic of inviting the Others to the ceremony was not as harmonious as the one agreeing to have the Others attend the fishing festival or the one to induce the two young men.

This would be an unprecedented event. It was a time when the ancestors were called.

A time of deep ceremony.

The discussions went back and forth and, in the end, Grey Fox Running with the support of Silent Hawk and Red Oak used his clout as leader to push through an agreement.

A few days later Taelo, Golden Hawk and Burley Bear began their journey up the beach to the home of the Others.

They were making the trip to invite them to the ceremony.

Burley Bear seemed to have new energy in his step and did a fine job keeping up with the two younger members who seemed to have wings on their feet. Even then it took more than a week for them to travel up the coast to the stream leading back to the living area of the old ones.

To their surprise, the entire Clan was awaiting their arrival and had planned an evening's celebration of their return.

"Tell us about your winter's journey, through the mountains and the valley of the Buffalo," Broken Spear asked with a gleam in his eyes.

Taelo never ceased being surprised at the knowledge the old ones seemed to have. He was not sure how they did it but somehow, they could glean information from one's mind.

Taelo surprised the old ones by telling the story in their language. He carefully recited the story of their travels and unselfishly embellished Burley Bear's part of the story.

Burley Bear not only walked on the snow in his snowshoes, but they were so well made that he left no prints in the snow where he walked.

The Clan of Others began hooting and stomping the ground.

When he made the sled, he went down the mountain side so fast that he ran into two buffalo. They flew up in the air and on the way down he skinned them and loaded them on the sled before returning to his campfire.

Golden Hawk and I were so mad that we made him pull that sled for three days all the way back to the Elk Clan on his own.

This brought the Clan to their feet as they continued their hooting in appreciation of the story Taelo was telling.

Taelo held up his hand and asked the gathering to listen to one more feat of the Burley Bear.

On our return to the Elk Clan, Burley Bear was swimming in the water by the beach. A giant shark was attracted by his thrashing about. When it came to investigate the noise, the shark got so disoriented by the sight of Burley Bear in the water that it swam up onto the beach to where Golden Hawk and I were standing.

At the same time Burley Bear, seeing the size of the great shark ran out of the water screaming in fear.

The scream was so loud that it brought the entire Elk Clan to the beach but even more amazing the scream was so powerful that the shark died of fear.

Who in his right mind would want to face and fight someone so large and ugly?

By this time, the hooting and the stomping of feet made it impossible for Taelo to continue.

Burley Bear was standing and laughing, the Clan of Others went wild.

Golden Hawk spread a dozen buffalo hides out in front of Burley Bear, placed the shark skin on top of them and then spread the shark teeth for everyone to see. They had given the jaw of the large shark to Burley Bear and had left the smaller teeth embedded.

The entire Clan stopped and looked on in disbelief as they took in the prize Burley Bear had brought back with him.

The elders had enjoyed the stories, and all passed food or drink to Burley Bear. It was clear they were proud of his accomplishments and the fact he was so well accepted by the New Ones.

His status was now of a hero among Clan of Others.

Burley Bear stood up and waved a finger at Taelo. He was a little overwhelmed by the stories Taelo had shared.

It was his turn, and he could tell stories as good as or better than Taelo.

He had the Clan on their feet when he told of Taelo walking through solid rock.

They were hooting and stomping in appreciation when he told about Taelo and Golden Hawk running down their buffalo and letting the buffalo run into and spear themselves. His insistence that this was true and the way the two hunted only made the hooting louder.

Burley Bear really had become quite a good speaker and storyteller.

The evening was a great reunion and at its close, Taelo extended his invitation to the Others to attend the Elk Clan induction ceremony for himself and Golden Hawk.

A hush fell over the Clan of Others. Never in their history had they been invited to a ceremony. There was no Clan memory to guide them in making this decision.

Broken Spear had warned them of such an invitation and still they were shocked.

"We are honored by your invitation. You must give us a few days to discuss this. We have no Clan memory to address this situation," Broken Spear replied with a certain look of confusion.

He knew other members of the Clan were reacting in a similar fashion.

This was a similar reaction to the invitation Burley Bear had made for them to fish in the cove, but it was much more important and held a meaning far beyond fishing on the beach.

"Well, I think we have surprised them. We will need to talk with Burley Bear and see if he can talk to them. He has gotten use to our brash and forward ways," Taelo shared with Golden Hawk.

After the story telling broke up, the two cornered Burley Bear and asked him to talk with the Clan elders and make certain they understood that both of them wanted them present at the ceremony. Burley Bear agreed to do so and to make sure the elders understood the importance of the Others being there.

The elders told Taelo and Golden Hawk of their plans to induce Burley Bear into the circle of adults.

This was great news to all three of the young men. They went out on a walk to enjoy the good news and discuss their good fortune.

A month later, members of the Others and the new ones met on the beach and for the first time in the history of either Clan, they sat together to usher Taelo, Golden Hawk and Burley Bear into the council of elders.

Each Clan gave the three, membership in each other's circle of adults.

"Tonight, each Clan has induced these three into the circle of adults leading their Clan. This makes us kindred Clans and makes it a responsibility for each to look out for the other. I believe the three have already demonstrated that by doing so everyone receives benefit. I propose we become partners and help each other weather the storms and any hard times we may face," Gray Fox Running said standing in front of both councils and giving his message in both tongues.

Broken Spear stood up and called forward a young woman and her new child.

"This is the first child born to our Clan in more than ten springs. Most of us cannot remember the cry of a child. When it was born an eagle screamed overhead. Tonight, we are naming this child Scream of the Eagle in honor of Taelo who has guided this Clan to a new life.

We know our time is short, but we are honored to join you as partners for the remaining time we the Clan of Others have," Broken Spear spoke.

To everyone's surprise, Burley Bear translated the speech into the tongue of the new ones. Though it was clear Burley Bear's throat struggled, the words were clear and understandable. By this act his stature, in the Clan of Others and in the Elk Clan as well, went up dramatically.

Each of the young men was led into the circle of elders where their contributions were described, and they were praised for their good work. They were honored for their leadership and for their support of the two Clans. The old ones followed a similar ceremony.

Taelo was given the added name meaning to guide or leader of men. Golden Hawk was given a name meaning brother to Taelo. Burley Bear was given the extra name of protector. Each Clan gave the same name though there were different words in each language.

Taelo was taken a little by surprise since he never thought of his feats as unusual. He was always himself. This genuine self-effacing quality is what made him so effective and unknowingly powerful. The ceremony went on all night until the crack of dawn.

Taelo, Golden Hawk and Burley Bear walked along the beach watching the sun come up over the mountains to the east.

"Life has been kind to us. We must be thankful our two Clans have chosen to work together. Let us vow to always chose to do what is honorable, just, and fair to all concerned," Taelo proposed as they stood looking out to sea.

20 Golden Harvest

Grey Fox Running, Silent Hawk, Red Oak, Broken Spear and Quiet Fox spent a full week in discussions on the relationship between the two peoples. This experience was new to both Clans.

Broken Spear and Quiet Fox explained how hard it was for the Others to accept change because they were regulated more by their memory of what was done before.

Grey Fox Running explained how the Elk Clan members had to overcome the fears based on the stories of how fierce the old ones were in battle.

Both sides knew they were more alike than different. Both groups were focused on the wellbeing of the Clan and its families. Both wanted only to be prosperous enough not to suffer cold and hunger each winter. Both peoples were guided by similar principles.

This understanding bound them and led them to the agreement to work together.

"It is time we shook up all the other Elk sub-clans. I would like to extend an invitation to the Others to attend our fall Elk Clan meeting," Grey Fox Running invited the leaders of the Others.

Grey Fox Running had talked this over with all the Elk Clan elders for quite a while before making such an offer. The elders of the Elk Clan felt that having the Others attend would indeed shake up the overall Elk Clan leadership and refresh their way into the future.

Broken Spear discussed this with the Clan of Others. It was Burley Bear who encouraged the Clan leadership to accept and after a long discussion they decided they would attend the meeting. This was unprecedented for both Clans.

For the rest of the summer the two Clans shared their knowledge and many of their Clan secrets. It was surprising how many things the old ones knew but did not use because they found it hard to accept doing things differently or because they had decided to stop doing something. And yet many of these things the Others had stopped doing were of tremendous value to the Elk Clan.

The Others were especially good at processing and treating leather. They were able to soften it and make the leather smooth and pliable. However, they kept secret of how to get the leather a brilliant white color.

Many of the Elk Clan members brought their raw leather to get treated by the Others so they could have pieces of white leather with which to work.

The payment for this was half of the leather and the meat that could be wrapped with it.

This was reasonable because the Elk Clan had a valley full of buffalo as the source of their leather.

Burley Bear, Taelo and Golden Hawk inseparable before, now worked with new energy, harmony, and purpose. They led a hunting party into the valley of the buffalo. Most had moved out but throughout the summer some stayed and provided a substantial bounty for both Clans.

Neither Clan would suffer any hunger in the coming winter. The summer hunting alone had provided the necessary reserves.

There was a huge amount of leather being harvested because of the abundance of the Buffalo. New clothing was made for everyone. Extra outfits were made in anticipation of the trade with the other Clans in the fall.

The sea provided colorful stones and seashells with which to decorate the jackets and dress clothing. Every afternoon the women would sit looking out to the sea and make and decorate the clothing. Their designs were intricate and inspired by the brilliant country around them.

The stones, shells and pieces of antler were expertly used to make buttons and patterns. They also mixed the leather of various animals to create textured shirts and jackets.

The fish trap continued to supply an abundant number of fish. The construct fascinated the members of the old ones. This was a new capability for which there was no memory for the Others. They wondered how Taelo and Golden Hawk had thought of and constructed such a huge fish trap. They, however, had no trouble in participating in the spearing of the fish in the trap.

The production of dried fish took on the feel of a well-designed production system.

From morning until noon fish were speared from the fish trap.

Then the fish were cleaned and staked out so they could be put out to dry. The steaks of fish were rubbed with salt and when thoroughly dried were tied together with fiber twine, in bundles of four.

The fishing went on throughout the summer and the supply of fish was so plentiful the Clan would be taking a great amount to share with the other Clans.

Salt was in constant production. A shallow flat area, covered with flat rocks, had been doubled in size. This was filled with seawater and allowed to dry. The salt was then carefully scraped off and put in woven fiber bags. This was tedious work but until the Clan found a salt quarry it was the only way to get salt. Though this was hard work, it provided an abundant supply of salt.

This salt would also be valuable in the fall trading.

Blueberry bushes covered the ridges on the spit. When they got ripe the entire Clan went out and gathered blueberries.

These were eaten fresh. They were also cooked and mixed with other greens to make a relish to put on the meat and finally they were dried so they could be used throughout the rest of the year.

Once again, the abundance surprised the older members of the Clan. This was a time of plenty. No one could remember having such good times.

Periodically, Taelo, Golden Hawk and Burley Bear would disappear for a few days. No one knew where the three went but they would appear a few days later fresh and relaxed.

The three had kept the cave with the warm water a secret. They periodically retreated to their cave to relax.

They planned to share it with their parents in the coming winter but until then, they would enjoy it as a retreat for themselves. They always took a good supply of food and relaxed in the hot pool, looked out over the valley of plenty and discussed different philosophical ideas.

"Those three have a secret place they periodically retreat to. It seems to do them good. I wonder where this place is and what is there," Grey Fox Running said one day to Red Oak?

"Well, I would say they deserve it. Those three have made a huge difference in the well-being of the Clans.

They have brought two very different people peacefully together, have found a supply of meat, they have developed a way of fishing so effective we have to stop fishing, or we catch too many," Red Oak replied.

"I agree. Those three have indeed provided the Clan with a new way of living," Silent Hawk added.

The summer and early fall became a rhythm of gathering food, making various implements, fishing, diving along the cliff for various sea animals. Life for both Clans was enjoyable and prosperous. The hot springs at the Others became a favorite place for families to go to enjoy a few days of relaxation. This interchange of members of the Clans brought the two Clans even closer together.

The two Clans would go to the Clan meeting with more goods and food to share than ever before. They had decided everything they took to the Clan meeting would be left for the Clan to divide. They would leave all their winter stores behind and have it guarded by a few warriors.

Taelo, Golden Hawk and Burly Bear explored the valley below the residence of the Others and found it had an abundant supply of dewberries and blackberries. They led various members out to these patches so the berries could be harvested.

Burley Bear made the discovery of a large honey tree. This was marked for harvesting later in the season after the bees had a chance to collect the late harvest blooms.

The Others had come to enjoy bathing in their hot water spring. They recalled the Clan had in the past made a variety of bath oils.

The making of scented oils was re-introduced to the Clan membership by Broken Spear.

Soon a variety of these bath oils were being made. It became somewhat of a contest to see who could make the oil with the best aroma. They presented a generous amount of these oils to Taelo and Golden Hawk to bring back to their family and Elk Clan members. They also prepared enough to trade in the fall meeting.

Taelo especially liked this specialty of the Others. After a hot bath he loved to rub on the various scented oils. He, Golden Hawk and Burley Bear took a supply to their hide away to use when they retreated there.

21 The Hunting Team

Change was in the air for the Elk Clan. The leadership of the Clan took on a new flavor as the women exerted their influence. They had observed how the women of the Others had the same and sometimes the more commanding positions in the leadership council. They were not yet in the position nor had they the experience to take on those positions, but they were extremely active in the matters of the Elk Clan.

When Taelo suggested the Valley of Plenty might make a better home for the Clan, the women were the ones to decide the current site should be their spring and summer quarters to complement the fishing and making of salt and the winter quarters would be made in the valley.

A group made up of women and men went to the valley to locate the best place to make their winter camp.

A large lake was located at the entrance to the valley. It was just a small distance away from the river.

The higher ground on the western side was where they decided to put the main lodge. The individual lodges would be built toward the mountains rising above the valley to the west.

The small river or stream feeding the lake ran from the warm water cave Taelo, Golden Hawk and Burley Bear had used as their personal hide out.

They had taken their families to the cave and shared the location with the rest of the Elk Clan.

From the vantage point out the opening of the hot water cave, White Swan was able to see the entire area and make small adjustments to the plans for the village. She was able to place all the homes and the main lodge well above the flood plains that were very recognizable from above.

The valley would be a secure winter home for the Elk Clan.

Though the valley seemed to promise a bountiful supply of buffalo, the Elk Clan members were still sensitive to the fact that they had just faced a possible winter of starvation. It would send out its long hunt teams to secure their winter meat supply.

The hunting teams were organized and sent their various directions. The Elk Clan and the Others split up the territory, so they would not hunt against each other.

Burly Bear joined Taelo's group and a few of the more adventuresome young men of the Elk Clan joined the Others in their hunt. Taelo had encouraged this with some of his young friends saying they would learn a lot from the Others.

Another interesting situation came up when several of the young women spoke up and wanted to go out with the hunting parties. This was hotly debated by some of the elders.

It was one of the women from the Others who finally swayed the group. Through Burley Bear, who had become the interpreter between the two peoples, she explained many women of her clan hunted and they also fought in any attack on the Clan's camp. This was known and few dared attack their camps because the women were especially fierce in defending their children.

She went on to point out that, it made the men feel better when like now they went away on the necessary long hunts. They felt confident their women were well equipped to protect themselves and the camp.

Women did not always go on the hunts but all of them had done so one time or another to learn the ways and to toughen themselves to the rigor of the hunt and prepare themselves as leaders in the Clan.

After this session, several young women who were brave enough to do so, joined the same group Taelo and Golden Hawk were in.

The leader of this hunting party, Little Otter, looked at his group, Taelo, Golden Hawk, Burly Bear and three young women, Quiet Rabbit, Talking Wren, and Busy Bee and let out a small groan. With this team, he figured his hunting chances were as dead as a cold rabbit.

A few of the doubting elders had talked to Little Otter and had let him know not much game was expected from his hunting party. However, it was his task to keep them safe.

Though Taelo, Golden Hawk and Burley Bear had repeatedly proven themselves as hunters, there was still some doubt among some members of the Clan and with the women on the hunting team they felt the team would not do well. Some thought Taelo and Golden Hawk were always lucky and were not sure what they would produce when out on a regular hunt.

Grey Fox Running had discussed this dissension among the leadership with White Swan.

"Make sure the young women do not get dissuaded but go with Taelo. I think the Clan will be surprised with the outcome of this hunt. I know Taelo and Golden Hawk well enough and trust they will guide their hunt leader to new heights of achievement," White Swan advised Grey Fox Running.

Grey Fox Running had no doubt and both he and Red Oak made sure the memberships of the hunting parties were as White Swan had advised.

White Swan took Taelo aside and explained the politics and the doubts being discussed. She had made a habit of informing him of the politics of the various situations throughout the Clan. She was always amazed at Taelo's measured and mature responses or advice.

It was no different this time.

"I have raced with these young women as we grew up. They are almost as fast as I when it comes to running. I will teach them to bring down the buffalo as you taught Grey Fox Running. They know the sling, and we will gather small game while we run and play. We will account for ourselves as good as the rest and my goal is to be much better," Taelo replied.

Taelo discussed this with his team.

"The elders do not expect us to catch much game. Little Otter has been told the only thing expected from this team is for him to keep us safe.

I think we should set a goal to out hunt all the other teams and from the first week and every week we should send more game home than anyone else," Taelo said as he talked to the group.

There was general agreement from all the team members. The young women in the group felt a special kindred with Taelo for his confident attitude and his respect for their ability.

The day arrived for the teams to leave, and Little Otter led his team out in the direction they had been given. Taelo immediately recognized it as the least desirable area for hunting. Burley Bear, being the slowest runner was in the lead. Taelo caught up with him and shared the bad news with him.

"If we go northward, we will come by the far end of the valley where your Clan is situated. Perhaps we can visit for a day and then go east of the valley.

The hunting there may be better than where we have been sent," Taelo shared with Burley Bear.

Taelo had spoken all of this in Burley Bear's language. He was better at it than Burley Bear was with the language of the Elk Clan. Having this command of a second language was useful, as now when he could talk to Burley Bear without worrying about Little Otter overhearing.

Taelo next jogged along with Little Otter, who in contrast to his name was quite large. He was as large as Burley Bear but was hairless as compared to him.

Little Otter was the name given him as a child and no one had given him a better name yet.

Taelo conversed with him and let him know the team knew not much was expected from them. He let Little Otter know the team wanted to prove the elders wrong. He also shared with him the area they had been given to hunt was sparse in game since it was more desert than anything else.

Finally, he suggested they alter the hunting area a little and go farther north and east than had been assigned. This would take them beyond the desert to a range of mountains Taelo and Golden Hawk had seen but had not yet visited.

Little Otter was a little overwhelmed with his team. They were not the meek and mild group he had been led to think they would be. Instead, they were active and assertive and needed little guidance. He found if he was to remain in charge, he would need to change the way he had intended to lead this team.

He knew they had the worst hunting grounds and personally resented being given this poor area. The idea of visiting a rich hunting ground and doing well attracted him.

He had also heard so much about the camp of the Others. Visiting them was an attraction he could not pass up.

He agreed to Taelo's suggestion.

Little Otter and Burley Bear were about the same size and running was not their strongest suite. The two traded the lead back and forth.

Taelo and Golden Hawk taught the use of the sling to bring down small game as the team jogged along. Soon the women in the group were hitting the rabbits almost as well as Taelo.

Every evening, they ate well.

The women were much better cooks than the young men. They taught their skills on how to cook the rabbits and other small game.

Taelo made sure that those who did not cook helped before and after the meal.

Little Otter was taken at how well the team functioned. He began to think that perhaps they could do better than expected.

On their third day out and close to the home of the Others, Taelo spotted an elk and immediately signaled Golden Hawk and the two dashed out. Golden Hawk went the opposite direction to Taelo. The rest of the team did not even notice the two disappear until they were gone.

Suddenly, the elk jumped across the trail ahead of the jogging team and almost immediately Taelo crossed behind it. He drove the elk to where he hoped Golden Hawk was waiting.

As the elk jump over a fallen log, Golden Hawk drove his spear in from below.

The two let out a whooping war cry and the rest of the party came to where the two were celebrating.

The team spent the rest of the afternoon skinning and preparing the elk. This was their first large kill. The liver, heart and tongue were wrapped and kept in a cool place.

The remainder of the carcass was cut up into sections and then wrapped in the hide and put on a travois.

Early the next morning the group set out to the camp of the Others. They were considerably slowed by the travois. They arrived to a waiting group of Others. The camp had been warned by Broken Spear of the hunting party's arrival.

Taelo greeted Quiet Fox and presented the Clan with a gift of the elk meat. This and the team membership impressed the Clan leadership.

Taelo introduced Little Otter as the hunting party leader and made it clear he was in charge of the hunting party.

"I see your Clan has adopted our way in how you organize your hunting party. Each of you has a female partner. We will see if there is someone to accompany Burly Bear," Quiet Fox said as he took in the hunting party.

This interpretation caught Taelo by surprise and he looked again at the young women members of the hunting party. Taelo did not want to correct Silent Fox's assumption about the relationship of the team members.

Instead, he said, "That is up to Burley Bear. We have come by to see you and then to proceed east of your valley in hopes we find some good hunting. If we are successful, we will send some food your way. How does your hunting go this year?"

"Our hunting teams are out and have been sending back a steady supply of meat. There are two groups who are hunting our own valley and doing very well. There is one group north of here and another East of here. You may encounter them if you go that way," Quiet Fox replied.

"We will look for them as we travel, perhaps we can celebrate by hunting together if we meet," Taelo continued as the hunting party was led into the Clan's quarters.

Broken Spear greeted him and asked him to sit with him for a while. After everyone had gone away, he spoke from his seat by the heated spring.

"I dreamed of your coming. Your team will do well this year. You will find our hunting team and save them from some danger which I can't see clearly nor understand.

There is a disturbed spirit I can't grasp or understand. Be careful this danger will be a threat to you personally. When confronted with this danger you must act quickly and decisively. If I understand more, I will let you know," Broken Spear said quietly as he looked at Taelo with concern in his eyes.

"Thank you for this information. I will look out for the hunters and to their well-being. I will make sure my actions are swift and focused," Taelo replied in the tongue of the Others.

"I see Burley Bear has become a teacher as well as guardian. His relationship with you has saved him from becoming a bully and pest of the tribe. It was a good day when you hit him on the head," Broken Spear said with a chuckle.

"He indeed is a good friend. His strength has become the talk of our Clan. However, his wit and intelligence has also been recognized," Taelo said fondly as he thought of his large friend.

Burley Bear had guided the rest of the team to the campfire designated for their stay. He and Little Otter, who except for the lack of hair was the same size as Burley Bear, gave out the gifts of meat. The tribe was impressed by the matching size of the two.

Except for their looks they could have been brothers. The two worked well together and both were smiling and talking to the Clan members as they distributed the elk meat.

"What were the two of you speaking about," Little Otter asked in curiosity when Taelo joined the group?

"Broken Spear is the seer of this Clan. We don't have anyone like him in our Clan. He sees into the future. He was sharing with me that we will run into a dangerous situation. When it occurs, we must act swiftly, and we will overcome it. Broken Spear however could not tell me exactly what the danger we face might be," Taelo shared with the entire team.

Quiet Rabbit, Talking Wren, and Busy Bee were amazed at the cave of the Others. The fact they had a hot spring was something to envy.

"You found this place for this Clan," they asked Taelo?

"Yes, I was shown the way by my elk ancestors and an eagle in the sky," Taelo replied.

"I am going down to the hot spring to bathe, everyone better enjoy the evening and get a good night sleep. We begin a long journey tomorrow," Taelo said as he took his things and went down to the spring.

"Can we come with you," Talking Wren asked trying to embarrass Taelo?

"Everyone is certainly welcome. The more the merrier," Taelo replied with a grin.

He turned and walked confidently to the pool where he stripped down and entered the warm water.

The next morning the warming rays of the sun shining into the overhang awakened the visitors. The young Elk Clan women were envious of the excellent location Taelo had found for the Others.

They would dream of the warm water spring and luxurious bath they enjoyed the evening before. This place was an ideal home.

Quiet Fox came over to the group and introduced a robust and good-looking young woman of the Others.

He looked at Little Otter and said, "I would like you to accept Meadow Flower as another member to your hunting party. I know you feel your team has been organized in such a way you will fail. Instead, Broken Spear foresees your party being the most successful. Meadow Flower is strong of heart, strong of body and she is to be Burly Bear's partner someday."

Taelo translated this to Little Otter, who let out a small groan. He was not yet sure this was going to be a good hunting trip, but he figured one more woman would make little difference.

"I am pleased to have her with us. I hope she can be ready to leave in short order," Little Otter replied with a forced smile.

His heart was heavy with the burden of having what he thought would be the weakest hunting team.

After Taelo had replied to Silent Fox that he was pleased with the arrangements, he began to get his things ready to depart. He was just getting everything completed when Burly Bear came by and told him Broken Spear wanted to talk to him.

"We are about ready to leave, hurry up so we can get under way," an irritated Little Otter called after him.

Taelo left the group and went to see Broken Spear.

Broken Spear was sitting out in the early morning sun, and he spoke as Taelo approached.

"In my dreams, I saw you in great danger. You were trapped and were trying to get out of some cave or hole full of water. You must go in the opposite direction. It will seem to be the wrong way, but it is the way to save your life. Go down in the water, it will lead you to another opening where you can get out.

One last thing, there may be someone with you. You must take immediate action if they fight you. It was a very confusing vision. The spirit is deranged. It is not a normal predator. I cannot see what it is." Broken Spear informed Taelo.

Taelo thanked Broke Spear. He told him he would use this information and do the best he could to protect the rest of the team from this threat.

He then returned to the hunting team just in time to take up his things and say farewell to the various members of the Clan.

Burly Bear's parents were present, and a self-conscience Burly Bear was giving his mother and father a hug before joining the group.

"What a softy, the biggest among us is the one whose mother worries most about his well-being," Taelo, teased Burley Bear as they began their jog away from the camp.

22 The Hunt

*T*he team set out with Burley Bear setting the pace. Meadow Flower turned out to be faster than both Burly Bear and Little Otter. She kept up very well and presented no problem.

The other three women began to teach her their language, and they began to pick up the language of the Others.

The three Elk Clan women had seen the special treatment and respect the Others gave Taelo and Golden Hawk. They wanted to be able to understand this Clan directly versus having the language interpreted. Each day as they were running or picking berries, they would learn a few words and bantered back and forth.

Meadow Flower had a good sense of humor, and she and the other women were soon joking with each other as they tried to learn each other's language.

Each day when they stopped, Little Otter would be surprised at the amount of small game the group had caught as it traveled.

303

There was always enough for a good dinner and leftovers to serve for breakfast.

He was beginning to enjoy his team and was beginning to feel they would do well. At least they would do better than he had at first feared.

On the fourth day of travel, they were going along a ridge when they spotted three mastodons coming up the valley. Little Otter wanted to hunt them immediately, but Burly Bear objected.

"They are only three. Broken Spear says soon they will all be gone.

Broken Spear has told us to enjoy seeing them and only hunt them from the larger herds. We should not hunt this small herd," Burley Bear explained.

The hunting party watched as the three mastodons, a male, a female, and a young cow, went past below them. The male let out a blast as if to thank them for letting them go.

Little Otter was a little put out, but Taelo explained if Broken Spear had seen the end of the mastodons, then they should heed his words and enjoy seeing the animals as they journeyed on their way.

Little Otter looked at his hunting party and decided he was in charge in name only and only the Elk Clan elders thought he was in charge.

The hunting party continued their travel along the ridge they were on toward the east. They traveled another day and then as they came over a crest of the trail a huge lake surrounded on the top side with a stand of tall green pine mixed with an occasional towering oak and a wide valley bending around it to the east and then going north met.

Taelo commented on the grandeur of the area and pointed to a small stream just in front of them that trickled down the mountain side.

They began following the small stream. It seemed to be leading them to the lake they had seen. Periodically other small streams would join into the one they were following.

Soon they were traveling along a small river. At a bend, where the river made a pleasant pool and several large trees dominated a flat spot on the bank, Taelo stopped.

"This is our first hunting camp. I recognize it from my dream last night. Tomorrow morning, we will kill three bison when their herd comes down to the lake. We shall make our camp under that big tree and sleep up in the limbs. I will show you how to make a hammock sleeping place in the trees," Taelo announced.

He felt a shiver go down his spine because he had also dreamed a saber tooth lioness would trap him and he would have an adventure whose end he could not see.

The hunting party went about gathering wood, arranging their camp, and watching as Taelo took some green willow saplings from the riverbank and made a flat sleeping spot between two limbs, about twenty feet above the ground.

"Why are we making our sleeping place up in the tree," Burly Bear asked?

"That is a great question," Little Otter said patting Burley Bear on the back as Golden Hawk translated.

"In my dream, a large bear will come and greet us. She will be followed by a pack of wolves. A saber tooth lioness will follow the wolves. The lioness will chase me to a cave not far from here.

In the cave I will run into the mother bear, she will chase off the lioness but will trap me in the cave. We are sleeping in the tree so we can survive this group of predators. Do any of you object," Taelo said with a grin?

After Golden Hawk had translated, they all began gathering the willow branches and making their beds.

"Is Taelo pulling our leg," Meadow Flower asked Burly Bear.

"Maybe a little, but Broken Spear warned Taelo of some danger on this trip," Burly Bear replied as he worked at making something strong enough to hold him safely in the tree.

He was taking Taelo seriously.

Quiet Rabbit, Talking Wren, and Busy Bee were having a similar conversation and asking Golden Hawk if what Taelo had said was true.

"Well, if anything, Taelo has left out the more dangerous or worrisome parts. Make sure you make your sleeping area strong and able to withstand wind and storm," Golden Hawk replied.

He was worried about what Taelo had said and would talk with his friend later. He wanted to be ready to help when the crisis arose.

All of them watched as Taelo made his sleeping area and copied the way he brought his leather cover over the top from one side. This left one side partially open but made the whole sleeping structure rainproof.

Taelo had pointed out the various branches with potential to make good sleeping areas. He made sure the four women had the higher locations Golden Hawk, Burly Bear and Little Otter were spread evenly around the tree on the lower limbs.

Any predator climbing up the tree would face this first level from each side.

Taelo was nervous about his dream and about Broken Spear's warning. He was worried about the hunting party members.

In his dream several of them were in trouble and what happened to them was not clear. The order of things also was jumbled.

Additionally, there were other members of old ones. The dream just did not make sense.

Taelo suggested each of them should keep their spears up in the tree with them. He himself had all his belongings hung up in the tree around his bed area. He had tied a rope to his limb and used it to climb down from his perch.

The evening dinner consisted of fish from the river, rabbit stew and a few greens which were found along the riverbank. The banter was light, and the discussion turned to their hunt. All of them were eager to begin hunting in earnest. It would be the first time for the young women, and they were nervous.

The night passed without incident and early the next morning Taelo was up before everyone. The sun was yet to come up. He took a bath in the river and then started the fire to warm up and get the camp ready for a quick breakfast.

He went out to scout the area around the lake. When he returned the camp was bustling and everyone was finishing breakfast.

"We should be able to bring down several buffalo today. There is a large herd on the far side of the lake," Taelo shared with the other members.

Taelo asked who had hunted the buffalo before. He knew that the young women had not. He asked because he wanted the team to openly discuss the hunt.

He suggested Little Otter take charge and split the group up into two teams.

He was sensitive to the fact Little Otter was supposed to lead the party, but he was not going to leave anything to chance.

Little Otter appreciated Taelo passing the lead over to him.

"I would like to put the fastest of the women with Taelo. Then I will put the next fastest with Golden Hawk.

The last two will match up with Burly Bear and me. We know we are the slowest.

We will match a fast team with a slow team. The job of the fast team is to mortally wound the buffalo. The slower team will run down the wounded animal and finish it.

Both jobs are critical and dangerous.

The slow team must be careful the wounded animal does not turn and attack them," Little Otter counseled.

He was pleased Taelo had turned the matter over to him. He had been afraid Taelo would try to take over. Little Otter now saw why Taelo was so highly thought of by all who associated with him.

Taelo could have just as easily have said what had just been said but he turned it over to him.

"Let's have a race to that far tree and back to see how we will assign you women," Little Otter continued.

The four women lined up and on Little Otter's signal they raced to the tree and back.

Quiet Rabbit was a full ten yards ahead by the time she got back to the camp. She had wanted to hunt with Taelo and had used every ounce of speed she had.

Busy Bee was second, and Talking Wren was next by several yards and was almost passed by Meadow Flower as they neared the end of the course.

"OK, Quiet Rabbit, you are with Taelo.

Busy Bee you will be with Golden Hawk.

I would like to have Meadow Flower with me but until we can communicate better it is too dangerous. So, Meadow Flower you will go with Burly Bear and Talking Wren will go with me.

Burley Bear will back up Taelo and I will back up Golden Hawk. This should give us a well-balanced approach.

Let's get our gear and get to the hunt.

Each team will discuss what is about to happen and how they will handle different situations.

Before we leave, we will need to cut two small trees to form the main part of a travois and smaller willow branches to make the carrying platform," Little Otter instructed as he thought how much he would have preferred the quieter Meadow Flower with him.

He would have to listen to Talking Wren all day long and he knew she would talk.

Once each team had the material for their travois and they had organized the tools and other things needed to skin the animals and to prepare the meat, they set out along their side of the lake.

Taelo and Burley Bear went around the south part of the lake.

As they walked, Taelo explained what would happen and how he planned to bring down the buffalo, "We will first work together to split two or three young buffalo from the herd. Once they are away and out to the side, I will run up alongside them and place my spear to their chest and the ground at the same time.

This will cause the buffalo to plunge the spear deeply into themselves. If we are lucky and get two or three the first time, our hunt will be over for the day. If we only get one, then we will try for another.

Once the animal is wounded it will be the job of Burley Bear and Meadow Flower to make sure the animal is brought down.

We will need to be aware of what the other teams are doing so we do not interfere with them.

Quiet Rabbit, this time your job will be to carry two spears for me. You must keep up with me and be ready to give me the spears.

Perhaps the next time you will want to place the spears. However, we will need to practice this together before you try it on a buffalo. I practiced with my father for over a year before he allowed me to try the first time. I was very young and not strong enough earlier. We will know how long it will take you once I see how you do in practice.

Do not worry. Golden Hawk will have the same speech for Busy Bee."

Taelo explained this in both languages so there would be no confusion. Burley Bear understood and had hunted with Taelo before. He explained to Meadow Flower that she would see an amazing way of hunting the buffalo.

"Only because of Taelo's speed will we be able to hunt so easily. I think that Little Otter will be amazed at what Golden Hawk will do. He has not seen the skill of these two amazing individuals," Burley Bear shared with Meadow Flower.

A similar discussion was going on in the other team as Golden Hawk explained how the hunt would be organized.

Little Otter thought Golden Hawk was just trying to show off. He had not seen anyone do what Golden Hawk had just described.

It was not long before they came out on the far end of the Lake where the herd was grazing in the early morning sun. The wind was blowing from the herd toward the two groups of hunters. This made their approach easier.

"We are the second team. We will work the buffalo we select away from the herd, but we will wait for Golden Hawk to make the first attack. Then we will follow. In this way we will keep from running into the other hunting party," Taelo explained.

Slowly, Taelo worked four young animals away from the rest of the herd. He was able to get the animals well away from the herd before they saw Golden Hawk begin his sprint toward the group of buffalo he had culled out.

Taelo nudged Quiet Rabbit and began his run at the nearest young bull. The bull jumped and was just getting to his top speed when Taelo placed the spear. The bull went down almost immediately.

Taelo was already bearing down on the second animal, a young cow. He repeated the act of placing the spear and having he animal spear itself.

The remaining two young bulls had now reached full speed. Quiet Rabbit, running as fast as she had ever run, was struggling to keep up with Taelo.

He grabbed the two spears from her and then to her amazement he accelerated to catch up with the two young bulls.

Quiet Rabbit continued to run as fast as she could, but she could not keep up.

Taelo reached the third young bull and repeated the placement of the spear and immediately sprinted on ahead.

He was now on a personal mission. He raced on to catch up to the fourth animal. It had now become a contest of will and Taelo wanted to get this last animal. It had turned and was running up hill for the tree line.

Taelo knew he had him. He waited until the bull was just reaching the tree line and then rushed forward and placed the spear. The bull fell just shy of the edge of the forest.

Taelo checked to make sure the bull was dead and then turned to look back along the trail of fallen animals.

Quiet Rabbit came staggering up and then she too looked back along the trail of the fallen animals with Taelo.

She bent over and then went to her knees as she worked to catch her breath.

"What an unbelievable run. How could you run so fast and then still have energy to place the spears," Quiet Rabbit said between breaths as she bent over trying not to be sick as she sucked in every searing breath.

She now understood Taelo's apprehension of having her try to spear one of the animals. She was not sure she could have gotten the first one and she knew she would never have been able to get four.

She got up and followed as Taelo slowly walked back along the path he had just finished running.

"It became a contest of wills. I was determined to use all four spears.

Usually when Golden Hawk and I go out we take turns bringing down the animals. Sharing the load makes it a little easier.

I hope in practice you will pick up this skill quickly, then we can let you take the first one or two and I will concentrate on the last animals," Taelo explained.

"Having seen how it is done, I can appreciate why I must practice. I was a little upset when you first told me I would have to wait," Quiet Rabbit confessed.

Now she was not sure she would be able to do it.

By the time, the two made it back to the second bull where Meadow Flower was waiting, Taelo saw Burly Bear assembling the travois.

Taelo looked up the valley where the hunters on the other team were doing the same thing. He could see three animals Golden Hawk had downed. He wondered if there was a fourth. He knew Golden Hawk had culled four out.

The two teams had agreed to meet halfway between them. This would allow for the least amount of work for the hunting parties.

The last bull Taelo had killed was almost at the perfect spot.

"Now the hard work begins. We must drag the animals up to the tree line, gut them, skin them, and then prepare the meat. We need to get them up into the trees before dark," Taelo explained to Quiet Rabbit.

Taelo arranged a pulling harness for each of the four. It was an arduous pull to the edge of the forest. They brought their second bull up to the edge of the forest and pulled it to where Taelo thought would be a good spot to hang him. The other hunting group soon brought their first animal up.

Little Otter was overwhelmed at the kill. "I have never seen anything like it. Golden Hawk brought down four buffalo," he said to no one in particular.

He was excited and agitated. He now felt they had a chance to match up to the other parties.

When you have your animals up here please begin. Don't wait for us, we have four, yes four of them to drag up here," Little Otter gave instructions to Taelo's team.

Taelo walked over to Golden Hawk and clapped him on the back and congratulated him on his four kills.

Meadow Flower quietly asked Burly Bear why Taelo did not tell everyone he too had taken down four buffalo.

"I think because it will be a surprise when the rest realize we have eight animals," Burly Bear replied, "He will not boast about his skills, but he never lacks in confidence."

With Burly Bear and Meadow Flower's superior strength, Taelo's team worked faster than Golden Hawk's team. They had their four carcasses quickly hanging in the trees before Golden Hawk's team had brought up their fourth kill.

They were cleaning up the livers, hearts, and kidneys and cutting up the intestines they would keep.

They had also brought out wood for the fires they would need for the night. Meadow Flower had already started to cook a late afternoon lunch.

Talking Wren, who noticed the four hanging animals quietly, joined in the preparation of the lunch. She knew this would be a surprise for Little Otter and she was waiting to see his reaction. This was one time she would be quiet and enjoy the surprise.

It was obvious, Quiet Rabbit and Busy Bee were exhausted from the hunting run.

"Perhaps some of you could begin to help us, after all we have four animals to skin," Little Otter began, and then he noticed there were already four buffalo hanging in the trees. He looked around and realized there were four more still to be gutted and hung.

Golden Hawk laughed, "Well, my friend it seems you too have had a good day, and you have yours already gutted. I suppose now your team will take a nap, while we get out animals ready."

"No, we will help, but seriously, look at the herd. Notice the large bull toward the middle. Now look at the cow just this side of him. See the late calf. The wolves will have it in the next day or two.

I am going out and bring it up here for us to celebrate with," Taelo said with a wink at Quiet Rabbit.

"Who on my team wants to go with me," Taelo asked?

"I will go with you," Quiet Rabbit spoke up quickly. She was tired but she wanted to experience the thrill of the hunt again, besides, she wanted to hunt with Taelo again.

"I think she has her eyes on him," Meadow Flower said quietly to Burly Bear, who just grunted in response.

Taelo prepared two spears. Put a short length of rope around his neck and then grabbed two small square pieces of leather, he gave one to Quiet Rabbit. He also carried a coil of rope.

As they walked down toward the herd, Taelo explained to Quiet Rabbit the spears were only for an emergency. They would catch the young calf and tie his legs together. Then they would use the rope and lead it back to camp, so they would not need to carry it.

Near a lone tree, Taelo dropped the coil of rope, and he had Quiet Rabbit leave her spear. Taelo put the leather over his shoulders and began to crawl out toward the mother and her young calf. He could tell the calf was about four months old and he knew it would be culled out by wolves in no time. He was surprised it hadn't already happened.

The going was slow. The afternoon sun was nearing the horizon before Taelo had worked his way out to the calf. He then began to move the mother and calf out toward the edge of the herd.

The group on the hill had a perfect view of the herd and even though they knew the target of Taelo's hunt they often could not see him. They were impressed with how subtle and precise his action and movement were.

Taelo used his spear with a rabbit hide tied to the end to signal the cow the way to the edge of the herd. Once he got her there, the cow immediately sensed danger and wanted to move inward, but Taelo kept moving the calf away from the herd. The mother followed as Taelo got the calf clear of the herd.

Taelo suddenly jumped up, leaving his spear behind and ran straight at the calf. The calf had just started to react when Taelo caught its head, twisted it, and brought the calf down. He immediately caught a hind leg and a front leg and tied them together with the rope around his neck.

The mother buffalo looked on, began her attack but backed away when Quiet Rabbit came up and shouted and waved the leather she was carrying.

"Well, done Quiet Rabbit, you probably saved me from having to either run for a tree or kill the cow," Taelo praise her.

Quiet Rabbit was pleased. She had been afraid of the cow and had acted on instinct. Taelo's approval relieved her. Quite Rabbit ran over to the tree and retrieved the extra spear and the rope.

Taelo made a simple head harness from the rope and put it on the calf. He then untied the legs of the calf and immediately began leading it toward the edge of the forest. The calf tried several times to run but finally settled down and followed Taelo.

"What in the world is Taelo up to," Little Otter exclaimed as he first watched the calf being taken down and then the harness being put on.

"Well knowing Taelo, he will have the calf talking to him and probably its mother giving him her blessings," Burley Bear said as he too wondered what his friend was up to.

"This calf is fairly large, perhaps it can help us transport the meat back to the Clan," Taelo said thoughtfully as they walked up the hill toward where the hunters were processing the eight buffalo they had killed.

Taelo shared his idea with Little Otter. "It sounds a little crazy to me, but if you can get it to pull one of the travois, I am all for it.

Because of his size, Little Otter was always being asked to pull a travois and the idea of not having to do it excited him.

All afternoon they processed the meat and then moved the carcasses halfway back to the original camp. The calf helped a little, but he was a little too jittery to be useful. Taelo took him the rest of the way to camp and built a small pen to keep him in.

The team went to their main camp and feasted on grilled buffalo tongue. This was a treat they all enjoyed.

Taelo fortified the enclosure for the calf and then went up to his sleeping quarters and fell immediately to sleep. The rest of the group very quickly followed his example. They knew the next day held a full day of getting the meat prepared for smoking and drying.

The night passed uneventfully and the next morning the group was up early and discussing how to proceed.

It seemed all was well.

A few days later the entire load of hides, semi dried meat and some fresh meat was loaded on a larger than usual travois and attached to the young buffalo. Little Otter and Talking Wren would return with the load of meat. Once they had delivered it, they would return with the young buffalo. They planned to use him again for the next load.

The journey home took Little Otter and Talking Wren fourteen sun cycles. Talking Wren lived up to her name and Little Otter thought his second name should be Little Otter the deaf.

He was amazed at the strength of the young buffalo and fed and treated it well. When they finally made the beach and were walking along the water the young calf seemed to get new energy, and they made excellent time. As they approached the camp the Elk Clan members came out to greet them.

"The camp has moved into Taelo's valley. We are here to make salt to take to the main camp. However, we will take your meat and process it, so it is ready for winter. Then we will transport it down to the main camp when we take the salt down.

We go once every fourteen sun cycles with the salt," explained one of the elder warriors as he took in the strange sight.

Everyone marveled at the calf, and they were amazed this team had brought in so much meat. They told Little Otter and Talking Wren no other team had sent back any meat so far.

Little Otter thought about the members of his team and realized he had the best hunting team in of the Elk Clan.

23 The Rescue

*T*aelo and the rest of the team decided to rest for a couple of days before going back on the hunt.

The warning by Broken Spear had not materialized. Taelo was nervous about the fact nothing out of the ordinary had occurred.

He would remain vigilant!

On the last day of their declared rest period, three members of a hunting group of the others straggled into camp. They were exhausted and desperate. They explained they had been hunting when they came across an overly aggressive saber tooth. It attacked part of the party. It then stalked them as they were trying to clear its territory. The three had left the wounded hunters in a cave.

They had fought the saber tooth all the way back to Taelo's Camp. It was somewhere in the area close by.

Taelo made sure the three hunters had a good dinner and then helped them make their beds up in the tree. The tiger might be able to climb, but if he was as big as the hunters claimed, then it probably could not climb very well.

Taelo made sure anyone going to the edge of the camp was escorted. The entire team was on alert.

They stoked the fires and then climbed up to their beds.

Taelo had set a watch, and each person would sit awake for three hours and pass the watch to the next person.

He climbed into his enclosure and went to sleep.

In the dark of the moonless night, A putrid odor awoke Taelo. He heard nothing but sensed danger close at hand. Swiftly and silently, he moved into a fighting crouch.

Deadly claws whisked through the space he had just vacated. Uncharacteristically, the saber tooth had climbed silently up the tree.

Taelo automatically thrust the spear into the tiger's mouth.

The angry roar was heard for miles around!!!

The occupants in the tree all were immediately awake. They were not sure where their adversary was.

Suddenly, pushed off balance, Taelo and the lion fell from the tree.

Both lay stunned for a moment.

Taelo recovered first and jumped up and ran toward the lake. He knew he was at a disadvantage on the ground. In the lake he would have a fighting chance.

He also wanted to get the lion away from the camp to ensure the safety of the team. He would make his stand near the edge of the cliffs towering above the lake on the mountain side.

This would give him the option to dive off to escape the lion.

The saber tooth was rapidly closing the distance. Even Taelo's speed was not enough. Taelo realized when he reached his destination, he would need to turn immediately and fight the tiger.

He dug deep and came up with one more surge of energy and speed.

Burly Bear jumped out of the tree and shouted at the top of his voice and threw a spear toward the tiger.

The tiger hesitated for a moment but then took up the chase after Taelo. This hesitation gave Taelo a slight margin.

Burly Bear picked up his spear and shouting at the top of his voice was chasing behind the tiger trying to distract the animal.

What he would do if he succeeded had not crossed his mind.

Confusion reigned in the camp. The various camp members were trying to sort out what had happened and what was going on.

Quiet Rabbit had seen Taelo running out of the camp with Burley Bear close behind. She grabbed her spear and ran after Burley Bear. She quickly caught up with him and then went out in front.

She picked up the shout and was making almost as much noise as Burley Bear. She was quickly a hundred yards ahead of Burley Bear. Her only thought was to help Taelo.

She was running faster than she had ever run before. What she would do if she caught up to the tiger and Taelo had not crossed her mind. She just knew she had to help Taelo.

She heard the roar of the tiger somewhere ahead and then there was only a still silence. She found more speed and ran fearlessly toward where the sound had come from.

Burley Bear soon joined her. The two tried to find the trail but there was nothing. They both shouted for Taelo but there was no reply. They went along the edge of the cliff that overlooked the lake but saw no sign of either the tiger or of Taelo.

At the last moment just as the tiger pounced, Taelo turned and brought his spear up. Taelo's spear found its mark in the center of the tiger's chest.

He was not sure this action was going to be enough to save his life. In reflex the tiger was reaching out with her sharp claws.

Suddenly the ground gave way and both he and tiger were falling. Even as he was falling, Taelo instinctively used his spear to position himself above the tiger. He looked into the eyes of the maddened animal.

The black at the bottom of the fall came into view. He hoped it was the water that the seer had mentioned. Then the impact took his breath away.

The impact of the water drove the spear all the way through the tiger.

Taelo hit the tiger and then fell into the water and went down into it for what seemed like eternity. He came up with his, shark tipped hand spear ready to fight the tiger. However, the impact and his hunting spear had done its job. The tiger was floating dead on the water.

Taelo looked up the chimney that had saved his life. The walls were smooth, with no visible foot or hand holds. He could barely make out the opening high above him.

He was alive and trapped.

Taelo relaxed and took in his surroundings. The faint light from the opening at the top gave just enough illumination to let him see in the tunnel. He let his eyes adjust to the relative darkness. He knew he was in trouble unless he could figure a way out.

The tiger was still floating with Taelo's spear through its body. The spear seemed to provide just enough buoyancy to keep the body afloat.

It was too bad he would have to leave the carcass here. He would have loved to have the skin. Perhaps if he got out quickly, he would be able to lower himself down from the top and haul the tiger out. It was huge; it probably outweighed him by several hundred pounds.

He then recalled Broken Spears guidance about going down to another passage.

Golden Hawk and the remaining hunters had arrived at the cliffs and were scouting around and calling Taelo's name. But there was no sign of him, and no one found the new hole opening into blackness and the water below.

"I am sure he is alright," Burly Bear said as he continued to look for Taelo. He was sure Taelo was close by. He could feel his presence.

Taelo remembered Broken Spear's words. The way out is under the water. He had failed to tell Taelo there would be some thirty feet of water. Taelo took several deep breaths and then dived into the water.

The visibility was poor, but using his hands, he found an opening near the bottom leading out of the funnel. He went along a horizontal tunnel until there was light from above. He was fighting for air as he rose through the water expecting to come out in the lake.

Instead, he came out in a pool located in a large cavern. The opening of the cavern was about twenty feet above the lake.

Taelo was about ready to get out of the water when a roar caused him to freeze. There on a shelf above the water lay the huge mother bear who had visited Taelo on the beach.

"It is good to see that you are well," Taelo said in a conversational tone. He went to the far side of the pool and slowly got out. He was hoping the bear would let him out of the cave.

"I only need passage out of your cave. I did not mean to disturb you and will leave you alone once I have left," Taelo continued his banter as he backed slowly to the edge of the cave opening.

The big bear gave one more roar and then lay her head down in disinterest.

Taelo turned and walked out along a trail leading from the cave. He made his was upward and headed up the cliff.

The members of the hunting party were spread out along the cliff still trying to locate Taelo.

Quiet Rabbit was calling his name in desperation!

Taelo walked up behind her and quietly answered her.

Quiet Rabbit turned and gave Taelo a hug.

"What happened?

Where did you go?

Are you alright," she asked Taelo in rapid fire?

She called out to the rest of the hunting party.

The whole group returned and exploded with questions.

"I learned from an old medicine man if you grab the teeth of a saber tooth and pull them sideways out of its mouth, it will leave you alone. I remembered this as I ran. I turned and waited for the saber tooth to catch up and grabbed the teeth one in each hand. I am sure you all heard the roar of pain as I pulled the teeth from her head," Taelo said as he looked at his teammates.

"Then, since I was a little sweaty, I walked to the edge of the cliff and dove off and went for a swim. I swam across the lake and back and here I am," he said with a bow.

Burley Bear started laughing when he realized Taelo was telling them a mate's tale.

Quiet Rabbit wiped the tears from her eyes. She was not sure whether they were tears of joy or whether she was mad at Taelo for making light of such a serious situation.

"Who would like to help me bring this tiger into camp," Taelo asked?

The entire camp followed him to the hole at the top of the chimney. The group realized they had all walked by the top of the tunnel several times. However, unless one climbed up the slight rise surrounding the chimney it was not visible.

Quiet Rabbit looked down the deep hole. It seemed very frightening, but she volunteered to be lowered into the tunnel to tie the rope to the tiger.

When she got down to the water, she saw the huge tiger still floating. Its size was unbelievable. Quiet Rabbit tied the rope around the tiger and then tugged on the rope.

The tiger was slowly raised.

Quiet Rabbit stayed to the edge of the pool. She realized how isolated she felt and wondered how Taelo had gotten out of this situation. It was obvious he had not climbed out.

It took a good hour of pulling, holding, and pulling some more to get the tiger to the top of the chimney. It must have weighed five hundred pounds. Finally, the group was able to pull the tiger clear of the hole.

This feat would not have been possible without the help of the members of the Others.

Taelo immediately dropped the rope down for Quiet Rabbit. Burly Bear made pulling Quiet Rabbit seem easy. She was light as a feather in comparison to the tiger.

"That was brave. Thank you for going down so I could have the tiger hide and head," Taelo said as Quiet Rabbit was lifted from the hole.

"How did you get out," Quiet Rabbit asked in a low voice?

Everyone stopped to hear Taelo's explanation.

"When I saw I had killed the tiger, my spirit soared. Before I knew it, my feet were on the ground" Taelo replied with the same twinkle he had earlier.

"Yes, and if we look closely, we will see wings on your feet," Burly Bear said gruffly as he and several others picked up the pole to which they had tied the tiger.

23 The Rescue

That morning after a good meal. The three hunters from the other hunting party were given food and supplies. Burly Bear, Meadow Flower, and Quiet Rabbit went with them to help and to tend to the wounded.

"Return to us as soon as possible. If the one injured can no longer hunt, bring those who can hunt back to our camp. They can hunt with us, and we will make sure they are able to contribute their part to the Clan," Little Otter commented.

Little Otter took his hunting party father east and there in a large valley they found many elk. Hunting elk took more skill then running down the buffalo but within three days, the group had several elk hung in the trees. They were processing the meat as fast as they could.

They were able to pull back all the meat on a large travois pulled by the young buffalo that had become a constant companion of Little Otter. It followed Little Otter everywhere he went.

They had just returned when Quiet Rabbit followed by Burley Bear, Quiet Meadow and four hunters from the Others walked into camp.

Burley Bear was pulling a travois with one of the hunters laying on it.

Taelo greeted them and guided them to the area around the campfire. He recognized Rolling Stone who had been one of the warriors on the beach when they had found the whale.

Burley Bear let everyone know that Rolling Stone's new name was Saber Scar.

Saber Scar smiled and pointed to Quiet Rabbit. He recalled that he was delirious by the time Quiet Rabbit arrived. He was sure he was on his death bed and just wanted to be left alone but she proceeded to wash his wounds that went to the bone and in several areas to the other side.

He pointed to the neat stitches that closed the gashes across his chest. There are more than two hundred stiches on the outside and she tells me there are a few on the inside.

I hope to tell my children about the miracle lady of the Elk Clan.

"We were just getting ready to take our next load of meat back to the Clan," Little Otter commented.

"I will take this load back. I can take them back to our cave and then take the load on south to the Elk Camp," Burly Bear volunteered.

Little Otter suggested Burley Bear take the load of meat to the Clan of Others. The Load of meat would make up for the loss of one hunting party.

He was glad to have the opportunity to do some more hunting with the team.

He now had the confidence that his team would show themselves quiet well.

"By the time you return we should have another load to take south," Little Otter said in closing.

The next morning the hunting party loaded the travois up with most of the meat they had hunted.

"When you return, come by here. We will leave our kill here and then travel a few more days east," Little Otter spoke up.

His hunting party was doing much better then he would ever have imagined. He was learning how to lead them and proud of being with this team.

Taelo commented to Golden Hawk that Little Otter had found his confidence and was becoming a good leader.

<u>*24 Return to the Valley*</u>

*T*he Hunting continued to be bountiful. Taelo suggested to Little Otter that the team move south as they hunted.

Golden Hawk made the point that they should end their long hunt and return home.

Talking Wren added that their team had already sent more meat home than any other hunting team. Three large loads of meat had been sent back to each of the two Clans.

Burley Bear stopped at the top of the hill that they were all coming up and stated that he thought their hunt was at an end.

The rest of the team came up to where he had stopped. At first it was hard to register the sight. The far mountains silhouetted by the light blue sky and snow caps formed the frame with the dark green of forest tops rising above an undulating mass of dark brown forms that seemed to have worms wiggling randomly above curved white spears.

Little Otter was the first to speak and ask Burley Bear if this was a big enough herd for them to hunt.

Quiet Rabbit suggested they take one young male as she made the point that one would be more meat than they had sent back to the Elk Clan so far.

Taelo and Golden Hawk agreed with Quiet Rabbit and decided they would travel down along the herd and look for a place they could make a trap for such an animal.

"Let's see if there is a narrow valley or canyon somewhere ahead where we can drive one into. We will tell the rest of the team to follow along the ridge, and we will scout ahead for the place where we can trap the animal," Taelo said to Little Otter.

"May I accompany the two of you," Quiet Rabbit asked when she heard what they were going to do?

"Yes, you may. I just want you to know we will be running almost the entire day," Taelo replied. "Does anyone else want to come along," he asked?

There were no takers. They all knew they would not be able to keep up.

The three set off running along the side of the herd. It was early afternoon before they found a suitable valley or canyon. Golden Hawk spotted a short, narrow passage that came to a dead-end after one bend. It was perfect if they could guide a mastodon to go into it.

Taelo and Golden Hawk decided to spend some time preparing the narrow passage to trap the mastodon.

He asked Quiet Rabbit to go back to the hunting party and guide them to this place as quickly as possible.

He stated that he and Golden Hawk would spend the rest of the afternoon preparing the trap. They would be ready to trap a mastodon and would do so if the right one wandered into their trap area.

Quiet Rabbit left immediately with the promise of getting the team back before sunset. She made Taelo promise not to do anything too dangerous.

Taelo and Golden Hawk cut about twenty long poles and cut a point into one end. They put these with one end in the ground and the other end pointing up into the passage. The mastodon would be able to walk past them going into the passage but would not be able to walk back if it tried to turn back out of the passage.

They put two poles on one side and a matching pair on the opposite side of the passage. These poles were just far enough apart so the mastodon could pass between them. They put five sets of four about ten feet distance from each other.

After the entrance, they set up a series of poles about half the height they estimated the mastodon to be and put in poles with sharpened points so the animal would not be able to move forward, sideward, or backward. This would be the point where two or three of the hunters would drive spears into the mastodon from the sides.

By the time they were done the late afternoon sun was casting long shadows. The herd was still making its way slowly past them as it seemed to flow up the valley.

Together the two went down the valley to decide which animal to cull out. They spotted one of the younger, smaller bulls at the edge of the herd and decided to try to slowly move him out away from the rest.

They approached him from behind and waved a piece of leather to move the young mastodon to the edge of the herd. Then at the critical moment, when the passage was close at hand, Golden Hawk moved up between the bull and the herd.

The young bull reacted exactly as Golden Hawk desired him to and moved toward the entrance to the passage.

The two got the young bull past the first set of guide poles and stopped. They were not going to push the animal any farther until the rest of the hunting team arrived.

Quiet Rabbit was the first to arrive. She had alerted the team, and they were coming behind her, but she knew that Taelo and Golden Hawk would act before the sun began to set.

She told the two that the team would arrive just as dusk was setting in.

"We will stay here across the end of the crevasse. Hopefully, the mastodon will move slowly into the trap and will not try to back out. If he tries to escape, we will try to wound him to keep him from escaping. We need to be very careful. These animals are powerful and when frightened they can cause unbelievable damage and harm.

The spearing will require great strength. We will let Burly Bear and Little Otter do the initial spearing to bring down the mastodon.

The rest of us will try to distract the animal so the two can get a good throw and follow through," Taelo explained to Quiet Rabbit.

His explanation comforted Quiet Rabbit, since she was worried about Taelo and Golden Hawk acting on their own to down the mastodon.

She had run back to keep them from taking any hasty action against the animal. She had underestimated Taelo's and Golden Hawk's level and logical thinking. They were very careful and serious.

The young bull mastodon moved slowly up the crevasse. Every time he tried to back up the pointed poles would poke him. He slowly moved forward only to find he was more constricted than before. Finally, he was in the main trap with spears poking him in every direction he tried to move. He stood still and seemed content to just stand in place.

Taelo, Golden Hawk and Quiet Rabbit had been moving slowly up the crevasse and moving the pairs of pointed spears up into position behind the mastodon. Should it somehow be able to turn around, the mastodon would face a wall of spears blocking its escape.

The rest of the team arrived as the evening was taking on that grey black appearance where nothing seemed exactly real. It was hard to see.

Taelo decided it would be too dangerous for the team to try to take down the animal so late in the day.

Burley Bear, Little Otter and the rest of the team agreed.

They decided a camp at the top of a small knoll would be a safe location.

Taelo sat for a long time looking at the stars twinkling in the black fabric of the night sky. He welcomed the presence of Quiet Rabbit who true to her name sat by silently by his side.

He looked around and found that the rest of the members of the team were doing the same.

He knew that hunting together had bonded them to each other and he saw that each had found the one they wanted to sit with.

The next morning Taelo explained who on the team should spear the mastodon. Burly Bear and Little Otter agreed with the two of them driving the spears in from the side. Burley Bear would spear for the heart and Little Otter from the other side for the lung.

They each sharpened a spear. They approached the mastodon from the side.

Taelo and the rest of the team distracted the bull by getting out in front of it and waving small pieces of leather.

The mastodon tried to back up but was trapped by the extra pointed poles behind him. These poles caused him to panic, and he lunged forward into the pole in front. At the same time both Burly Bear and Little Otter ran their spears full force into the mastodon from the side.

Little Otter's spear glanced off a rib. His forward momentum put him in danger of falling into the pit when Talking Wren grabbed him by the hair and pulled him back up hill.

Little Otter let out what sounded like a war scream as he fell back uphill on his butt.

Talking Wren's action had saved his life. He looked at her and holding the top of his head where it felt like his hair had been ripped out, he thanked her for saving his life.

"Perhaps, she was not so bad a person to partner with," he thought to himself.

Meanwhile Burly Bear's spear found its mark, went between two ribs and into the heart. The mastodon gave out one more cry and collapsed.

Taelo let out a cry of victory and thanked the ancients for giving the young bull a quick and painless death.

Except for the incident with Little Otter the kill had been easy and very clean.

Taelo pointed at Talking Wren and shouted praise for her quick and decisive action.

The kill represented three times the amount of meat the team had sent back so far. Two thirds would go to the Elk camp and one third to the Others.

The skinning and preparation of the meat took two weeks. At the end of this time one travois, pulled by hunters from the Others' camp took a load of meat to their camp. A much larger travois, to be pulled by the now, almost tame bull was loaded with the meat to pull to the Elk Clan camp.

Even then there were four other smaller travois, each loaded with a variety of meat, hides and other foods the hunters had gathered. These other foods included some fish, and many plants and roots.

Taelo, Golden Hawk, Little Otter and Burly Bear sat over the evening meal to discuss the best way to go back to the valley along the river. Taelo thought if they continued down the valley they were in, they would hit the river and then be able to travel west. They decided two hunters would always scout out ahead of the party and mark the best way the loaded party should travel.

Burley Bear would follow the valley in the direction the Mastodons were traveling and then close to where they had hunted the first buffalo around the lake he would turn to the west.

In the morning, they each went their separate ways. They would get back together once they had delivered their hunting spoils.

Golden Hawk and Busy Bee went out as scouts first. The going south followed the natural direction of the valley. It was the westerly direction Little Otter was worried about. They had several tons of meat to transport. This would make a climb up the mountains extremely challenging.

The first day they only made ten miles down the valley. Golden Hawk and Busy Bee came back and let the party know the valley proceeded for another ten miles beyond.

Taelo and Quiet Rabbit went out the next day and proceeded south, southwest in search of a way out of the valley or to the river. They moved in a steady jogging rhythm. They were well matched in stamina and carried on a conversation as they moved along.

Quiet Rabbit had learned a tremendous amount of hunting lore and the two practiced some of the skills Taelo described.

The two practiced the language of the Old ones and Taelo shared his belief the old ones were dying out and Broken Spear had foreseen their demise.

Taelo on the other hand learned a few additional things about plants and even if he knew about them, he would listen politely to Quiet Rabbit give her explanation. He had learned the art of listening which gave him the ability to think through what he heard and allowed him to encourage others. It also caused the people with him to talk more and share more of their perspectives.

A tall cliff closed the end of the valley. However, there to its right was a gradual rise and then it went down to another small valley. This valley was the beginning of a spring flowing to join a small creek. They would be able to follow these small streams down and hopefully they would come to the river.

The two returned to the camp late into the night with the good news.

The hunting team traveled for almost a week on a south, southwest course. The streams did flow together to form the river, and the river was heading west. This convinced Taelo it was the same river he; Golden Hawk and Burley Bear had followed the winter before.

Golden Hawk and Busy Bee came back to camp one day with the news they had found the Elk Clan camp. The hunting party was only two days away.

When they were one day out, a scout from the Elk Clan camp found and greeted them. He was amazed at the amount of meat and other things to eat the hunting party was bringing in. The other hunting parties had returned but they had only done marginally well. The first two loads of meat Little Otter's party had brought back, were about the equivalent to what all the others had brought in. What he saw now dwarfed the others.

The scout stayed with them for the remainder of the day and then went ahead of the party to let the camp know the last group was returning. He was excited to let them know how much this last team was bringing in.

A loud round of welcomes came from the members of the Elk Clan as the team pulled in the main travois and the four auxiliary ones. They had come back as the best party of the four sent out.

"Little Otter, you have done extremely well. You will be known as a great hunt leader," one of the elders said.

"I am the weakest hunter of this team. It was the teamwork that made it possible for us to bring home such a harvest. Every member has become a top hunter and someone who I would want by my side in case of trouble.

Both Golden Hawk and Taelo are superb hunters and fearless leaders.

Burley Bear is the strongest of us and knows no fear.

Taelo, the speaker to bears and the slayer of saber tooth tigers performs magic when he hunts.

"You have brought in the safety margin for our Clan this coming year. We will be able to share with the rest of the larger Elk sub-clans and still enjoy our margin of safety. If the buffalo return to the valley then we will indeed be a wealthy Clan. Tonight, and tomorrow night we will celebrate your return and listen to the stories each of you must tell," Grey Fox Running announced to the entire camp.

He and White Swan exchanged a hug of pride as they watched Taelo, Golden Hawk and the rest of the team move into the center of the camp.

24 Return to the Valley

The early fall passed at a comfortable pace until it was time for all the sub-Clans of the Elk Clan to get together once again.

25 Meeting of the Clan

Grey Fox Running and Red Oak led the Elk Clan members up the beach away from their camp. The Clan was getting an early start and planned to be the first to arrive at the valley for the Clan meeting. He wanted to claim the area on the far side of the lake. That area would provide the space for both the Elk Clan and the Clan of Others.

He knew that all the other Elk sub-Clans would have an initial negative reaction about having the Clan of Others as part of their meeting and wanted to control the interactions of the two cultures.

Taelo, Golden Hawk and Burley Bear went out ahead as the Elk Clan and the Clan of Others met and came together on the beach. They would turn to go northwest toward the meeting valley.

The two clans were coming together at the location where Burley Bear had chased after Red Oak and his team only a few moons before.

Burley Bear made the point of walking over to Red Oak to thank him for being such a good leader. They both had a good laugh as they recalled that chase event.

Silent Hawk, the leader that had stepped aside to put Grey Fox Running in the leadership position of the Elk Clan leader, had been selected to lead the two Clans back to the Elk clan meeting valley. This journey was one of renewal for the Elk Clan. They had left the valley on starvation rations and were now returning early because they were now so rich in goods that they were slowed by them.

A few days later, the Elk Clan came to the valley where Taelo and Golden Hawk had killed their giant dire wolves and Brave Deer, and his hunters had fought the rest of the dire wolves in hand-to-hand combat.

Brave Deer and his team and Taelo and Golden Hawk stood together as they recalled their experiences.

This time the two stood with Burley Bear their new friend from the Others. He was impressed by the size of the dire wolf hides that Red Oak, Taelo and Golden Hawk held up.

Busy Bee, Brave Deer's daughter, commented to her two closest friends, Quiet Rabbit, and Talking Wren that she now had a much greater appreciation of Taelo's and Golden Hawks capabilities and that the night they had returned with the two giant dire wolf hides now meant so much more than it did at that time.

Silent Hawk commented on the dramatic change the Elk Clan had experienced in such a short time.

Later they stopped at the Honey Tree and collected enough honey that every family of both Clans had two small bags.

The sharing of the honey was a continuing sign of how close both Clans had become.

The procession was a strange sight. Tall smooth-skinned people walked with an easy gait alongside of the broad, hairy people walking with an awkward somewhat stiff one. This was a contrast in human design.

Though different in appearance and some customs, it had become apparent to all in both groups they were more the same than different. They embraced their common beliefs and foundational principles.

Both clans brought a huge amount of extra food and other valuable supplies. They had baskets, leather goods, tools, spears, clothing, and specialty foods to trade with the other clans. The leather work of the old ones was unique and intricate in design.

Taelo, Golden Hawk and Burley Bear had come with a supply of their own things to trade and share. They had made several sleds and snowshoes. They had speared several more sharks and had a supply of arrows made with the teeth. Additionally, they had used several of the larger teeth to make the spears for trade purposes.

The three young men were the only single males doing this kind of work and were looked upon curiously by some. However, Taelo and Golden Hawk knew there would be items at the clan meeting that they would want, and they planned to have the currency to be able to get these items. They enrolled Burley Bear who immediately joined them in the preparation for trading.

Secretly the three had also created as series of carvings designed to be stacked one on top of the other. There was a base representing mother earth. On top of it stood a large Bear with a notch cut on the ear, a Deer, a Fox and together an Eagle and Hawk. This made a very impressive totem.

The three were going to present this totem to the entire Clan. For both people it represented the unity of nature. This had been a project they had spent their time on when they went to their hide away.

They had made a large travois to pull it to the meeting center. Little Otter and what everyone now thought of as his buffalo, had been recruited to pull the travois. The journey convinced them the totem would permanently stay in the valley.

They certainly were not going to pull it back.

The entire procession stopped and took in the valley. The dark green pines stood like sentinels holding the far snow-capped mountains at bay from the long oval dark blue lake.

The yellowing cat tails on the far-left bank shielded the far side of the lake where they planned to camp from the rest of the flat valley floor on the other side of the lake.

And in the distance, they could follow the tumbling path of the small river as in entered the valley to feed the lake.

The light blue sky, large tumulus clouds slowly drifting by and the gentle breeze of the early afternoon seemed to pull the two clans forward.

Grey Fox Running was pleased that they were the first to arrive and they would have the place he had planned.

Taelo, Golden Hawk and Burley Bear cleaned up the area where the council always had their seat. They set up their totem and covered it with a large hide. They would unveil it as a surprise gift to all the sub-Clans. They had kept the entire effort secret from everyone. Only the three of them knew what it was.

Wise Owl brought in the Elk Horn Clan two days after the arrival of the Elk Clan and the Clan of Others. He saw that the area on the far side of the lake had already been taken. He chuckled at having been displaced. He was early enough to have a place down by the lake just across from those on the other side.

He went over to greet Grey Fox Running and see how the Elk Clan had fared. He was greeted by Grey Fox Running, Red Oak, and Silent Hawk at the point where the small bridge sat in the middle of the river. There he was introduced to Quiet Fox, leader of the Others.

Wise Owl was surprised to see that the Elk Clan had brought a group of Others as large as their own group. He understood immediately why they had chosen to be on this side of the river. He also noted all were healthy and they had an enormous amount of food and goods on display. It was apparent Grey Fox Running and Red Oak had performed the magic they had been sent to do.

"It is good to see the Elk Clan has done so well. Who are the friends you bring with you," Wise Owl said as he greeted Grey Fox Running, Red Oak, Silent Hawk and Quiet Fox of the Others?

He was intrigued by the situation and was very interested in how it had all come about. He was sure this was going to be an interesting and historic gathering for all the Elk sub-clans.

"It is good to see you my friend. I would like to introduce you to Quiet Fox of the Others. We have joined our two Clans in friendship and bring them with us to introduce them to the rest of the Elk sub-clans," Grey Fox Running said and then repeated the introduction to Quiet Fox.

"I am honored to meet Wise Owl. Taelo and Golden Hawk have told me many stories of the Elk Horn Clan and its wise leader," Quiet Fox spoke in Wise Owl's language.

This surprised Grey Fox Running who did not know Quiet Fox had been getting lessons from Taelo, Golden Hawk and Burley Bear.

The three were standing on the bank of the river beaming with pride. Quiet Fox was their pet project.

"I would ask you to help in the introduction of the Others to the rest of the sub-Clans. We have prospered and done well by working together. We have invited the Others to this meeting as a sign of friendship. They have brought gifts to share and goods to trade," Grey Fox Running continued the introduction.

"You have my support. This should be one of the more interesting gatherings we have held for as long as I can recall," Wise Owl said with a chuckle.

Gray Fox Running had instructed each family to prominently show the wares they had brought so all could see.

Broken Spear and Quiet Fox had given similar advice to the group of Others. Their pure white leather with its intricate bead work was especially of interest.

Each arriving sub-clan had a different but surprised reaction. The entire Clan was speechless !!!

A silence had fallen as each sub-clan understood there were Others among them.

There was a rise in the acrimony felt toward the main Elk Clan. Representatives from each of the other sub-clans came forward.

"What is the meaning of this? Why have you brought this group of Others with you," one of the elders from one of the sub-clans asked?

"They have become honorary Elk Clan members at our invitation. They attended my son's induction into adulthood and named the first child born to their Clan in over ten summers after Taelo. They have worked hard with us to reap the bounty the ancestors have sent to us. They are our brothers, and we honor them so," Grey Fox Running replied slowly and eloquently to the leaders who had come across the river to confront him.

"We have brought the best of our stores to share with you. We could not carry all we have. What we have brought will be shared with all. We have much excess food if it is needed. We wish our brothers and sisters of the other sub-clans only good tidings, but you must honor our friends as your friends," Silent Hawk spoke in support.

There was some grumbling among the group from the other sub-clans, but it was obvious the Elk Clan which had left in desperation and on the verge of starvation had returned with an abundance none of the other sub-clans could match.

They were accepted more from an inability to provide a counter proposal as to why the Others could not participate.

At the Elk Clan leadership welcome meeting, Wise Owl stood up and spoke in support of Gray Fox Running and pointed out to all, when the Elk Clan left the valley last season, most thought the Clan had little chance at survival.

Now the Elk Clan had returned seemingly the richest among all of them. This turn in fortune and their newly found friends all pointed to the Clan being led by the ancestors.

There was some grumbling, but the representatives returned to their sub-clans with the news of the wealth displayed by the Elk Clan and the fact the Others were friends and would stay.

As was the custom, the elders and leaders from each sub-clan came together for their first business meeting on the following evening. The Elk Clan continued its assault on tradition. It arrived with its group of elders now consisting of both male and female members. Including the Others in the Clan leadership circle by itself would have been enough but having women in the leadership circle was an additional challenge.

"Are there any other surprises you plan to pull on us?" a member of the Elk Hide Clan asked in a tone of disgust as he stood and looked over the arriving group.

"Brother, have I offended you in some way. Please accept my offering of young buffalo hump, the tongue and heart of the same animal prepared with salt from the sea and cooked together on a flat stone in the way of the Others," Gray Fox Running said in a loud and proud voice as Taelo, Golden Hawk and Burley Bear carried the cooked items on thin flat slate slabs in for all to share.

They put the items on tripods as the Others had shown them to make.

This surprised all in attendance, but all came forward to try the food whose aroma and flavor seemed to tease their palates. Several of the elders commented that they had never tasted anything so wonderful.

Taelo, Golden Hawk and Burley Bear then crouched in the shadows outside the circle of elders.

Broken Spear could feel their presence and was enjoying the discomfort felt by some of the elders from the other sub-clans. It was interesting to notice that women were not welcomed or accepted in the circle of elders of the new ones. This was strange to Broken Spear since women were the primary leaders of elders in the circle of the Others. They usually lived longer then the men and were around many more years. It made sense to have the women provide this continuity on a leadership team.

"And why are women included in your circle of elders?" another representative asked loudly.

"This is something we learned from the Others. In the Clan of Others, women hold equal power with the men. They have more members on the council of elders. We are learning from them and have found the women add a balance previously missing in our planning discussions. We have changed our meetings to include our women elders," Grey Fox Running replied.

A murmur went through the group of elders. How would such a situation be addressed? If they acted against the Elk Clan, they would face their own angry women. If they accepted this change then the women of all the sub-clans would want similar privileges.

Why had this happened?

Who had given the Elk Clan the right to turn the world on its head?

The elder men quickly realized there was but one solution. In frightening rapidity, the world around them was crumbling. This day, the Elk Clan had walked in and turned the world as it had been known and lived for so long, upside down. The stability the Clans had known for an unknown period was on its head and change was thrust unceremoniously upon them all.

The word spread rapidly throughout the sub-clans.

The food turned out to be a good idea. Its preparation had been purposely planned, and the cooking had been very meticulous. This was the best food the Elk Clan and the Clan of Others knew how to prepare. The women had made the point that it was hard to argue after a good meal.

"Let us take a moment, share the food, and drink we have brought. Then let us sit down and talk about the coming year and what must be done to ensure we all prosper," Grey Fox Running proposed.

"I agree with my good friend and look forward to these new ideas. It is clear the Elk Clan, the first clan, has been renewed, refreshed, and enriched. The rest of us should listen and learn from them.

Let's finish enjoying this delicious smelling food and the conduct business," Wise Owl of the Elk Horn Clan said as he put his arms around Grey Fox Running's shoulders.

"Was that the kind of help you were looking for," Wise Owl said quietly to Grey Fox Running.

"Yes, thank you for speaking up. I do not want to create a permanent problem. I do want change to take place," Grey Fox Running replied.

From the dark surrounding the Council of elders, Taelo, Golden Hawk and Burley Bear enjoyed the moment. They had been instrumental in bringing this change to the Elk Clan and now to all its sub-clans.

Both Grey Fox Running and White Swan sat looking at each other proud in their knowledge of Taelo, Golden Hawk and Burley, sitting in the dark sharing this moment of change, being the fuel and instruments of this historic moment.

Grey Fox Running spoke to the entire gathering of Clan leaders and repeated something Taelo had shared with the Elk Clan when he was induced to the Elk Clan as an adult, "Change is important if we are to grow as a people. In our lives only, change is certain. Without change we cannot grow or prosper. To feel comfortable with change we must all be humble learners. Humble learners handle the discomfort of change in a positive way."

After everyone had something to eat, Grey Fox Running stood and announced Taelo, Golden Hawk and Burley Bear had each been inducted into the circle of full adults and warriors. He shared all the adventures and contributions the three had made.

He closed by pointing to the mysterious item covered with a hide.

"Taelo, Golden Hawk and Burley Bear have made a gift to all the Clans. They have done this in secret. Even I have not seen this. They will now unveil their gift and present it to the council of elders," Grey Fox Running said in closing.

Taelo, Golden Hawk and Burley Bear came forward.

"It has been our pleasure to work on this gift to all the Clans and to the council of elders. It represents the union of the people, the animals, and our mother earth. It shows we are the same in thought, the same in heart, the same in spirit," Burley Bear spoke in the language of the new ones as Taelo, and Golden Hawk pulled the covering from the totem carving they had made.

There was a general murmur of appreciation and wonder at the quality of the work.

"The base represents the mother earth. You see the waves of the sea, the mountains, the trees, and sky," Golden Hawk continued in the tongue of the Others as Taelo translated to the language of the new ones.

"Next is the bear. This is a powerful totem for both peoples. Notice this one has a piece missing from its ear. This is the bear who created Broken Spear," Burley Bear spoke in his own language and Golden Hawk translated.

This same bear visited and spoke to Taelo on the beach this past year as it protected him from a pack of sixty wolves.

"Above him are our fox and wolf brothers. They are both our competitors and as we can see by looking around, they are becoming our companions. One is my father, and the other is the leader of the Others," Taelo said in the language of the old ones and Burley Bear translated to the language of the new ones. They had rehearsed their speech and cross translation. They wanted to make the point both peoples were equal.

"Above are the birds of the sky, a swan, a pheasant, a hawk and at the top an eagle. The lion is the one Taelo and the eagle flew with several years ago. They are all connected," Golden Hawk finished. The eagle at the top had its claws in the nose of a mountain lion and the hawk, the swan and the pheasant were carved in a spiral up the side of the lion. A spear protruded from the side of the lion.

The leaders gathered around the tall totem pole standing at least three spears high. The work was very well done. It was unlike anything seen before by anyone in either of any of the Clans.

This was taken as a sign by all the leaders they were being sent a message from the ancestors.

"The leaders of the future speak to us of the past and present. They are adventurers, they are inventors, and they are the masters of change. I speak to you as one who is old and who was broken so I would be able to see and understand. This is a symbol of unity and of the wholeness of nature," Broken Spear said in the language of the new ones.

This was a surprise to everyone but especially to Taelo, Golden Hawk and Burly Bear. They were very close to Broken Spear, and he had not let them know he was learning the language of the new ones. Broken Spear looked at the three with a twinkle in his eyes and winked at them.

After the first meeting, things proceeded in a more normal way. Trade among the various sub-clans went on in a vigorous manner.

Taelo, Golden Hawk and Burley Bear each did a brisk business in trading their shark teeth and shark teeth arrows and spears for various articles they desired.

When it came the time to share and redistribute the food supply, the Elk Clan had food to give to all the other sub-Clans. This was the final sign the partnership with the Others was valuable and would continue.

And so Taelo, Golden Hawk and Burley Bear began a long and enduring friendship. They were young men, who were recognized for their leadership, their ingenuity, and their honesty. The new stories added to the collection of both Clans included their many adventures. The stories told were memorable and the stories yet to come would continue to build on the solid accomplishments already achieved.

The End

Preview of: *The Golden Feather*

1 Spring by the Sea

*T*aelo, Golden Hawk and Burley Bear accompanied the Elk Clan and the Clan of Others back from the first combined and very successful meeting of all the Elk Sub clans and the Clan of Others.

The three were the prime motivators of the cultural change taking place in both peoples. The Elk Clan and all the sub clans now had women on the Council of Elders. This was an adoption from the practice of the Clan of Others where women made up the majority of the membership in their Council of Elders.

Taelo was pleased that both White Swan, his mother and Quiet Pheasant, Golden Hawk's mother were members of the Council of Elders.

363

Preview of: The Golden Feather

His father, Grey Fox Running, the leader of the Elk Clan joked about the fact that he now had to take direction on how to manage the Elk Clan and how to behave in his personal lodge from the same woman.

The bond among the team led by Little Otter on the first Elk Clan mixed gender long hunt continued to strengthen and grow.

They often retreated to the hot water pool and cave by the top of the waterfall cascading down several hundred feet into the Valley of Plenty.

The team operated as a unit. They were bonded by the mutual respect and the experience of looking out for each other during one of the most successful long hunts in the Elk Clan's memory.

They were to learn they were bonded by language, by principle, by their capabilities and as predicted by Broken Spear, the seer of the Others, by a bond that would carry them through their lives.

Taelo's and Golden Hawk's accomplishments and unselfish sharing of the wealth they could have accumulated for themselves was woven into the stories now told by the Elk Clan and the Clan of Others. They openly shared the most prolific honey tree with the entire Elk Clan. They generously shared the shark teeth taken from a huge shark they and Burley Bear fought and killed.

Preview of: The Golden Feather

The young buffalo bull Taelo rescued became Little Otter's constant companion and the first draft animal the clan had ever utilized. He was the reason Little Otter's team was able to pull two thirds of a Mastodon killed during the long hunt back into the Valley of Plenty.

Taelo and Golden Hawk guided the Clan of Others to a new home and the food they needed to survive the first winter.

Burley Bear, a member of the Others, with the looks of and almost as large as the giant brown cave bear, became their best friend, protector, and partner. He was the older brother both Taelo and Golden Hawk looked up to both physically and intellectually.

The past winter the three had made their joint journey into adulthood. Taelo and Golden Hawk were the youngest members of the Elk Clan to be given the honor of being called hunter and warrior.

Their induction to this position was a joint ceremony between the Elk Clan and the Clan of Others. Burley Bear, Golden Hawk and Taelo were inducted by both Clans to the position of hunter and warrior.

The first newborn to the Clan of Others in almost ten winter cycles was named, Scream of the Eagle, in honor of Taelo.

The two clans had speakers that had learned the language of both Clans.

Preview of: The Golden Feather

Taelo's team as they were referred to all spoke both languages and were equally welcome and accepted in both Clans.

Taelo, the source of change once again surprised the Clan by rescuing and raising a wolf pup he found wandering lost in the forest. The wolf now almost full size, named Lasher, followed him everywhere. The bond between the two was immediate and mutual. Taelo had spent much of his time bonding with and training Lasher. The two were inseparable. At night Lasher slept next to Taelo. The wolves had previously become familiar, but they always stayed on the periphery of the camp. Now there was one among them.

Golden Hawk and Taelo were walking slowly along the beach. The two friends were on the way to meet the rest of their group for their weekly dinner by the sea.

They and the rest of the team had recounted, retold, and polished their hunting stories more times than they cared to think about. They had contributed their fair share of the work to keep the clan fed and clothed throughout the winter.

The early spring breeze promised warmth and brought the fragrance of flowers from the cliffs above the bay.

Taelo, Golden Hawk and their hunting team friends had endured the winter in the Valley of Plenty and the hot spring cave at the top of the falls. This spring the move to the beach camp was an effort they had spearheaded and led.

Preview of: The Golden Feather

They surprised the entire clan by cleaning all the beach side lodges and the main lodge prior to everyone's arrival.

They had also set up the fish trap in the bay and caught one large fish for every home. These events always caught the clan by surprise because Taelo's whole team seemed to do as they pleased. They, however, always ended up contributing in some significant way to the clan.

The team had also become more then friends. They had paired off and were young lovers. After a long winter they were all ready for some new adventure. Their long hunting experience had changed all of them. They were more daring, more confident, and restless.

Red Oak and Grey Fox Running, fathers, and uncles to Taelo and Golden Hawk sat in front of the main lodge of the Beach summer camp.

"Look at those two. They are inseparable. I think they will come up with an excuse to leave us for the season," Grey Fox Running shared his observation with his best friend Red Oak.

"I think you are right. Golden Hawk has been restless. Quiet Pheasant has been worried about what the entire hunting group is up to," Red Oak continued.

Grey Fox Running and Red Oak were lifelong friends. Together they had pulled the Elk Clan back from the edge of disaster and ensured the clan had food for the winter. They had brought it from near starvation to become one of the wealthiest clans of the Elk Clan group.

Preview of: The Golden Feather

Taelo and Golden Hawk were their sons and were just as close friends as the two of them.

"Look how Taelo's wolf follows the two everywhere. Taelo has an uncanny way of making animals work for him.

Last fall it was taming the young buffalo calf and putting it to work pulling a travois.

Now he has trained the wolf to hunt with him and obey signals as well as voice commands," Red Oak commented on the strange new feature in the camp.

The two commented that they would help their two young hunters in every way they could.

In another part of the camp, Quiet Pheasant was talking to her older sister, White Swan.

The two had some very different and interesting observations.

"Taelo and Golden Hawk are discussing some new journey. This time they will end up taking their friends with them. Have you noticed how tightly the hunting team has bonded," Quiet Pheasant commented?

"Yes, and it is clear to me that I have already lost my son to Quiet Rabbit, and you have lost yours to Busy Bee. The four of them are always together. They seem perfectly matched," White Swan said wistfully.

She was quite pleased with the outcome of the match making the two of them had arranged.

"It turned out just as we planned. So why the sigh," Quiet Pheasant said.

She felt exactly the same way.

The two had maneuvered the young women and ensured their placement on the hunting team. It had all worked out exactly as planned. Now as mothers they were feeling the loss of their young men.

"You know the surprise is the bond between Little Otter and Talking Wren. That is the odd couple. I would never have made that match," White Swan said with a chuckle.

"Well, I enjoyed the fact the Others assumed they were all matched pairs and immediately added Meadow Flower as another hunting partner. They wanted Burley Bear's mate to hunt along with the rest of the team," Quiet Pheasant replied.

She too was happy with the outcome.

"The Others seemed to have been right in their assessment," White Swan said putting down the blouse she had been decorating as she looked down the beach to where Taelo and Golden Hawk were just joining the rest of their team out on the large tooth boulder.

Thank you for reading this far.

Continued in the: The *Golden Feather*

https://www.remwriter95.net/

Preview of: The Golden Feather

About the Author

Ronald E. Mueller
remwriter95@gmail.com

Ron grew up in what is now Flint River State Park in Southeast Iowa. The 170-year-old house Ron lived in is built into a hillside. It faces a 125-foot-high cliff towering over the little Flint River. The house and the land talked to him about; the passing of time, the struggle to conquer the land, the struggles people faced and the wonder of nature.

He climbed the cliffs, crawled into the caves, dove from the swimming rock, collected clams from the bottom of the pond, gigged and skinned frogs for their legs. He trapped muskrats for fur, hunted raccoon in the dead of night, and with only a stick hunted rabbits in the dead of winter.

His young life was outdoors, and nature tested him.

He walked to a one-room stone schoolhouse uphill both ways. A stern but warm-hearted teacher, Mrs. Henry was instrumental in shaping his character as she shepherded him from the fourth to the eighth grade.

It was a great way to grow up.

Ron graduated from Burlington, High School, went to Vietnam in the Navy. He graduated from The University of South Florida with a master's degree in engineering, worked for thirty-eight years for Procter and Gamble, traveled around the world thirty times.

He has remained happily married for more than fifty years. His daughter and his two sons are all successful and his three grandchildren have all graduated.

His wife has humored and supported him as he became a full time became a professional storyteller.

His experiences intertwined with snippets of fantasy lend themselves to the adventures he leads the reader through.

Books by Ron Mueller
Fiction Series
The Taelo Series
The Early Years
The Golden Feather
Journey of Discovery
Dangerous Passage
Condor Clan Slingers
Circumvention
The Journey of Sages
Future Leaders Journey
Taelo Collection

A Taelo Story
White Swan and Quiet Pheasant
The Child's Name
Floating Cloud
Quiet Rabbit
Busy Bee
Little Otter & Talking Wren
Broken Spear
Burley Bear & Meadow Flower
Taelo Story Collection

The Alex Evercrest Series
The River Front
The Girl on The Grill
Missing
Maggot
Racist
Votive Candles
Windy City
Country Road
Pool of Blood
Sins of the Daughter
Body Parts
The Skull Collector
The Vanishing
The Shadow Fighter
Moonshine
Grief's Trajectory
The Magic Touch
Northern Lights
Alex Evercrest Heroine
Alex Evercrest Collection Two
New Direction
A Family Affair
Disruption
The St. Lebuinnus Church Murder

A Brian O'Neil Novel
Hawaiian Phoenix
Moon Curser
Death Broker

The Problem Solver Series
Solutions
Drug Lords
Border Crosser
The Problem Solver Collection

Science Fiction

The Savitar Series:
Journey's End
Savitar
Confluence
Savitar Series Collection

Bram Nielson Series
The Fold
The Message
Fold Wormhole
Negative Fold
Ripples in Time
Bram Nielson Collection

Single Science Fiction Books:
Current Past and Future
The Event
The Door
Viajante 7

https://www.remwriter95.net/

Character names and Roles

Taelo   Main Character through all series

White Swan   Taelo's Mother
Grey Fox Running   Taelo's Father
Golden Hawk, Taelo's cousin and best friend
Quiet Pheasant, Golden Hawks mother, sister to White Swan
Red Oak   Husband to Quiet Pheasant - Lifelong
                              friend of Grey Fox Running
Quiet Rabbit   Eventually Taelo's mate
Fast Skimmer   Quiet Rabbit's father
Silent Pool   Quiet Rabbit's mother
Floating Cloud   Quiet Rabbits Grandmother
Busy Bee   Eventually Golden Hawk's mate
Brave Deer   Busy Bee's Father
                              One of the Main hunters for the Elk Clan
Little Otter   Leader in the first long hunt for the Taelo
team
Talking Wren   Eventual mate to Little Otter
Little Pebble   Busy Bees Mother
Wise Owl   Elk Hide Clan leader, Council Leader.
Grey Weaver   Elk Hide Clan, storyteller.
Silent Hawk   Initial Leader of the Elk Clan
Sharp Beaver   Hunter in Brave Deer's team
Soft Down   Minor character when the elk clan reach the
beach.
The Others
Broken Spear   Seer of the Others was Long Spear.
Tall Fern   Broken Spear's early mate.
Silver Arrow
Quiet Fox   Leader of the Others
Little Doe   Wife of the Others Leader
Burley Bear   Of, the Others Taelo's protector and friend
Meadow Flower   Burley Bear's mate
Saber Scar   Originally Rolling Stone got new name
                              after being attacked by a saber tooth.
Marigold   Sister of Meadow Flower Saber Scar's
mate

Around the World Publishing, LLC

www.ingramcontent.com/pod-product-compliance
Lightning Source LLC
Chambersburg PA
CBHW060313100726
47907CB00002B/383